ENJOY THE READ!

Elephants Cry

A COLD CASE MYSTERY

BRUCE FLOOD

 FriesenPress

Suite 300 - 990 Fort St
Victoria, BC, V8V 3K2
Canada

www.friesenpress.com

ISBN
978-1-4602-8999-0 (Hardcover)
978-1-4602-9000-2 (Paperback)
978-1-4602-9001-9 (eBook)

1. Fiction, Mystery & Detective

Distributed to the trade by The Ingram Book Company

Acknowledgments

I'd like to express my appreciation to an agent who shall remain nameless. With his guidance and the need to develop my story, I was able to reconstruct and rewrite a novel of interest.

I am very grateful for the encouragement given to me by many individuals I call friends.

To fellow teacher Tyler Schaefer, thank you for your photography and computer savvy

A special thanks to my 2014-15 grade 7 class at Listowel Central P. S. who had to endure my first reading.

Enormous gratitude goes out to my proofreader and editor Kathryn Boyd for her excellent feedback and recommendations.

Finally, love and thanks to all my family.

for my wife Jane,
who makes
life magical

prologue

"Is this Paradise?" the elderly man asks himself.

The late afternoon sky is azure apart from a delicate swirl of white cloud in the deep distance. The sun is beaming bright and a gentle, cool breeze caresses his skin. The sounds of songbirds singing in the trees fill the air and his nostrils flare with the fragrant scent of saffron flowers. There was a thunderstorm earlier. This is the season when it rains mid-day almost every day just enough to keep the dust subdued for a short while.

Positioned by his office window overlooking the compound, Major Hawkins glances at his pocket watch and a confused expression casts over his weathered face. The hunting expedition is returning to camp a few hours before the usual time. With thoughts of something gone horribly wrong, Hawkins detects the agitated state of the safari ranger as he slaps the dust from his pants with his hat and marches towards the main building.

The portly Major is a retired veteran of the British forces and now represents the SoAfCo Group that organizes and operates hunting expeditions in Nambia, just west of the Kalahari Desert. The safari ranger, Luc Boudreau, is a rugged individual who also spent some time in the military.

It thunders only this time it's the stomping of boots on the porch. Boudreau storms into the office and plops down in a chair. "That McPherson kid is a complete idiot!" Shifting his weight to the edge of the seat, the ranger's disgust is obvious. "He shot too early! He killed the wrong elephant!" Boudreau takes a deep breath and concludes, "What an asshole!"

Major Hawkins moves discreetly away from the window to comfort his veteran employee. "Calm down, Luc. What seems to be the problem?"

Slouching wearily back into his chair, Boudreau attempts to collect himself and his speech becomes less dramatic. "I'm calm. I just hate dealing with jerks like that." The ranger continues to call McPherson every name under the sun. "The guy is such a loser."

Hawkins wants a full report on the cause of Boudreau's unfamiliar conduct. "Why don't you tell me all about it? What happened to get you so upset?"

"Okay!" answers Boudreau. "I'm calm," he repeats while taking another deep breath. "I might as well start from the beginning."

The camp was a hive of activity hours before sunrise. Two young men wearing combat outfits waited by the front gate. Their faces beamed with excitement while a third man dressed in traditional safari garb stood nearby. He was older and considerably less enthusiastic. Boudreau shouted instructions to his tracker. The tracker, known as Jabu, directed the scouts in his Bushman language and they readied to embark.

It was the wet season and there would be waterholes along the southern edge of the pan. The elephants would be there. A spectacular and rewarding hunt would be guaranteed. When all was ready, Boudreau gave the order and the hunting expedition led by the tracker set out on foot into the darkness.

As dawn broke, the eight-man safari snaked their way through the flat lands of tall, yellow grass. The scorching sun transformed the early morning into a sweltering sauna. It would be an hour before they would reach the verdant jungle and the shelter of shade trees. When confronted by a dense wall of rainforest, they would be compelled to hack their way through the lush foliage with machetes and slog their way through the forest floor of thick, red sludge.

By mid-day, darkness fell. A flash of lightning illuminated the black skies followed by a thunderous bang. Within seconds, the fury of a tropical storm erupted and members of the expedition cowered like trapped animals in a pitfall.

"Jabu!" the taller of the two young men called ahead to the tracker. "How long do these rains last?"

The tracker slowed his pace reluctantly in response to Bryce McPherson's concern. "Yes, bwana, the rains will end soon. We must keep going." Jabu continued to wield his machete and move forward.

Again, the clash of thunder and one of the scouts crouched on impulse. With eyes as wide as saucers, he gazed at the tree tops wrapped in shifting gusts of torrential rain. Thunder was thought to be a powerful deity amongst his people and the sky a source of danger. Death by lightning was not uncommon to this region. The safari managed to keep in stride.

Boudreau, who travelled directly behind the tracker, slowed his pace. Wanting to chat with the older gentleman who tagged along, he allowed Bryce McPherson and his chum to slide by.

"Mr. Barnes isn't it?" the ranger asked the older man as he approached.

Spencer Barnes was a stately Englishman who proudly met the needs of his employer. He had been hired by the McPherson's as a house attendant and was given the assignment of steward for their reckless son. Tagging along was part of his employment.

"At your service," replied Barnes.

"Who is this McPherson kid?"

3

Bryce McPherson was the heir of good fortune. His family emigrated from Scotland to North America in the 50's. His father, Andrew, had influence in the steel industry and frequently sent Bryce on adventures just to rid of him for short periods of time. Young McPherson tended to be overly aggressive and manipulative, and often acted without compassion. He treated Barnes like a menial servant.

"He's a bit of a pain I'd say," answered Barnes.

"How's that?" asked the ranger.

"Young McPherson is spoiled and arrogant," Barnes replied. "I pity the girl who gets herself involved with him."

It had been thirty minutes since the rains stopped when the procession finally came to a halt at the far limits of the jungle.

"There!" the tracker calmly whispered as he pointed ahead.

Members of the expedition huddled around Jabu and gaped into the open expanse. In front of them was the most magnificent, awe-inspiring land creature on the planet. The stream was swollen by the rains and at least sixty elephants gathered about the water's edge bathing and sunning themselves. Each family formed a distinct group and several moved gracefully through the golden grass away from the hunting party. The closest group was only a few meters from reach.

The ranger reached over and prevented McPherson from raising the gun barrel. "Easy does it."

Elephants do not have far ranging eyesight, but their sense of smell is unparalleled and their hearing has more capability than humans. Sensing danger, the elephants began to stir.

All of a sudden like a great whirlwind, a young matriarch charged in their direction and stopped short of the trees. With eyes fixed on the intruders, she lifted her noble head and a deafening trumpet burst shattered the heavy silence. She wouldn't have ventured any further. It was a warning to stay away from her family.

Bryce McPherson in his own mind was the only being of importance and rules of management never applied to him. Often acting on impulse and without seeking anyone's approval, he decided to execute. The elephant gun raised and erupted with a thunderous sound.

The matriarch had lifted her trunk high a second time and was hit in the exposed area of the neck. She reared on impact and blood spewed from the wound. Like a thunderbolt, a second shot flashed from the gun and ripped a hole in her chest. As she crumbled to the ground, elephant screams from the herd filled the air. The frightened animals scattered, save the fallen beast.

The jubilant hunter wheeled around. "Did you get it, Ian?" Bryce shouted with excitement. "Did you get the kill on tape?"

Ian Wilcox was a boyhood chum who tolerated his friend's haughty behaviour. "Relax, man! I got it!" He tapped the video camera held in his right hand. "It's all here!"

McPherson dropped the gun and slid a leather belt from his pant loops. He put it to his face and swung it up and down like an elephant would its trunk. Bryce put the belt to his groin area and pulled it vigorously back and forth as he approached the dead animal. This act of masturbation was accompanied with the lyrics of a recent song by the Rolling Stones.

"I'll never be your beast of burden. I've walked for miles, my feet are hurting." McPherson sang with exaggerated modulation. "All I want is for you to make love to me."

He whirled the belt over his head and then whipped the dead elephant several times. The video camera rolled and McPherson's performance continued. He sank to his knees as if humbled by his accomplishment. Bryce looked to the heavens, cupped his hands together and conveyed the act of prayer.

"Cut!" a voice called out like a director would on a movie set. "That was a great piece of work, man!" Wilcox placed the video camera down and clapped his hands in appreciation of a job well done.

Spencer Barnes shook his head in disapproval of young McPherson's sadistic display and Luc Boudreau retreated

several meters into the woods in an attempt to gain his compo-
sure. Ian Wilcox retrieved a bottle of whiskey from his back-
pack and joined his buddy for a celebration of triumph.

The hunt was conclusive. Two scouts with machetes removed
the tusks while McPherson and Wilcox continued their celebra-
tion. The safari would soon slither into the jungle and snake
their way back to camp. The revelers would soon follow after
the thrill of the kill subsided. The carcass would be left behind
to rot.

A tall figure appears in the doorway of Hawkins' office and raps lightly on the wooden framework.

"Come in," invites the Major.

Boudreau spins around in his chair to acknowledge the visitor. "I felt like grabbing the elephant gun and blasting a hole in that McPherson kid, Mr. Barnes!"

"I agree," admits Spencer Barnes as he enters the room. "Sometimes I feel like murdering the bastard myself."

Chapter 1

Detective Jack Reinhardt sips from his coffee mug and gazes from the fourth floor office window at the winged gargoyles perched atop the tall building across the street. Always fascinated by these mysterious creatures, he often imagines them blinking their demon eyes as they come to life. With staunch faces and a lust for blood, they spread their dormant wings and powerfully swoop down to wreak havoc on the city.

Reinhardt is a special duties officer with the police department and in charge of a team that deals with unsolved crimes of murder. In his late forties, he is unmistakably affected by his job as a 'cold case' detective. Although in great physical shape, his face reveals the wear and tear of arduous duty and many a sleepless night. Grey around the temples and pronounced wrinkling in the cheeks are all signs of work related tension and stress.

The detective lowers his sights to the sidewalks below. The Federal Building where he works is located on Main Street in the city core. It's just after eight o'clock in the morning and people, mostly business-types on their way to work, are scurrying in every direction. Just as Reinhardt takes another sip from his mug, he is startled by a presence in the room.

"Good morning, Jack!"

The voice belongs to Detective Richard Newland who has been Reinhardt's partner in crime for three years. He's an amusing looking fellow and somewhat appealing at the same time. His hair is crayoned in orange and matching freckles highlight his ever-smiling face. To call him clownish would describe both his appearance and personality.

Newland accompanies Jack by the window and peers at the activity below. "They look like they're on speed. We should go down and arrest them all."

The detective jokes, but there is some truth in what he is saying. Drug trafficking and exchange on the street is prolific in this city and on the rise.

Simultaneously, the detectives contemplate their position of struggle to enforce law and order. Newland snaps out of his trance first and remembers why he came.

"Chief wants to see us in ten minutes."

"Okay, Richard. I'll be right there."

Jack is the only person on staff excluding the chief who calls Detective Newland by his given name. The rest of his coworkers call him Dick. Some say it's because of his short stature and calling him Dick is short for Richard. Others jokingly say it's the way he performs in the workplace. Either way, Newland is very accepting and actually prefers Dick as a moniker.

Detective Reinhardt peers from his office window once again. From his vantage point, he can see a few blocks south on Main Street where a midway of novelty shops, bargain houses, kinky boutiques and sidewalk huskers will soon come to life. This section of downtown has been a haven for homeless beggars, a hangout for undesirables and a major problem area for the police force.

Reinhardt remains in his reverie for a couple of minutes until Dick sticks his head in the doorway. "C'mon, Jack! The chief is waiting!"

"I'm coming!" Jack sets his coffee mug on the desk and joins his partner.

The two detectives walk the familiar walk to the office of their superior. Upon reaching their destination, Dick raps lightly on the door and a low voice from within instructs them to enter.

Chief Inspector Conrad Burgess is Head of Investigations. His office is furnished with an over-stuffed leather couch and two matching armchairs. The chief sits behind his mahogany desk and one of the armchairs is occupied by an unfamiliar and curious looking fellow. Both Burgess and his visitor rise for introductions as Reinhardt and Newland enter the room.

Gesturing with hand motions, the chief announces, "Jack and Richard, I want you to meet William Cooney of the Glasgow City Police."

Following a round of handshakes, Chief Burgess directs everyone to have a seat. "Jack, do you remember the Bryce McPherson homicide? It rocked the city about twenty-five years ago and never did get solved."

Reinhardt ponders for a moment and then remembers. "Yes! I was a rookie patrolman when it happened."

"The victim's parents were quite influential people in the community at the time and they want to reopen the case," Burgess informs his men. Acknowledging his visitor, he adds, "Detective Cooney can fill you in better than I can."

The Scotsman quickly responds to his cue. "The McPhersons moved back to Glasgow about a year after their son's murder. Mrs. McPherson is very ill right now and she wants her son's remains flown back to Scotland where they can eventually rest together in peace."

Cooney speaks with a strong Scottish accent which needs close attention to be understood. While the visitor from overseas continues with the McPherson's wishes, Detective Newland is candidly rolling his eyes.

"The McPhersons are much aware of the advancement in forensic technology," says Cooney. "Since their son's remains are to be exhumed, they want to reopen the case and possibly bring closure to their long ordeal."

The Scotsman's lines have been well-rehearsed and, judging by his animated mannerisms, it would be painless to assume that this detective is a spare part and expendable. As well, his short stature, hair colour and freckles are similar characteristics to those of Newland. Detective Reinhardt finds the likeness quite diverting and grins.

"You think this is amusing, Jack?" asks Chief Burgess.

"No sir!" Reinhardt replies with a hint of embarrassment. "It's just." He stops in mid-sentence to look at Cooney, then to Newland and back to Cooney again. "It's nothing."

Taking a moment to gather himself, Jack continues, "The McPherson case should be very intriguing. I'll get my team on it right away."

"Fine," responds Chief Burgess. "I trust you'll get Detective Cooney acquainted with our procedures, get him settled in and make good use of his expertise?"

"Yes, of course," returns Reinhardt. "Richard here can be Detective Cooney's personal attendant."

A semi-concealed expression of anguish crosses Newland's face and William Cooney is all smiles. "I'd fancy you calling me Coon," says the Scotsman. "All my mates back home call me Coon."

Jack attempts to minimize another smirk. "Yes, well, let's get started." He rises from the couch and reaches across the desk to shake his boss's hand. "Thanks Chief!"

This prompts a chain reaction of handshakes and the three detectives file out of the office.

Huddling in the hallway, Jack makes the call. "Richard, show Detective Cooney…"

The Scotsman quickly interrupts, "All my mates back home call me Coon."

"Well, we want you to feel at home," reassures Jack. "Show Coon around the station and introduce him to some of the team," he instructs Newland. "We'll meet in the conference room in about an hour." Checking his wristwatch, he adds, "Say ten o'clock."

"Ten o'clock," repeats Dick.

Cooney is amused by Dick's quick wit and he giggles.

Jack is all too familiar with his partner's sense of humour or lack of it. He just shakes his head and starts back to his office.

"Right this way," Newland directs the Scotsman. "The tour is about to begin."

Cooney points his finger and corrects his tour guide. "That's left."

"Right you are," agrees a smiling Newland.

Proceeding down a hallway, Dick asks, "How much do you know about cold cases and the work our team will be doing, Coon?"

"I haven't had much experience investigating," admits Cooney.

Newland's internal light goes on as he recognizes this shining opportunity to dominate a coworker. "Well, let me tell you, Coon," he begins. "It's like following a recipe. There are things to do first, you know, to get ready. Then, there are things to add until everything is put together. And then, it's done. You follow?"

Cooney looks confused as they enter an open area. The office pool is a large space filled with desks occupied by workers engaged in their specific duties. Around the perimeter are rooms and offices with glass fronts. All but one office, that is.

Newland and Cooney walk by the first room on the left and their attention is diverted by a thumping noise coming from within. A worker is banging on the Xerox machine.

"Percussion maintenance," Newland tells the Scotsman. "He's hitting the machine to make it work. That's Polanski. He probably has his football pool jammed in there and needs to fix the problem before he gets caught."

Cooney pretends to understand. "Aye."

Detective Newland points straight ahead to the corner office where another employee busily pecks on a keyboard. "That's Howie Hirsch. He's our alpha geek."

Cooney looks confused once again and Dick realizes he will have to explain most of everything to this visitor from across the giant pond. "He's our computer whiz! He's the most technically proficient nerd in the department."

The Scotsman nods in understanding. "We call them ram lovers and sheep shaggers." His remark causes Newland to snicker.

Continuing their stroll around the office pool, Cooney points to the office without a glass front. The name on the door reads Captain Maddox. "What's he like?"

Captain Troy Maddox is second to Chief Burgess in command and he oversees all activities of the office pool.

"He's a seagull," answers Dick. "The kind of boss who swoops in, chirps a lot, shits on everybody and flocks off."

Cooney lets out a resounding roar of laughter which causes Newland to bellow with laughter as well. Drawing the attention of everyone in the immediate area, they don't appear the least bit embarrassed by their outburst.

"That's a cracker!"

"A lot of people think I'm funny," Dick tells him, "although a few people think I'm a mutation of some kind."

Dick Newland can be annoying and brash, and somehow lovable at the same time. That's the way it can be with a team of workers. You're with each other for the better part of each day and you learn to tolerate one another. You become friends. Dick's tongue-in-cheek randomness has exposed his quick wit, but usually merits groans from his audience.

"I think you're funny," says Coon.

Newland puts his hand on the shoulder of his Scottish friend and they proceed down another hallway. Ahead of them is an employee banging on a pop machine.

"Percussion maintenance?" asks Cooney.

Dick nods his head up and down emphatically. "We're going to get along just fine, Detective Cooney!"

"Call me Coon. All my mates back home call me Coon."

"And you can call me Dick."

"Aye, Dick!"

Jack sits at the large conference table with a pile of papers in front of him. He has been familiarizing himself, as much as he could in an hour, with the McPherson case. His secretary places files on the table at each vacant chair.

Jill Rosseter is an integral member of the team fulfilling many more duties than her title suggests. She's in charge of the hard copy files and does most of the prep work in reopening a case.

The next member of the team to enter the conference room is alpha geek Howie Hirsch. Oddly handsome behind thick rimmed glasses, his duties include computer data files, research and analysis, and implementation of all the marvelous functions of computer software.

"Morning, Jack!"

"How you doing, Howard?"

"Just fine, thanks!"

Moving closer to the secretary, Hirsch asks, "How's your day going so far, Jill?" He's liked his coworker for a long time and thinks of her as a beautiful nerd girl that no one gives notice because she wears conservative clothing and always has her auburn hair in pins.

"Fine," she responds frigidly. Jill is all business as she continues to distribute folders.

"Have a seat, Howard," invites Jack. "Richard and Vera should be here any minute."

Hirsch assumes one of the vacant spots at the table and Detective Reinhardt adds, "Our team will have a detective from Scotland assisting us in this particular case."

"A detective from Scotland!"

The voice belongs to an attractive, middle-aged woman entering the room. Dressed in a white lab coat, Dr. Vera Hampton is a forensic pathologist and the team's laboratory connection. "Must be an important case, Jack?"

"There is some urgency to this case. We'll get started as soon as Richard shows up with our guest."

"So, what's he like?" asks Jill half-interested in the visitor.

Jack smiles. "I'll let you be the judge of that."

Dick and Coon make their way towards the conference room where the team anxiously awaits and Dick is explaining the finer points of detective work.

"It's like cutting a path to where you want to go. You hack through obstacles in your way. You know, like stumbling blocks. Just when you're about to arrive at your destination, something else gets in your way."

Newland finishes with his words of wisdom just as they reach the conference room. Shoulder to shoulder, Dick and Coon get stuck in the doorway. Their resemblance is uncanny. The wardrobe of each man is non-practical and the disarray of colour scheme just adds to their goofy and playful nature. It's a comical sight and team members struggle to hold back their chuckles.

"Come in guys and let's get started. Everyone, I'd like you to meet William Cooney of the Glasgow City Police." Jack senses an interjection and immediately adds, "He would like it if we called him Coon."

"All my mates back home call me Coon."

It's awkward for Jack to articulate Detective Cooney's preference of name as he presents the team's newest member. "Coon, I'd like you to meet everyone."

Following introductions, all members of the team sit and Jack is ready. "Okay, let's begin. As I was just saying to Vera, there is some urgency with this case. The body of the victim in question is being exhumed and flown back to Scotland. We need to take this opportunity to do some further testing on the remains, put some pieces together and solve a crime."

"Another murder mystery, Jack?" asks Vera.

"Definitely," answers Jack. "The victim's head was bashed in."

Howie Hirsch asks, "How old is the stiff?"

"The murder occurred on the night before Halloween twenty-five years ago," replies Jack. "Bryce McPherson. It was all over the newspapers. This is big stuff!"

Dick is always raring to go and he pumps a fist. "Let's do this!"

"Bring the boxes up from cold storage, Jill." Reinhardt wiggles his finger at Newland and Cooney. "The guys here can help." He turns to Dr. Hampton. "We'll get samples to the lab as soon as we can, Vera. The remains should arrive within a day," Jack tells the pathologist.

The doctor rises from her chair and says, "We're pretty busy, Jack! I'll see what we can do and keep you posted."

"Thanks, Vera!" he responds appreciatively as she leaves the meeting with her case file.

Detective Reinhardt hands a piece of paper to the computer whiz. "Howard, here's a list of names I want you to run through. See what you can come up with and we'll meet back here same time tomorrow morning."

Hirsch nods in acceptance. "You got it, Jack!" Standing and turning to leave, he acknowledges the secretary, "See you later, Jill!"

Without making eye contact, Jill responds with a simple, "Bye!".

"Here's a package Jill put together for each of us," Jack tells his men referring to the case files in front of them. "We need to start right away, so get reading." Fiddling with a pile of papers on the table, Jack continues, "After you help Jill with the boxes, Richard...."

Jack is interrupted by Newland. "Call me Dick. All my friends call me Dick."

Reinhardt isn't a bit surprised, but he is somewhat ruffled. "Okay, Dick! When you've finished helping Jill, see that Detective Cooney gets settled in." He immediately corrects himself, "Coon." Jack shakes his head. "This is getting confusing!"

Dick and Coon appear entertained by their leader's perplexity. They look at each other and snicker like kids playing a trick on someone.

"Come with me, gentlemen." Jill clears her throat of her cynical remark. "We've got some boxes to retrieve."

*

A young man pulls red coveralls over his svelte and athletic frame, steps into a pair of black rubber boots and closes his locker door. Justin Lombardi is a part-time labourer of sorted classification at the Municipal Zoo and he is preparing for his late-morning shift.

Leaving the locker room, he ventures outdoors and pauses for a moment to absorb the sights and sounds of his workplace. He loves his job and everything about it. Attending to the animal pens will be his first duty of the day.

Justin collects his cleaning instruments and bucket of sanitizer from a storage shed and proceeds to the monkey cages. The Capuchin monkeys have priority. These lovable fur balls seem to shit more often than any other species on the planet and their cages need constant consideration.

The young zoo employee opens a lock and starts into the first cubicle of confinement. A part of him wants to free the denizens, but a larger part of him understands the importance of zoos. These institutions provide the opportunity for people to enjoy animals of the wild and the Municipal Zoo ensures the best possible care and treatment for its inmates.

A monkey jumps onto Justin's arm. "Hello, Chico! What are you up to?" All of the animals are personalized and invested with an individual identity.

The monkey looks at him wide-eyed and paws at his sleeve. Anyone with substance procures happiness and indulgence when observing the comical antics of these creatures.

While scrubbing the bowels of a second row of pens, Justin senses a presence and lifts his head to see the grotesque face of a woman staring at him from the opposite end of the screened cage. Justin is startled and he knocks the bucket of disinfectant all over the place. Fumbling to set the bucket upright, he looks up again and the woman is gone. He scours the immediate area, but she is nowhere to be seen. With heart still racing, he sponges at the bottom of the monkey cage.

Someone approaches and asks, "Have an accident, Justin?" Peter Simpson is one of the senior employees at the zoo and Justin's immediate supervisor.

"Holy shit, Pete!" exclaims Justin as he squeezes a wet sponge over the bucket. "Who is she?"

"Who's who?"

"You know." Justin's hands are trembling as he continues to wipe up the spill. "The woman with the red face and elephant tattoo."

Pete looks in all directions without a sign of the woman in question. "Was she here again?"

"Her face was just inches away from mine!"

"Gruesome, isn't she?" His boss snickers. "It's a wonder you didn't shit your pants."

"No kidding!" Who in the hell is she?"

*

The red-faced lady makes her way to the rear of the bus. Appalled by her appearance, many of the passengers turn their head away as she trudges past. Many feel her presence unnerving and best ignored.

She doesn't carry any bags and she's not filthy and stinky. Her clothes are ill-fitting - woolen sweater a few sizes too big; baggy dungarees; tight sneakers with toes trying desperately to escape through the material. She wears white gloves, the kind worn to church on Sunday although her gloves have taken on the appearance of everyday abuse. Her head is covered with a dark coloured kerchief which hides much of her grey hair and envelopes a most disturbing complexion. Her wrinkled face is entirely painted red and the tattoo of an elephant is visible on her forehead. Eyes the colour of agony certainly conceal secrets of a tragic human being.

The red-faced lady sits alone and silently converses with imaginary friends on either side of her. Her lips are moving without sound and she is highly entertained by the topic of conversation. She giggles and attempts to cover her smile with a soiled white-gloved hand.

The bus doors opened and three giggling teenagers boarded. They jostled their way to the rear of the bus and plopped down in the back seat where they continued to giggle. The girl on the left was blonde, good-looking and very bubbly. The girl on the right had light brown hair and was barely cute. The girl in the middle was strikingly beautiful with dark, curly hair and almond-shaped eyes that added to her look of innocence. She played with the trinket on a gold chain that dangled from her neck. It was a recent gift from a male admirer.

"What if he asks you out?" questioned the girl on the right.

"Are you going to go out with him?" the girl on the left asked.

The girl in the middle turned red with embarrassment and covered her smile with one of her hands. She was wearing white gloves.

"Well, you like him, don't you Anna?" asked one of the girls.

"I think he's a hunk, don't you Anna?" asked the other girl.

Her friends kept firing away with more questions and the three girls giggled.

"I have to go!" The girl called Anna rose from her seat and grabbed for the handrail by the side door. The bus slowed and came to a stop at her regular point of departure. Anna turned to face her friends. "He's all right, I guess."

"I'll phone you after supper!" yelled the blonde girl.

"I'll phone you as soon as I get home!" her other friend shouted.

Anna descended the steps and waved from the sidewalk as the bus pulled away.

The red-faced lady coughs and rises from her seat. She grabs for the handrail and the bus comes to a stop. She gets off and waves at the bus as it pulls away.

Proceeding down the sidewalk by degrees, she walks with leaden steps and undignified slouch. The old woman lives in a low-income housing complex just around the corner where her ponderous journey will end.

She moves at a snail's pace along a stone pathway that leads to her single room apartment at the rear of the neglected building. She opens the door to unit #6 and enters. There is no need to use a key because the lock mechanism is faulty. Once safely inside, the red-faced lady activates the deadbolt.

A snow white cat makes its entrance into the same unit through a torn screen in the open window.

"We're home now, Dorothy!" the old woman says to the cat. "Come and I'll get you something to eat."

Chapter 2

Jenny Reinhardt is in front of the television set and rolling on the couch like a playful kitten. School is over for the day and the energetic youngster is flipping through the channels while her mom prepares supper in the kitchen.

"What time is it, Jenny?" a girl's voice echoes from the top of the stairs. Jenny's older sister Shannon is racing to get ready for her date.

Pressing the 'guide' button on the remote, Jenny shouts, "It's 4:38!"

The little girl continues her channel surfing until she notices an elephant with her two babies. The infant elephants make her giggle as they romp about and stumble into their mother.

It's a documentary film on elephants being killed for their ivory and the program narrator describes the events with sickening dislike. "One of Africa's wildlife treasures is doomed if the lawbreakers continue the slaughter."

Jenny's mood soon changes as she watches in horror.

Shannon flies down the flight of stairs and launches herself into the family room. She's on her way to the kitchen, but slows down when she hears the narrator's comments coming from the TV.

"Our film crew captured the brutality of poachers butchering these glorious animals."

Realizing the program isn't suitable for a twelve year old, Shannon orders her younger sister to turn it off.

Carol Reinhardt is by the sink chopping onions with a small paring knife when her older daughter enters the kitchen. Swallowed by the irritating essence of the pungent tubers, Carol looks at Shannon with a lachrymose expression and asks, "Going so soon?"

"I know you're going to miss me but you don't have to cry, mom!" Shannon giggles as she organizes her backpack. Then, she informs her mom that Jenny is in the other room watching elephants being murdered."

Carol sets the paring knife on the counter and replaces it with a tissue. "Put on some cartoons, Jenny!" she shouts. Wiping the tears from her eyes, she asks Shannon, "What about supper?"

Shannon and her boyfriend attend Wednesday night classes at the university. She plans to pick him up at the zoo and go to a restaurant for something to eat before school. "I'm going out with Justin."

Carol walks to the refrigerator and opens the door. Stooping to retrieve a head of lettuce from the crisper, she attempts to smooth the frown lines on her forehead with her free hand. "What time will you be home?"

"I'll probably go to Justin's for a while after school. No later than eleven." She gives her mother a kiss on the cheek. "Love you!"

Just as Shannon leaves by way of the side door, Jenny wanders into the kitchen and tugs on the white fringe of her mother's lime green apron. "Mom?"

"Go wash your hands for supper. Your dad will be home any minute." She spins her younger daughter around by the shoulders and taps her on the behind. "And turn off the television set."

Without being able to ask her question, Jenny skulks from the kitchen like a scolded puppy.

Dragging the back of her hand across her forehead once again, Carol lifts her ginger coloured hair from her eyes just as the side door opens. It's her husband home from work and they immediately gravitate to each another. Jack places his hands around his wife's thin waist, pulls her in and gives her a big kiss on the lips.

"Can I get you anything before supper, Jack?"

"A glass of wine would be great." He reluctantly releases his hold and Carol wiggles free.

She moves to the kitchen counter and reaches for a glass in the cupboard. "The newspaper is on the desk in the den. I'll bring your drink in."

"Thanks, my love!" Jack slowly moves in the direction of his comfy chair.

*

Justin Lombardi hustles to finish business before his ride shows up. Tools of the trade have been returned to their proper places and he stops for a moment to peruse the work shed. Admiring his management and organization, he takes a rag from his coveralls and dabs his brow.

His father, Joe Lombardi, was a long time employee of the zoo until he passed away eight months ago due to illness. Justin had begun working as a junior curator at age thirteen and wishes to follow in his father's footsteps. Now, at age twenty-four, an opportunity for promotion is within his grasp. The young man has submitted his application for the position of Animal Care Specialist.

Justin leaves the work shed and walks across the compound towards the locker room just as the ringing of a telephone reverberates from one of the employee huts like a school recess bell.

"Justin!" Pete Simpson yells from the doorway of a hut. "The front gate just called. Shannon is here."

Justin is running late due to his encounter with the red-faced lady. He acknowledges Pete with a wave of his hand and quickens his pace to the shower room.

Shannon has been sitting in her green Cavalier chatting with the Keeper of the Gate, Philip Marlow, who is another senior employee of the zoo and former good friend of Justin's father. Her boyfriend finally approaches the exit gate and she smiles as his curly brown hair bounces with every step he takes. Justin quickly manoeuvres through a turnstile and runs to the car.

"See you tomorrow, Phil!"

"Have a good night, you two."

Opening the passenger door, Justin flings his backpack into the rear seat and jumps in. Leaning over, he kisses Shannon. "Let's go! I'm starving!"

Known for their excellent food, ambiance and retro décor, Checkers Pub and Eatery is a checkerboard design of black and white. The booths, stools and wall-hangings all contribute to a 60's flavour and a flashing jukebox is forever playing golden oldies. Justin and Shannon met here two years ago and have been dating ever since.

The restaurant is fairly busy. Patrons are being escorted to their tables as others arrive and wait to be seated. Servers are racing around with trays in hand while busboys clean and reset tables. Justin and Shannon are situated in a cozy booth by a window.

Shannon is an attractive brunette with a shapely figure worthy of all the complimentary double-takes from admirers and Justin considers himself a very lucky man. Reaching across the table and seizing both of her soft hands, he flicks his tongue at her as if Shannon is tonight's special on the menu.

"Stop that!" she whispers forcefully and a grin appears on her face.

Justin returns her smile. "We're going to get married some-day, you know?" There is a sparkle in his eyes that matches the one in hers.

"I know we are," she replies. "Shush! Here comes the waitress."

*

It's sort of a special event having her father home for sup-per during a week night. He works long hours and often comes home late. Jenny is sitting at the dining room table and impa-tiently awaiting the arrival of her parents. She has something very important to ask them.

Her parents finally enter the room and set the food items on the table. A routine is followed whenever they have a family supper. Family members join hands and say grace before dig-ging in. After a short period of enjoying their meal, conversa-tion between parents begins. When topics are exhausted, the focus then shifts to children with the oldest going first. Jenny is excited because the place setting across the table from her is empty.

Jack is busily involved with his heaping portion of meat and potatoes while Carol nibbles at her skimpy serving. Picking away at the vegetables on her plate, Jenny anxiously awaits her turn to speak.

"How was your day, Jack?" asks Carol.

Her husband cuts eagerly into his pork chop and answers with his mouth practically full of food, "We started a new case today." Opening a new case obviously has given him a huge appetite. "How was your day, dear? Did you get to the mall?"

"I decided to wait and go on the weekend," his wife answers as she pokes at a small piece of meat with her fork. "I went to the post office and the grocery store. I did some on-line banking." She pauses to recollect. "Oh, and I washed my car."

While parents continue to discuss their day's activities, Jenny begins to fidget in her chair. Her father detects her agitated state and asks, "What's wrong, Jenny?"

"I need to ask something," she replies. "I tried to ask mom before supper, but she was too busy."

"I'm sorry, sweetie!" Her mom sounds very apologetic as she reaches for her daughter's hand. "What did you want to ask me?"

Finally, it was time for the little girl to ask her question.

"Do elephants cry? I was watching TV and some bad things were happening to them."

Carol vaguely remembers. "That's right! Shannon said you were watching something you shouldn't have been. What bad things did you see?" There is a worrisome tweak in her voice.

Jenny tells her parents of a man shooing a mommy elephant and of the baby elephants looking real sad and making strange noises.

"Don't watch stuff like that, Jenny," her father says using a caring yet stern expression. "You'll be having bad dreams again."

Her mom feels responsible. "It's my fault, Jack! I should keep a closer eye on what she's watching."

Her parents seem to be drifting away from her question, so Jenny asks again, "Do elephants cry?"

Carol gently squeezes her daughter's hand and smiles. "I don't know if elephants cry, honey! Do you know, Jack?"

"Well," Jack replies. "I've heard something about animals and how they can show emotions. Why don't you ask Justin? He'll know for sure."

Turning to her mom, Jenny pleads with urgency, "Please, can we go to the zoo on Saturday?"

"Sure!" her mother answers with a smile. "Let's not talk about bad things on television any more. Who wants dessert?"

Gathering a few dishes from the table, Carol marches into the kitchen.

*

A waitress dressed in black and white sets the baskets of food on the table in front of Justin and Shannon. "Enjoy!" she says before walking away.

"This looks great!" Lifting his burger with both hands, Justin adds, "And so do you!" Examining his girlfriend amorously, he sticks out his tongue and plunges it into the bun.

Glimpsing about, Shannon whispers with a hint of assertion, "Stop that! Someone might be watching!" She loves the constant attention and she smiles at him once again.

Shannon waits until Justin has devoured a good portion of his food before asking, "You said on the way here that you had some good news to tell me."

Justin's memory is jogged. "You know that position I applied for last week? Well, I haven't been officially promoted but Pete Simpson can't keep a secret."

She reaches across the table to grab his hand and she feels the softness beneath the calloused exterior. "What did he say?"

"Here's the deal," starts Justin. "I have to go to work early on Saturday. The zoo is getting a new elephant from out west somewhere and they want me to help unload. Pete heard from a reliable source that, if I handle myself favourably, I'm a lock for the job."

"Who's the reliable source?"

"The big guy himself," Justin tells her referring to Samuel P. Crawford, Director of the Zoo and head administrator.

"Wow! That's great, Justin!" She squeezes his hand tightly. "Are you happy?"

Justin wears a wide smile. His love for animals is inherited from his father and he plans to devote the rest of his life to the zoo. The answer to her question is obvious.

"Come on! We better get to school," he says.

Justin and Shannon are on their way to the university. Shannon is in her first year of an Arts program majoring in English. She takes an Anthropology class on Wednesday nights as an extra credit and she hasn't any plans for a future career as yet. Justin is in his final year of Psychology and Behavioral Sciences and currently studying the aspects of human life.

The Cavalier comes to a stop in the school's parking lot and they get out of the car. Grabbing her book bag from the back seat, Shannon asks, "Do you know what your class is about tonight?"

"Thought I told you. We find out about our term paper." Justin fetches his backpack. "What about your class? Whose bones are being unearthed tonight?"

"I have no clue!" she tells him. "Mr. Thompson our instructor, I think they dug him up." Chuckling, they walk hand-in-hand towards the school entrance.

The front foyer and immediate hallways are packed with young minds going every which way, and Justin and Shannon budge their way in.

"What's the game plan?" asks Justin.

"Meet me in front of my classroom at butt break."

Butt break is a term used by students for their thirty minute recess. Justin and Shannon haven't smoked a day in their lives.

"Okay! I better get to class." Justin gives his girlfriend a loving kiss. "I want to be there when Sinclair-Smythe's makes his entrance."

"I hear he's a bit of a kook."

"He's unusual," Justin admits. "See you at butt break and I'll tell you all about it then."

After another quick kiss, Shannon watches her boyfriend hurry off to class.

*

28

Jenny's bedroom has a work area where she does her school assignments each night after supper. Slouching over her desk with head in hands, her math books are resting untouched. She can only think of elephants being brutally murdered for their ivory tusks and the suffering of the baby elephants. Somehow, she knows they wouldn't survive without their mothers.

Her mom appears in the doorway and sees Jenny pondering at her desk. "Stuck on a math problem?"

"I'll be done in a minute!"

"Good!" says her mom. "I've started your bath."

Jack is flipping through the daily newspaper when Carol walks into the living room. He peeks over his reading glasses and watches her plop wearily on the sofa beside him. Cognizant of her wrinkles, she lifts a hand and rubs her forehead.

Jack sympathizes. "It must have been a tough day."

Carol is a few months older than her husband. They had met at an ice-skating party while he was attending police academy. It was love at first sight and they are still desperately in love. Jack sets the newspaper on his lap and puts his arm around his wife's shoulders.

"I just hope Jenny isn't bothered too much by that program she watched," says Carol. "You know how she wakes up crying sometimes."

"I think she'll be fine." Her husband is reassuring. "Do you want me to have a talk with her?"

She squeezes his hand. "I'll go up and read her a story after she has a bath."

"You are a good mom."

They engage in a loving embrace.

Chapter 3

The Human Behaviour class is held in a large auditorium with rows of seats graduating to the accesses and overlooking a broad stage. Black curtains at the back of the stage conceal whatever is behind. About one hundred and seventy students attend this night session.

Justin descends a flight of stairs and sits in the best available seat. Students rush into the auditorium behind him while others anxiously sit and wait for their instructor.

Dr. David Sinclair-Smythe possesses a flair for the unexpected and he is well-known for his stage performances. Some people refer to his conduct as being off-the-wall and eccentric. Both traits are prerequisites for teaching a course in human behaviour.

On one occasion, the doctor graced everyone with his divine presence by being lowered from the rafters dressed as an angel from heaven. Another time, a huge yellow weather balloon rolled onto the stage and came to rest. Suddenly, the balloon exploded with a deafening bang and like magic, there was the doctor. Just two weeks ago, Sinclair-Smythe set himself on fire and ran onto the stage in front of a horrified audience.

Attendants raced to his aid and sprayed him with extinguishers. Unharmed, the doctor bowed and waved to his appreciative students.

The room is filled with anticipation and some students are actually trembling with excitement. The lights dim completely and everyone sits in darkness. It's time for the show to begin.

A student with kinky hair and a bad case of acne sitting next to Justin gives him a tap on the arm and whispers, "Here we go! This guy is a lunatic!"

Music, or some sort of loud noise from the past, starts blasting from two huge speakers at either side of the stage. The curtain at the back of the stage opens slightly revealing a bright light and a lot of smoke. The silhouette of a punk rocker with a huge Mohawk gradually appears and the audience applauds with enthusiasm.

The auditorium lights turn on and the music mercifully stops. Sinclair-Smythe struts to the forefront while the audience, many standing, continues the ovation. He's feeding off their praise. Eventually, the applause dwindles and everyone takes their seat. A hush falls over the room. The doctor is in the house.

Sinclair-Smythe is dressed in a metal-studded vest, bondage trousers with bullet belt, and high-laced boots. He's sporting the tallest spiked hair-do ever erected and his face, neck and arms are covered with piercings and tattoos. His microphone is on and he's ready to preach.

"The voice you are hearing is me, Dr. David Sinclair-Smythe, your professor. My portrayal is David Sinclair-Smythe, a nineteen year old student masquerading as a punk rocker while working on a term paper."

The doctor swaggers around the stage in an arrogant manner sharing himself with everyone in attendance. "Here's the story behind my masquerade. I'm finally of legal drinking age and I'm partying downtown on a Saturday night with a bunch of friends. How I got to be on my own later, I can't recall. I do remember being very hungry. So, I wandered into a late-night pizza place, got a pizza and went back outside."

Sinclair-Smythe continues to move about the stage in lordly fashion. "As I proceeded along the sidewalk, I sensed something was about to happen." He looks at the dazed audience as if to ask, "What do you think happened?"

The students have been well-instructed in classroom management. No shouting out of answers or opinions. Hands must be shown. The doctor would recognize students in turn with a description. Names, of course, were not used. Once recognized, the student would approach the nearest microphone which several have been strategically placed throughout the auditorium.

Hands are now flying in the air.

"Right here in the funky red shirt." Sinclair-Smythe is pointing to a male student in the third row from the front who takes his place at a microphone.

"What happened was you were tapped on the shoulder by a lady of the night and told it would cost just fifty dollars for ultimate pleasure."

The audience responds with laughter and the doctor is quick to reply, "I should have been so lucky. And besides, ultimate pleasure was going for twenty bucks back then."

Laughing continues while eager students wave their hands.

The doctor points to one of the top rows. "Up there with the yellow sweater and hair to match."

A young girl races to the microphone. "An animal escaped from the city zoo and was on the prowl. It jumped in front of you and you were faced with a life or death situation."

"That happens downtown at night all of the time. It doesn't have to be an escaped animal from the zoo," he tells his audience.

Again, laughter fills the room as Sinclair-Smythe retrieves a stool from the side of the stage and returns to the forefront. He sits and continues, "Here's what happened."

A young David Sinclair-Smythe held a pizza like a waiter would a tray as he walked along Main Street late at night. All of a sudden, there's no pizza. A group of kids dressed in punk rocker outfits raced by and snatched it out of his hand. They ran halfway up the block and darted into a secluded alley.

His reaction time was delayed and it took a moment for David to realize just what had happened. He proceeded up the sidewalk to the alley and peered into the darkness. He watched while at least a dozen of these kids devoured his eight slice pizza.

"Hey!" David shouted into the black hole. The kids scattered like rats and disappeared into the cracks. "If I knew you were hungry, I would have given you the pizza. You didn't have to steal it!"

Just as he turned to leave, a deep voice from the darkness stopped him. "You would have given us the pizza?"

A tall figure emerged from the bowels of the alley. He was well over six feet and skinny as a rail. His head was shaved and his eyebrows had been replaced with several rings. His nose and lower lip were pierced as well, and shiny metal objects dangled from his waist belt. Most people would be intimidated or disgusted with his odious appearance.

"Yes, I would have given it to you."

"My friends are hungry," said the skinhead. "Can you get us another one?"

Dr. Sinclair-Smythe rises from his stool and moves methodically about the stage. "One of the temperamental dispositions I've developed over years of studying Behavioural Sciences is empathy," he tells the attentive audience. "Empathy correlates strongly with friendliness and I found this out with the skinhead. Here's this teenage kid, homeless and starving. I agreed to get him another pizza and we became good friends."

A spattering of hands wave in the air and the doctor motions for hands to be lowered. "Please, let me continue."

Sinclair-Smythe returns to his stool and is ready to share more of his story. "The skinhead's name was Big Mac. He was a year younger than I was, eighteen, and had been on the street for three years. The gang he ran with was known as 'The Family'."

The doctor looks very serious as he continues with his lecture. "Our streets are full of young runaways. Why?" He puts up two fingers. "Two significant factors are parental neglect and negative life events. Many kids that lack the support, encouragement, warmth and affection of their parents turn rebellious and they start rejecting 'normal' behaviour. Many kids who go through family separation or loss develop psychological distress and resort to drugs in order to relieve their emotional pain. In both cases, kids abandon the traditional lines of thought, values and experiences. They feel it necessary to embrace alternative ones."

Again, the hands of inquisitive minds soar high in the air. The doctor points into the crowd and announces, "The girl in the green."

Another aspiring collegian takes to the microphone. "What was Big Mac's story?"

Sinclair-Smythe replies, "I knew someone would ask that question and who could answer it more accurately than Big Mac himself."

A spotlight draws everyone's attention to the top of the stairs and they watch a tall gentleman descend the steps and join the doctor on stage. Many of the students recognize the man as Mike Wheeler, general maintenance foreman on campus.

"Most of you know him as Mike," the doctor says. "This is also Big Mac."

An attendant runs a second stool onto the stage during the applause. A microphone is clipped on Wheeler's lapel and he sits beside the doctor.

"I have to tell you," starts Sinclair-Smythe, "I've been trying to get Mike to do this for a few years now. Let's begin by answering the last question." He twists on his stool to face his friend. "What's your story, Big Mac?"

Mike Wheeler addresses the crowd, "When I was fifteen, my older brother fell when we were playing at a construction site and he died from his injuries. My parents put some of the blame for his death on me and they made me feel guilty. Not being able to cope with my home life after the accident, I ran away."

"You say you ran away from home," intervenes the doctor. "How did you hookup with your street gang?"

"Gangs on the street are always on the lookout for recruits. They find you!" Wheeler adds, "I was lucky that 'The Family' spotted me first and took me in."

"Why was that lucky, Mike?"

"You know the answer to that, David. You lived with us."

The doctor faces the audience. "I lived with 'The Family' for almost a month and it was quite a revelation. But, I'll talk about that later. First, to find out why Mike was lucky hooking up with 'The Family', we need to look at the dynamics of street gangs. Some gangs have deviant ideologies such as anti-authoritarianism and anti-establishment. Others align themselves with the social movement of anarchism, communism or neo-Nazism. These groups are directly associated with vandalism, violence and street crime. Big Mac's family, although some of its members had a critical view of the world, were primarily concerned with an individual's right to freedom and, of course, survival."

Mike adds, "We got into some mischief because we had a lot of time on our hands. We definitely had to beg, borrow and steal. We weren't violent and we never hurt anyone physically."

A male student in the front row reacts to the doctor's pointing finger and asks, "Who made up 'The Family' and what were their stories?"

"Kids came and went all of the time," answers Mike. "Some ran away from foster homes or abusive parents. Some got a taste of life on the street and ran back home. Many stayed for a very long time." He takes a moment to recall. "The oldest member of our family was A&W. Nobody used their real names. We used nicknames associated with restaurants and fast-food chains. Anyway, A&W was our leader and we followed his direction because he had the most experience. Members like Little Caesar, Subway Harvey and Wendy were there before I came and they were still there when I left."

Justin has been sitting in the audience intently listening to Mike Wheeler's story and he wants to know more. His hand goes up.

"Up there with the light blue jacket and all the curls." The doctor's finger is aimed directly at Justin who hustles to a microphone.

"How were you able to finally leave 'The Family' and the street behind?"

"That's a long story," says Wheeler, "but I'll try to make it as short as I can. Like David said earlier, we became friends. He would ask me questions about street gangs and I would ask him questions about his home life. David, without him knowing, had softened me up and I was ready to return home. He's the one responsible for getting me a job at the university." Wheeler is visually appreciative.

Sinclair-Smythe comes to the aid of his emotional friend. "Mike returned home and his parents welcomed him back with open arms. They were able to put the past behind them and become a conventional family again. The rest is history as they say."

Students in the audience acknowledge the perseverance of their visitor with a clapping of hands. Mike Wheeler smiles and the doctor waits a moment before continuing.

"Mike's story has a happy ending, but our streets are full of homeless kids who won't be so lucky." He rises from his stool and checks his wristwatch for time. "We've got some unfinished business to discuss. Your term paper."

A rumbling of voices filters through the room.

"Many years ago I sat where you are now," the doctor informs the students. "My assignment was a term paper on the 'Experimental and Psychodynamic Approaches to the Study of Groups'. With Big Mac's help, I was able to infiltrate a gang of street kids and complete my study. My journal entitled 'It's a Jungle Out There' was published and can be retrieved electronically from our school's homepage.

A serious look crosses Sinclair-Smythe's face. "It would be very dangerous to pull a stunt like I did nowadays. Street crimes have escalated and gangs are toting guns." In dramatic style, the doctor removes the Mohawk wig from the top of his head. "And there is no need for you to masquerade."

The teacher returns to his stool and is ready to divulge their assignment. "So far in this course, we have talked about themes and variations in psychology and how each relates to 'real life'. I want you to go out and find a 'real life' person. You will complete a case study analysis of this individual, male or female, by conducting an interview. Your paper will provide a summary of the interview, an assessment of social patterns directly associated with your 'real life' person, and, as a feature in your conclusion drawn from the interview, the theories currently being utilized to assess adult psychology. Some suggestions to get you started are printed on the task sheets."

Most of the students look confused and a rumbling of voices filters through the room once again. Sinclair-Smythe is successful in quieting the audience with hand motions and louder tone of voice.

"I know there are a lot of questions to be answered, but wait until you've had a chance to read your handout. It will explain everything in simple steps." He glances at his wristwatch again. "It's just about break time. Let's call it a night and bring any questions with you next week." The doctor points to the tables below each end of the stage. "Don't forget to pick up your handout before you leave. Have a good night!"

Students support their professor with a standing ovation before the mayhem of dismissal begins. Avid apprentices race to the front, greedily snatching sheets from the tables before heading to the exits. A few others ascend the stage to find out more of Mike Wheeler's story.

Justin waits for the commotion to diminish and then collects his handout. Making his way to Shannon's classroom, he'll persuade his girlfriend without much effort to skip the second half of her class.

*

Jenny tosses her dirty clothes and wet towel into a hamper and leaves the bathroom just as her mother ascends the stairs.

"Hurry up, sweetheart! It's almost nine and past your bedtime."

She scurries into the bedroom ahead of her mom and jumps into bed. Pulling the covers up to her neck, she nestles her head deep in the pillow.

Her mom enters the room. "Do you want me to read you a bedtime story?"

"I'm getting too old for bedtime stories, mom! Could we just talk for a little bit?"

Carol sits on the edge of the bed. "What do you want to talk about?"

"I'm still thinking of those poor elephants," Jenny tells her. "It's so sad. Somebody has to stop it from happening."

"There are a lot of things going on in the world that we have no control over, Jenny." Her mom ponders for a moment. "It's up to the government of each country to protect their animals from hunters. I think they try, but some countries are very large. It would be hard to catch all of them." Carol strokes softly on her daughter's forehead.

"Justin could stop them!"

"Maybe he could, but the zoo needs Justin to take care of the animals here." Her mom smiles. "Are you looking forward to going on Saturday?"

Mention of the zoo brings her daughter's head off the pillow. "Can we go early? I want to see all of the animals!"

"Sure we can! Now get some sleep." Carol leans over and gives Jenny a kiss goodnight. The little girl shifts her position and sinks her head back into the pillow as her mom turns the table lamp off. "Sleep well, Jenny!"

*

Justin reaches into the pocket of his jacket for his keys. "I'm glad you're with me," he says to Shannon. "I don't like coming home every night to an empty house."

Inserting the key in the lock, he opens the front door. This is the same house Justin and his father shared for as long as young Lombardi can remember.

Once inside, Justin drops his backpack on the floor, tosses his jacket on a chair and collapses on the couch. He's momentarily forgotten about his girlfriend standing in the doorway. Remembering his manners, he jumps back up.

"I'm sorry, Shannon! Let me help you!" Justin shuts the door behind her and takes the coat from her shoulders. "Can I get you anything? There's diet coke."

"No, I'm fine!" Shannon lowers herself onto the couch. "You were pretty quiet in the car. Is something bothering you?"

Justin sits beside her and sighs, "I really miss my dad."

Shannon is very affectionate and wants to help her boyfriend through this stressful time. She leans over and kisses him on the cheek.

"It must be hard for you."

"There was all this talk about families in class tonight. You know the maintenance guy on campus? Mike Wheeler is his name."

"Big guy?"

Justin nods. "He lived on the street when he was a kid and eventually went back to his parents. His story made me think about my situation, but I don't have a family to go back to."

"You have me!" his girlfriend is quick to point out.

Justin musters a smile. "I know, but you know what I mean."

She could never imagine what life would be like without her family. "Time heals, Justin! You'll get through this!"

"I guess so."

Shannon thinks this a good time to change the subject. "What about your term paper? You haven't said anything about your assignment."

Justin retrieves the handout from his backpack and returns to the couch and Shannon waits as he takes a minute to skim over the outline.

"I have to find a 'real life' person to interview. Here's a list of suggested people. Someone rich and famous; someone of different cultural background; someone in conflict or distress; someone dealing with health problems." An abrupt expression of surprise comes across Justin's face as though he has unearthed a treasure chest.

"What is it, Justin?" Shannon is eager to know the reason for her boyfriend's look of amazement.

"Someone with issues of identity! I know just the person!"

"You know someone with identity issues?"

"A woman who visits the zoo. Her face is painted red and she has the tattoo of an elephant on her forehead."

Shannon responds with excitement, "I've seen her at the mall! She's very strange!"

Justin is surprised. "You've seen her?"

"Some people call her the elephant woman."

Justin shakes his head in disgust. "I wonder why she looks the way she does?"

"I've heard a few things," Shannon tells him. "Some people say she's part of a religious cult. Other people say she snapped after losing her family in a fire and this is her way of mourning."

"Maybe she's hiding from something diabolical."

"Ooooo!" Shannon makes an eerie noise and giggles.

Her boyfriend smiles. "Well, I'm going to find out the real story of why the red face and elephant tattoo. I'm going to interview her."

*

Stirring in her bed, Jenny's mind is active with thoughts and images of bad things happening. She's half-asleep or half-awake and mumbling, "Somebody should stop them. Somebody should stop them," she repeats.

Suddenly, the little girl becomes calm as she slips into a deeper sleep.

Jenny feels peaceful as she flies in the clouds and gazes at the serenity of the landscape below. Her hair and nightgown flow while the cool breeze splashes lightly against her cheeks. Her flight will take her to a faraway place.

Sounds of tranquility will gradually change to noises of turmoil. There is a commotion below. Her help is needed and she descends her flight. With eyes fixed on a forested area, she swoops into the trees and races through the jungle with urgency until she sees a hunting party ahead. Bringing her flight to a stop, she hovers and watches.

Several men are crouching at the edge of the forest and looking into an open expanse. In front of them is a grey mass of elephants by the water's edge and a few elephants are meters away from danger. A matriarch charges towards the intruders, stops short of the trees and lets out a trumpet blast.

Just as the hunter readies to shoot, Jenny's tiny hand lifts the barrel of the gun into the air preventing a shot at the animal.

The hunter turns and sees a little girl in a flowing white night-gown surrounded by an aura of bright light. His glare turns to wonder.

"She only wants to be with her family," Jenny tells the hunter in a soft voice.

The hunting party watches the matriarch as she snorts and ambles away unharmed. A baby calf bounces alongside her mother happy because her mother has returned.

Chapter 4

With coffee mug in hand, Jack Reinhardt positions himself by his office window and gazes at the gargoyles perched atop the building on the other side of the busy street. At the same time, he's wondering what evils might have been released from the McPherson boxes when they were unsealed this morning.

Nowadays, cold cases can be reviewed more accurately and infinitely using DNA samplings. More facts can be found and more questions can be answered. Many cold cases, however, are permitted to slumber until a family member requests the case be reopened.

Criminal investigations had gone on for some time following the McPherson homicide. Daily newspapers revived or reviewed the shocking story for some time, but no additional information came forward and the case grew colder and colder. The puzzling murder of Bryce McPherson was finally sealed shut and embalmed in the basement along with the files of other unsolved mysteries.

Today, the case has been reopened. The body of Bryce McPherson is being exhumed upon the request of his parents. The lab will perform various tests on the remains and the detectives will rummage through boxes of files and crime evidence in hopes of uncovering the mystery.

Jack leaves his office and makes his way to the conference room where all team members except for the forensic pathologist have congregated. Everyone takes their position at the large table while the secretary, Jill Rosseter, begins handing Jack files from a box. He quickly leafs through each file, mostly pictures of the crime scene, and passes them on.

While files circulate around the table and team members examine the gruesome photos, Jack holds up a sheet of paper.

"I have a list here of samples Jill has already sent to the lab which includes sections of bloodied carpet and an elephant paperweight presumed to have been the murder weapon." He sets the list on top of a heap of files in front of him. "We have police records, transcripts, coroner reports and you name it."

Reinhardt eases into his chair and takes a moment before summarizing in a few words what is already known. "We've got a victim, rich guy who gets his head bashed in. His wife is at home in another part of the house and the house attendant finds the body."

"The butler did it," surmises Dick Newland.

William Cooney is quite amused and congratulates his mate on solving the mystery.

"He is definitely a suspect," says Jack. "What did you find out about him, Howard?" he asks the computer whiz.

Hirsch reads from his notes, "The butler's name is Spencer Barnes. He's still alive and living in the city." Reaching across the table, he hands Reinhardt a piece of paper. "Here's his address, Jack."

"Great! We'll look him up first," responds the detective as he sticks the piece of paper in his shirt pocket. "Anything on the victim's wife?"

"Anna McPherson maiden name Bello," says Hirsch. "She and her husband lived with his parent's until the time of the murder. She left town shortly after being cleared of any wrong-doing." He looks at Jack with a puzzled expression. "It appears as though she's dropped off the face of the Earth. I can't find her, Jack!"

"Sounds like a prime suspect to me," offers Jill. "Why wasn't she convicted of the murder, Jack?"

"She wasn't convicted because there wasn't enough evidence to bring her to trial," answers Jack. "The testimony given by the house attendant helped exonerated her of any crime."

Newland asks, "What about McPherson's best friend?"

Hirsch looks at his notes again. "Ian Wilcox. Still lives in the city. They know him downstairs, Jack. He's been run in for drunk and disorderly conduct, did some time for drug possession a few years back and he's been tested HIV positive."

"Sounds like a real loser," says Newland.

Howie hands Wilcox's address to Jack who stuffs it into his shirt with the other piece of paper. "Good work, Howard!"

"I read in the police report that the butler claimed he saw somebody running from the house on the night of the murder," says Cooney.

"We'll have to follow up on that claim when we talk to Barnes," Jack tells the Scotsman.

Asking for public assistance in solving crimes is common practice by the police force. Jack turns to his secretary and says, "Jill, inform the media and get the ball rolling there." He looks to the computer whiz and says, "Howard, see what you can do about finding Anna McPherson." He eyes Newland and Cooney. "We'll get our investigations underway and I'll contact the lab in a couple of days to see what forensics has come up with." Detective Reinhardt rises from his chair and announces, "Okay, everyone, we all have jobs to do."

Team members, all in acceptance of their assignment, get to their feet and prepare to leave. Jill will notify the television station, the radio station and the newspapers. A cash reward will be offered for information leading to the arrest and conviction of the person or persons responsible. Hirsch will hack away at his computer and try to unearth the whereabouts of Anna McPherson. Detectives Newland and Cooney will stick around and anxiously await further instructions from their leader.

"By the way, Coon," says Reinhardt. "I haven't had a chance to ask you how your first night's stay was."

"It was good, Jack," says Cooney. "I stayed at Dick's place."

"I thought he would be better off staying at my place rather than in a stuffy bed and breakfast," Newland tells his partner. "There's no way Coon could stay in a hotel downtown. The Glasgow City Police didn't give him much of an expense account."

"Are you sure everything is going to be okay staying at Richard's?" Jack immediately glances at Newland and corrects himself. "I mean Dick's place?"

"It will be just fine, Jack," Coon reassures him.

Reinhardt hoists a stack of files from the table and tucks them under his arm. "Are you guys just about ready to go for lunch?"

The detectives ride the elevator to the main floor. The door opens and they step into a spacious lobby. Marble floors, brass fixtures and decorative walls and ceilings add to the elegance of this majestic building.

"Hold the elevator." The commanding voice belongs to Captain Maddox. Cooney reacts to the order and prevents the door from closing.

"Keeping busy, Jack?" asks Captain Maddox.

"Just opened a new box this morning," replies Detective Reinhardt. "We're just on our way to lunch. What about you?"

"You remember Dr. Sinclair-Smythe?" Maddox is referring to the gentleman standing beside him. "We need his expertise in another case."

Sinclair-Smythe often assists the police with determining the criminal behaviour of psychopaths and sociopaths involved in murderous crimes. He and Jack have been familiar with each other since high school.

"Detective," says the doctor without extending his hand in greeting. "Criminal behaviour isn't my specialty, but I like to help out when I can." The doctor's conceit is quite apparent. "The elevator, Captain!" he summons.

"Yes, we better go," responds Maddox. "See you later, Jack!"

Cooney steps aside and allows the door to close behind them. The Scotsman is obviously taken by the Captain's imposing appearance. "So that's Captain Maddox!"

Walking towards the front exit, Dick wants to know, "Who was that asshole, Jack?"

"David Sinclair-Smythe. He teaches at the university."

"Thinks very highly of himself," says Dick.

"He's a shite," says the Scotsman.

Emerging through a revolving door, the detectives venture outside and into the congested sidewalk. It's just after twelve noon and workers on their lunch break wearing ID tags pinned to a lapel or dangling from a neck chain race about. The bustling city is home to a few million people and they all appear to be in the core area right at this moment. The lunch deli is two blocks upstream on Main Street and the detectives dive into the flow of bodies.

Detective Reinhardt finds it difficult to ignore the demoralizing sights and problems common to this big city. Less-fortunate souls stumble around with their permanent scars of hardship. Loiterers and laggards linger about in doorways. Garbage bins in alleyways fill the air with their nauseating odor. Buses pump exhaust fumes into the atmosphere as they pull away from transit shelters. The honking of cars and music blaring from store fronts all contribute to the pollution downtown.

The wail of an emergency vehicle and its blinking red lights alerts Jack. Newland is right beside him, but no William Cooney. Jack feels responsible for the safety of his rookie team member. "Where's Coon?"

Looking in every direction, Dick finally spots his friend peering into the display window of a novelty shop that specializes in party supplies and adult accessories. "Hey, Coon!" he shouts.

"I ain't no coon, muddafukka!" a deep voice rumbles from an alcove.

Dick is approached by a well-built black man wearing a muscle shirt, baggy trousers and a skull cap on his head. The detective desperately points in the direction of his Scottish friend and stammers, "I was talking to him."

Jack is about to reveal his police badge when Cooney arrives and offers his hand in friendship. "My name is Detective William Cooney," he tells the man. "All my mates back home call me Coon."

The man is confused by Cooney's bold behavior and strong Scottish accent. He takes a step back and wipes the front of his shirt as if to rid himself of an insect. "Get away from me foo' or I'll put a cap in yo' ass." Slowly turning away, the man mumbles several terminal threats and retreats to his alcove.

Jack spins around and quickens his pace towards the deli while Dick and Coon hurry to keep up. They are mindful of Jack's agitated temperament and Dick offers words of vindication. "Sorry, boss!"

Reinhardt wheels about and looks directly at William Cooney. "I'm sorry," he whispers, "but I can't get comfortable referring to you as Coon. Besides, we're liable to get knifed."

Cooney recognizes the detective's plight. "You can call me Willy. A few of my mates back home call me Willy."

"Anything but Coon," insists Jack.

Dick places an arm around the Scotsman's shoulder, smiles and concludes, "Willy it is!"

The cafeteria-styled deli is situated in a downtown mall and the mall is swarming with activity. The detectives contend

ELEPHANTS CRY

with a long lineup, purchase their lunch and find a table in the food court.

Cooney is delightfully engaged with a plate of corned beef and hash when Dick asks, "So, Willy! What were you checking out in the novelty shop window? You like that sort of stuff?"

"I fancy a magazine once in a while but I'm not a wanker," admits the Scotsman.

Jack interjects, "Could we talk about something else while we eat?"

"No!" grunts Dick and he gestures with his eyes. "Look behind you! Shit! Here it comes!"

"Ah, it's Jack and his little appendage." The voice is loud and effeminate. A black dude wearing a wide-brimmed hat, white chiffon blouse and yellow stovepipe slacks is all smiles. He obviously experiences gender confusion and doesn't appear the least bit concerned.

"Hello, Wizard!" greets Reinhardt.

"Ah, I see you're walking around with your Dick out again."

"You're very funny, Beverly!" Dick prefers to use Wizard's birth name when retaliating. There's been a war of words going on between the two of them for quite some time.

"Wizard, I'd like you to meet Willy," says Jack. "Willy, this is the Wizard of Ahs."

"Ah, you have a Dick and a Willy." He follows with an obnoxious laugh.

"The Wizard of Oz is one of my favourite movies," remarks Willy. "Do you fancy yourself as a wee wizard?"

Willy's Scottish speech has confused their visitor. "Ah, what did he just say?" Wizard asks Jack.

"It's not Wizard of Oz as in O Z," Jack spells it out for Cooney. "It's A H S because he always says ah."

"Au contraire, mon ami!" exclaims Wizard. "It's A W E S because I awe people with my knowledge and my brilliance and, of course, my presence."

51

The Wizard's delivery is very flamboyant and Dick looks like he's just bitten into a lemon.

"What do you want, Beverly?"

Ignoring anything Dick has to say, Wizard asks, "Anything for me, Jack?"

Wizard is on the payroll as a snitch and Jack often uses his street smarts when investigating crimes. "Nothing right now," the detective tells him.

Taking a peek at his shiny and cheap imitation Rolex watch, Wizard says, "Ah, time to fly." He starts to flutter away. "See you and your appendages later, Jack." His flight will take him through the crowded corridor and out of sight behind a kiosk.

"What a flamer!" Dick exclaims with disgust.

"Who is he or she anyway?" asks Willy.

Jack answers, "He's another member of our team."

"Bloody hell!" declares the Scotsman.

"You're catching on, Willy!" says Newland and then asks, "Where in bloody hell are we going next, Jack?"

"Let's go visit Spencer Barnes."

Chapter 5

Dick Newland navigates the unmarked police car around a corner. "What number is it, Jack?"

Detective Reinhardt fumbles for the piece of paper and pulls it from his shirt pocket. "Twelve twenty-six." He points. "It should be just up here on the right."

The car comes to a stop and the detectives examine the middle-class neighborhood. Spencer Barnes resides in a quaint home with a sun porch frontal. The yard is well-groomed and decorated with a shagbark hickory tree, two pagoda dogwoods and several flower beds.

Detective Cooney sits in the back seat and is impressed with the home's neatly trimmed appearance. "Not too shabby."

"What's the game plan, Jack?" asks Newland.

"You guys wait here while I go in. We'll put a tail on him later."

Police units have routine and protocol. Each has its leader and followers. Jack is in command of this unit and the front man who approaches suspects and interrogates witnesses. His men need to remain incognito when pursuing individuals associated with a crime. Dick and Willy will stay out of sight so they won't be recognized if ever seen by Barnes in public.

Jack walks up to the front porch and rings the doorbell. After a short juncture of time, maybe fifteen seconds, he rings the doorbell again.

"I'm coming!" shouts a voice from within. "Be patient!"

The door opens and Jack is confronted by a tall, angular gentleman with a pointed and narrow face. He has a wealth of snow white hair and his outfit is classy as far as house wear goes.

"What is it?" the man asks in a condescending manner.

Jack flashes his badge of recognition. "I'm Detective Jack Reinhardt, Mr. Barnes. I'd like to ask you a few questions regarding the death of Bryce McPherson."

Barnes protests. "I thought that was all over and done with a long time ago." The onetime house attendant for the McPherson's is visibly agitated. "I'd be hard pressed to remember any of the details, detective."

"The case has been reopened and I need to ask you just a few questions if you don't mind, sir?"

Dick and Willy watch as their boss is invited into the home of Spencer Barnes and they will wait patiently in the police vehicle while Jack interviews the butler.

Newland realizes that this is Willy's first stakeout and it won't be long before he gets a bit antsy. "This could take a couple of hours, Willy. Why don't you tell me all about how you became a detective?"

*

The Municipal Zoo was established in the early 1900's and, at present, houses about twenty-five hundred animals representing almost six hundred species and sub-species. The facility is divided into sectors, each representing a world biome and each biome having two or three exhibits. The exhibits themselves are world famous and bring great authenticity in their recreation of natural habitat. Young Lombardi is assigned to the African exhibits which include the African Jungle, the African Desert and the African Forest Trail.

Justin fills buckets with feed in preparation for his Thursday afternoon shift when he spots his supervisor, Peter Simpson. "Hey, Pete! Wait up!"

Pete twists around and glances at his wrist watch. "Finished school for the day already, Justin?" He notices the buckets of bird seed. "Getting ready to feed the fowl I see."

The zoo is home to scores of exotic birds ranging from the chattering Lory bird to the more subdued African grey parrot and keeping their names straight is a real challenge for the young employee.

"Say listen, Pete!" Remember yesterday when I saw the woman with the red face and I asked you who she is?"

"Yes, why?"

"Well, you didn't really answer me. What can you tell me about her?"

"Not much. She comes and she goes." Simpson is hedging and wants to change the subject. "You better get going and feed those birds, Justin. I can hear them squawking from here."

After a short while, young Lombardi is busy tossing seed into the chirpy ringneck parakeet cage when he senses an eerie feeling as if being watched. Closing the cage door, he takes off his protective eyeglasses and gives his eyes a rub. He squints and sees the red-faced lady by the hippo tank.

Aware of being detected, the woman is on the move with Justin in frantic pursuit. He sees her duck behind the zebra barn and races to catch up. When he gets there, she's gone. He runs to several locations where he notices a moving shadow. Each time, the elusive woman has vanished.

Justin stops his chase and scans the area. *There*! The red-faced lady is in full view at the exit gate. Running to catch her, he watches the woman pass through the turnstile and disappear around a corner.

Philip Marlow, Keeper of the Gate, is at his familiar post and patrolling the sidewalk by the guard house that separates the entrance and exit gates. Justin clutches the man's arm.

"Where is she, Phil? Which way did she go?"

"Calm down. Where did who go?"

"The woman with the red face!"

Philip Marlow points nonchalantly. "She's right there at the bus stop."

Young Lombardi gazes in the direction of Phil's gesture and watches as the red-faced lady boards the bus.

"Damn! I want to talk with her!"

"You want to talk with her!" He sounds surprised. "Why?"

Justin slows his breathing. "I want to interview her for my term paper."

"Is that all?" Phil sounds relieved. "You're doing a term paper."

Justin looks puzzled. "What do you mean is that all?"

"Oh, nothing."

Justin senses the gate keeper is definitely hiding something.

"What do you know about her, Phil? Come on and tell me."

"Why don't you ask Pete? He knows more than I do."

"But what do you know?"

"All I know," Marlow says, "is that she has a lifetime pass to the zoo. She comes and goes whenever she wants and she always rides the bus."

Having returned to his post, Justin has fulfilled his duties and is gathering up his buckets when he catches sight of his supervisor.

"Hey, Pete, wait up!"

Peter Simpson stops in his tracks and Justin hurries to him.

"Did all the animals have their feeding frenzy?" his superior asks.

"Say, Pete! I've got something important to ask you."

"What is it?"

"The red-faced lady. What's her story? Phil says you can tell me something about her."

Simpson realizes he has to tell the young man something. He places a hand on Justin's shoulder. "I'll tell you everything I know when we get inside."

The zoo supervisor and his young employee stride towards the main shed, and Pete will use this time to think of what to say. He leads Justin to the locker room and directs him to have a seat. Justin looks up at his boss and curiously awaits the answer to his question.

"The first time I saw the woman with the red face was a few months before your father died. I saw her only a handful of times until just lately. Now she's here every day."

Simpson appears somewhat reluctant to continue and Justin asks again, "Who is she?"

"I don't know," he replies. "All I know is she has a lifetime pass to the zoo. Your father arranged it."

"My father did!" Why would he do that?"

"I don't know exactly. You know how he was always helping people."

Justin is quite surprised that his father may have known this mysterious woman with the red face. "Did you ever see my father and her together talking or anything?"

"No!" His answer is emphatic. "She can't talk!"

Justin continues with his interrogation. "Are you sure about that? How do you know she can't talk?"

"Nobody around here has ever heard her say anything. She comes and goes and she avoids any human contact."

"It's like chasing your own shadow," Justin tells his supervisor. "I saw her earlier and wanted to talk with her, but she kept alluding me."

"Well, she can't talk so forget about it."

Justin is confused by Pete's insistence and wants to know more information. "Do you know why she paints her face red?"

"I know she's nuts!" determines Pete. "I'd stay away from her if I were you!"

Justin is quite disappointed that the red-faced lady may not be suitable for his term paper. At the same time, he's very suspicious of his supervisor.

"Are you trying to hide something from me, Pete?"

*

Dick and Willy sit in the police vehicle waiting for Detective Reinhardt to finish interrogating Spencer Barnes. Barnes is definitely a prime suspect in the murder of Bryce McPherson and Jack has been inside the house for over two hours.

Willy is in the back seat wearing earphones and tapping his fingers in time with the music. Dick is positioned behind the wheel reading the bio on Spencer Barnes and plucking unwanted hairs from his inner ear. Both men are startled by the opening of the car door.

"Let's go for a coffee!" suggests Jack.

His partners snap to attention. Willy puts the Ipod in his pocket and Dick turns the key in the ignition.

"So, what did the butler have to say, Jack?" asks Newland as the car pulls away.

Spencer Barnes hasn't changed his story from the original report he provided at the time of the murder. He told Detective Reinhardt that he was in his living quarters at the rear of the McPherson's house for most of the night and that Anna McPherson was upstairs in her bedroom. Bryce McPherson and his friend Ian Wilcox were in the den having a drink when they started to quarrel. Wilcox was livid about something and stormed out of the house. Hearing the two men argue, Barnes went to the den and saw Bryce alive. When he went to check on Bryce an hour later, Barnes found him dead on the floor and claims he saw someone running from the house.

"Did Barnes say anything about Anna McPherson and where she might be now?" asks Willy.

"He didn't say much about her except that she had nothing to do with the death of her husband. Barnes said that Anna left immediately following her ordeal and he hasn't heard from her since."

"Do you believe him, Jack?" asks Dick.

Detective Reinhardt found Spencer Barnes non-complacent during the questioning and somewhat evasive. "I think he knows more than he's telling us!"

Chapter 6

The Reinhardts live in a suburb several miles from the vast urban area of downtown. Community support has been a valuable asset in making their neighborhood a fairly safe and comfortable environment for everyone to experience. Jenny attends a school just a few blocks from home. Like many of the parents, Carol Reinhardt drives her daughter to school for her own piece of mind. Jenny was very quiet in the car this morning.

Jenny sits at her desk in the classroom. Friday morning announcements have been aired and her classmates are busy writing in their journals. The teacher, Miss Gilmore, is circulating and making sure that everyone is on task. Jenny's pencil isn't moving.

"Is anything wrong, Jenny?" asks Miss Gilmore. "You don't look very happy."

"I'm okay, Miss Gilmore. I might be a little tired, that's all." But there is something bothering the little girl.

Miss Gilmore motions with her index finger for the young student to follow her. Jenny responds and nestles next to her at the teacher's desk.

"I want you to tell me what's bothering you," whispers Miss Gilmore.

Jenny tells her teacher about the bad things that happened to elephants on the television documentary and of the dream she's had the past two nights.

"Somebody has to do something, Miss Gilmore!"

"Do you want to do something about it?"

"What can I do? I'm only thirteen. Well, almost thirteen."

"You could write a letter to a politician or a newspaper editor. You could make it the topic of your speech."

Jenny perks up. "My speech!"

"Public speaking is coming up in November. That gives you just over a month to work on it."

The idea of writing and speaking about elephants has Jenny anxious.

"I'm going to start this weekend. I can get my mom to help me and my sister's boyfriend. He works at the zoo."

Miss Gilmore tells the youngster that if she feels strongly about something, then she should do something about it and that it doesn't matter how old you are.

"Thank you, Miss Gilmore! I feel better already!"

*

"What time is it?" asks Willy.

Dick peers at his watch. "Almost ten."

Detectives Newland and Cooney have been staked out just down the street from the residence of Spencer Barnes for hours and impatiently waiting for some activity. Willy is in the passenger seat of the unmarked police car listening to his British tunes while Dick's eyes are fixed on the butler's home.

"Fasten your seat belt, Willy!" exclaims Dick. "It's show time!"

Cooney is wearing his earphones and needs a tap on the arm from his partner. Dick's finger directs Willy's attention to a black sedan backing out of the driveway.

"Is it him?" The excited Scotsman plucks the earphones from his head.

"Here we go!"

Willy is very anxious. "I wonder where he's going to take us?"

"The deal is to stay calm."

The Scotsman formulates his words. "I need to stay calm."

"We're not in any hurry. We'll just stay close and keep our eyes open."

"Keep our eyes open," Willy repeats in a calm voice.

Barnes leads the police away from his quiet neighborhood and onto a busy thoroughfare. As Dick settles in a few car lengths behind Barnes, he makes the observation, "You don't sound so Scottish when you're calm, Willy!"

When conducting police surveillance and tracking, everything is recorded – times; dates; routes taken; places visited; people contacted. William Cooney will be responsible for keeping these records in a daily chronicle.

"Where are we now?" asks Cooney. Looking ahead, he answers his own question and scribbles the name of the street from a large sign as they take an off ramp.

Newland follows Barnes into the core of the city and the sedan soon pulls into the parking lot of a large bank. Barnes enters the building while the detectives wait. After a short period of time, Barnes is back in his black sedan and the chase is on.

*

Forensics is the science that deals with the application of medical knowledge to legal questions. Criminal investigations were given a real boost with a stroke of genius by scientists in the field of genetics. Working with DNA and genetic testing have brought about closure to many cold case mysteries in recent years. The forensic pathologist, by examining crime evidence and body remains, can now uncover detailed information. A DNA fingerprint can be established through sample analysis and used to find a similar profile. Profile matches are strong evidence in the court of law. Suspects are identified and cases are solved.

The basement of the Federal Building includes the coroner's office and forensic laboratory. Dr. Vera Hampton is sitting at her desk and reading the coroner's report on the death of Bryce McPherson. She removes her glasses and rubs her eyes just as the elevator door opens.

"Good afternoon, Vera!" greets Detective Reinhardt. "Hard at it I see."

Dr. Hampton is a true professional and she is addicted to her work. "You know me, Jack!"

Reinhardt scours the area. Beyond a transparent partition and in the next room, he notices an autopsy in progress. A group of medical staff wearing white masks and protective glasses huddle over a fresh corpse. Tubes have been inserted into various incisions and vacuums suck liquid samples into clear containers. One of the interns drags a scalpel along the torso, plunges a hand inside and plucks the heart from the chest cavity.

Jack cringes as he makes the observation. "Looks like you're pretty busy down here!"

"We're swamped, Jack. I've hardly had a chance to examine your guy and all of the crime samples are still in the box. I'll start analyzing them hopefully later today." Dr. Hampton rises from her desk. "But I did find something very interesting."

She walks over to a stainless steel table where the decomposed body of Bryce McPherson is on display. Jack follows her and peruses the skeletal remains.

"This is what's left of him."

Vera slips on a pair of plastic gloves and carefully lifts the skull. "There's evidence of two blows to the head. One here," she says pointing to a slight mark on the front of the skull. The doctor gently turns the skull, picks up a bone fragment from the table and fits it into the base of the skull like a jigsaw puzzle. "A small piece of bone has been detached right here. This was the blow that killed him."

Detective Reinhardt concurs by nodding his head up and down.

Vera runs her index finger along a groove in the skull. "You can see the length of impact. He was struck with a long object."

"The coroner's report suggests McPherson was hit from the front and fell backwards hitting his head on the edge of a desk. You don't sound so convinced."

The pathologist smiles. "Not until I do some tests myself."

"Okay, then!" Jack starts for the elevator. "I'll leave you to it."

"I'll let you know when I come up with something, Jack!"

"That would be great, Vera!"

Reinhardt pushes the button for the elevator and Dr. Hampton walks back to her desk. "A sample of DNA from the victim's wife would be really helpful, Jack!"

"That's going to be difficult to provide. We haven't found her yet."

*

Spencer Barnes negotiates a few turns and parks his car on a side street. After fumbling for coins to put in the meter, he enters the metro bus depot. Dick double-parks in front of the building and puts on the flashers.

"Slide behind the wheel, Willy, and watch for Barnes to come out. I'm going in."

Newland hurries into the bus station where he catches sight of Barnes at one of the ticket counters. A transaction of some sort is made and Barnes walks towards the exit. Dick races to the counter and flashes his police badge at the clerk.

"The older gentleman who was just here, what did he want?"

The young clerk is startled. "He wanted an October bus pass. Is something wrong?"

Newland runs for the exit leaving the clerk with a stunned expression on his face.

Detective Cooney shoves over as his partner jumps behind the wheel. "Did you see Barnes come out? Where is he, Willy?"

"Stay calm, remember?" Cooney reminds him. "Stay calm."

Dick is perplexed and he glares at Willy. "Where the fuck is he?"

The Scotsman formulates his words once again. "He's back in his car and hasn't driven away yet."

Newland cranks his head around and detects the black sedan slowly pulling away from the curb. He wheels the police vehicle around and the chase resumes.

Barnes leads the police from the hub of the city in a northerly direction while Willy teases his partner for overreacting.

After a ten minute drive, the sedan negotiates a right turn onto a major street and Detective Newland does the same. With pad and pencil in hand, Cooney asks, "Where are we now?"

They are driving along the longest thoroughfare running east and west across the north end of the city. The Municipal Zoo is located at one end of this well-travelled route and the city's largest shopping centre is located at the other end.

The traffic is incredibly thick and Dick's pulse rate speeds up as he weaves in and out of cars in an attempt to stay close to Barnes.

"Keep an eye on him, Willy!" Dick beeps the horn at the slow moving vehicle in front. "Get moving asshole!"

Newland glances in the rear view mirror, speeds up and veers around the car in front of them.

Willy shouts, "Red light!"

Dick slams on the brakes. Activating the police siren, he proceeds ahead and drives cautiously through the intersection. Dick is frantic. "Where's Barnes? Do you see him, Willy?"

"I was watching for cars on either side of us. I don't see him."

"Shit!" curses Detective Newland as he slaps the steering wheel. "We've lost him!"

The black sedan turns into a rundown apartment complex. The small parking area consists of three vacant and seldom used spaces. None of the residents of these dilapidated one-level units can afford their own car. The superintendent of the building lives in a shabby detached unit and the other nine units form an L-shape that face an inner courtyard filled with weeds and stinking garbage bins.

Spencer Barnes gets out of his car and walks into the seedy courtyard. The proud Englishman moves with a loose jointed gait as he sidesteps deep cracks in the walkway.

A snow white cat rummaging through one of the garbage bins notices the invader approaching and hisses at him.

Barnes arrives at unit number six and tries the door. It's locked from the inside. He raps lightly on the door as he eyeballs the torn screen in the window. He knocks a second time. "Open up, Anna! I've got your bus pass."

The door unlatches and opens slightly.

Barnes looks into the eyes of the red-faced lady and he can see far beyond her grotesque exterior. "How are you, Anna?"

The woman answers with a cough.

"You haven't got rid of that persisting cough yet. Are you feeling okay?"

He is never invited inside and he never expects an answer to his questions. He hands her the bus pass and some money. "Well, I hope you feel better soon."

Anna accepts his handout without saying a word.

"The police were around yesterday asking questions. They're reopening the case. I'll take care of everything, so don't worry."

Without any reaction, the red-faced lady closes the door.

Barnes hears the click of the deadbolt lock and turns to walk away. The snow white cat hisses at him and enters the apartment through the torn screen.

*

The offices of administration at the Municipal Zoo are located on the second floor of the main building. Peter Simpson enters one of those offices and walks up to the secretary.

"He's waiting for you, Pete! Go right in."

Simpson smiles as he passes her desk and enters the director's office.

Samuel Crawford has been the head administer for many years and involved with much of the evolution the zoo has experienced. He sits at his desk where the gate keeper, Philip Marlow, stands by.

"Come in, Pete," invites the director.

Behind Crawford's chair is a wall of windows that provides a full view of the entrance gate and runway. Another wall is filled with video monitors. Surveillance cameras have been positioned in strategic locations around the zoo and the director is able to watch just about everything that goes on at this facility.

"I called you both in here so we can touch base," Crawford tells his good friends. "Have a seat."

While Simpson and Marlow comply, Crawford continues, "Anna has been coming here just about every day now and I saw Justin trying to catch up with her. Then he talked to both of you and I need to know what's going on."

Pete responds, "He's been asking questions, Sam!"

"Like what! What's he asking?"

"Justin wants to know who she is," answers Pete.

"You didn't tell him, did you?" asks Crawford.

Simpson is quick to answer. "No, of course not."

"There is a cloud of mystery hanging over the red-faced lady and I want to keep it that way, gentlemen. Remember our promises to Joe." The director looks confused. "I wonder why Justin is so interested in Anna?"

"He's doing some paper for school and he wants to interview her," answers Marlow.

"Did you tell Justin anything, Phil?"

"I just told him that she rides the bus and she has a zoo pass."

Pete jumps in. "You told Justin I knew something about her."

"Well, you see him more than I do!" says Phil.

"You don't tell him I know something!"

"Hold on!" Crawford stops his friends. "Let's not argue about this!" The director faces Simpson. "You and Justin went to the locker room. What did you tell him?"

"I told him she couldn't talk." Pete appears sheepish. "And I told him his dad had arranged for her lifetime pass."

"Why would you tell him that?"

Simpson hasn't a response and the three men deliberate for a moment.

"Okay!" summarizes Crawford. "Justin is working on a paper for school and wants to talk with Anna. So, let him. She can't talk anyway." He glares at Marlow and Simpson. "In the meantime, gentlemen, do not say a word to Justin."

Phil breaks a short silence and says, "It's a big day for Justin tomorrow."

Pete nods in agreement. "The new elephant arrives!"

"Let's hope everything goes well," says Crawford.

Chapter 7

Elephant exhibits nationwide are always among the most popular at zoos and the elephant community at the Municipal Zoo is growing in size by one. The new addition should arrive shortly after six this morning.

Buster is a five ton African elephant whose age is uncertain due to missing records. He has a history of fighting with other elephants, but there is no indication of any aggression towards people. Someone with authority considered the transfer and change of surroundings the best remedy for the elephant's pugnacity.

Years prior, the Municipal Zoo had incorporated an expansive wildlife sanctuary with a man-made lake for drinking and bathing. Built on twelve hundred acres, this facility provides lots of space and is the best choice for Buster's new home.

The sun begins to rise and a dim light casts over the zoo. Justin enters the main compound with two other employees and they make their way to the receiving area.

The air is brisk and all three are dressed in an orange nylon coat with heavy lining. Pete Simpson follows behind and will observe the operation from a distance.

The zoo's elephant trainer is currently attending seminars in Europe. In his absence, the assistant trainer, Al Markham, will supervise the new arrival. Justin and fellow animal attendant John Duscharne will assist.

The loading gate swings open and a security vehicle enters with hazard lights flashing followed by a truck with a flat-bed float. An enormous animal is squeezed between steel rails on either side of the float and is cobbled with massive shackles and thick chains. A leather harness around its head has a heavy corded bridle on either side and they are tightly fastened to the rails.

When the truck comes to a halt, the driver gets out of the cab, hustles around to the rear of the float and unhinges the ramp.

"Can I get some help here?" he shouts.

The zoo employees are eager to assist and they ready the ramp for Buster's descent.

An official-looking fellow gets out of the security vehicle and grunts, "Who's in charge?"

Al Markham answers, "I guess I am."

The man hands Markham a large key for the leg chains securing the elephant. "He's all yours!"

Justin has never encountered an animal this large and intimidating. The beast is about fifteen feet to the shoulders. Enormous and the colour of a storm cloud, the elephant sways its trunk from side to side like a pendulum. With each gruff snort, his steamy breath is like a puff of smoke from a fire-breathing dragon.

After the shackles and chains are removed, the restraints are eased ever so gradually and the elephant begins to backtrack slowly down the ramp. Al Markham uses a bull hook to gently direct the animal while Justin and his coworker John hold tightly onto the bridles. Unloading an animal this size is a delicate operation and the last thing the zoo employees want is a frightened five ton package.

The ramp creaks under Buster's incredible weight. The elephant grunts loudly several times and jerks his head. Al Markham tugs on the bull hook and Buster takes another step back.

All of a sudden, the elephant rears upward catapulting John Duscharne into the air. Justin is able to keep his footing and firm grip on the bridle. The security official and the driver of the truck shout obscenities at the animal and they quickly retreat to a safe distance.

Justin eyes his coworker wreathing in pain on the ground and notices the distress on the face of the assistant trainer. Taking immediate action, he positions himself directly in front of the elephant. While maintaining hold of his bridle, Justin grabs the abandoned bridle with his other hand. He pulls hard on both bridles and talks in a placating voice, "Easy, Buster! Easy does it!"

The agitated beast responds favourably and backs the remaining few steps down the ramp. Justin slowly releases a bridle and motions for Al Markham to hand him the bull hook. "Good boy, Buster." He softly articulates, "Easy."

Justin leads the elephant in the direction of the outdoor pen where the animal will be kept in isolation for a short period of time.

Pete Simpson, who has been an onlooker the entire time, is impressed with Justin's performance. He glances at the surveillance camera and gives the thumbs up. The director has been watching from his office the whole time.

*

Anxiously waiting in the kitchen for her mom to get ready, Jenny grabs a handful of dry cereal from the box on the counter. "Hurry up, mom!" she shouts with her mouth full.

The little girl spins on the stool like a dog chasing its own tail until a large hand lands on the top of her head. "You're going to loosen something up there if you don't slow down," warns her father.

Jenny stops twirling. "Are you coming to the zoo with us this morning, dad?"

"I can't today, sweetheart! Duty calls!"

Carol makes adjustments to her shirt collar and waist area as she walks into the kitchen. "Are you ready, dear?"

Jenny rolls her eyes as if to say, "What a silly question."

"I guess we're ready to go." Carol walks over and gives Jack a kiss as their daughter races to the side door.

"Have a good time at the zoo, Jenny," says her dad.

"We'll probably go to the mall after," Carol informs her husband. "We could be late."

Opening the door, Jenny hears the motor of a car. "Somebody just pulled into the driveway."

"That's for me," says her dad. "You girls have a great day!" Jack gives his daughter a kiss on the cheek and rushes out the door.

Carol looks at Jenny and asks again, "Are you ready to go, dear?"

Holding the door open for her mom, Jenny rolls her eyes playfully again. "Let's go already!"

*

The McPersons had resided in a posh subdivision comprised of huge homes owned by rich and influential people. Jack wants to inspect the layout of the place that shrouded the brutal murder and he's planned a visit. The police vehicle enters a private driveway and comes to a stop at the front entrance of the old McPherson estate.

The beauty of its architecture was inspired by European design and built to incorporate the natural element of an existing ravine and surrounding woodlands at the rear. The boundaries on either side of this prodigious manor are lined with assorted deciduous trees.

Jack needs to be reminded. "What's the name of the people living here now?"

Willy is prepared and reads from his pad. "Grogan."

Jack raps on the huge wooden door and a distinguished looking man soon answers.

"Are you from the police department? I've been expecting you."

"Mr. Grogan?" Jack offers his hand and the two men shake.

"Yes, I'm Patrick Grogan. Won't you come in, please."

The detectives enter the front foyer. Dick and Willy will observe and take notes.

Mr. Grogan speaks softly. "Your secretary tells me that you are investigating the McPherson murder." He peeks over his shoulder. "My wife Kitty doesn't appreciate that word as you can well imagine."

"Of course, Mr. Grogan," recognizes Reinhardt. "We won't take up much of your time. We just want to take a quick look around if you don't mind."

"By all means, detective. Take as much time as you need." With that, Grogan turns and leaves the policemen to their business.

The spacious foyer has a staircase that leads upstairs and branches to the left and right. Moving over to a pair of sliding doors, Jack opens the entrance to the den where the crime had been committed.

The décor has obviously changed, but the detective needs to examine the physical geography of the crime scene. The length of the room has to be a hundred feet with a large bay window at the front end and French doors leading to a patio at the opposite end. The wall across from the sliding doors has two stained glass cathedral windows that bookend a stone fireplace.

Willy writes in his pad and Dick paws the merchandise on a nearby table while Jack studies the surroundings. Strolling to the back of the room, Jack opens the French doors leading outside.

Dick and Willy wander behind their leader and soon join him on the patio. The backyard consists mainly of a delightful garden. The boundaries of trees render it impossible to see neighboring homes.

"I've seen enough out here," says Jack. "Let's go back inside. I want to try something." Dick and Willy tag close behind as Detective Reinhardt reenters the house.

"Stay here while I check out some of the other rooms," says Jack. "When you hear my signal, start shouting at each other like you're having a heated argument. Make it last for fifteen seconds or so."

Detective Newland responds by grabbing for his two-way radio and bobbing his head up and down like a marionette. "Okay, boss!"

Reinhardt leaves his partners in the den and closes the sliding doors behind him. He ascends the stairs leading to the upper level, veers left and locates the master bedroom where he sends the first signal.

"Okay!" Jack speaks into his walkie-talkie. "Make some noise."

Dick and Willy proceed with a convincing altercation that ends with the detectives laughing at each other.

Jack moves to another room in the upper level and sends another signal to his partners. He takes a moment to inhale the elegance of the upstairs before returning to the main level of the house. He enters the study where the home owner lounges on a sofa with travel brochure in hand.

"Excuse me, Mr. Grogan!"

Grogan peers over his reading glasses. "What can I do for you, detective?"

"Could you show me where the servants' quarters are?"

Rising from his chair, Mr. Grogan smiles. "We don't have any servants, detective."

He motions for Jack to follow and he leads the detective to an area at the rear of the house. Grogan opens a door, flicks a light switch and the room illuminates. "It's my wife's fitness studio."

Jack pokes his head into the spacious cavity. The room is equipped with the latest exercise machines, floor mats and mirrors on every wall.

"This used to be the living space for hired help." Grogan chuckles. "I can't quite afford the luxury of servants."

Detective Reinhardt sends another signal to his partners and waits momentarily. "Do you hear anything, Mr. Grogan?"

"No!" Patrick Grogan appears daunted. "Why?"

"Just checking on things," Jack tells him. "Thank you very much for allowing us into your home, Mr. Grogan." Reinhardt starts for the front of the house. "I think I've seen enough."

Reaching the front foyer, Jack sends one last signal. Voices can be heard coming from the den, but not loud enough to detect exact words. He slides the doors open and interrupts the bogus demonstration. "That's enough, fellas! Let's go!"

Jack turns and faces his host. "Thanks again, Mr. Grogan!" The two men shake hands before the detective departs with his partners tagging close behind.

Once outside, Jack tells Newland, "Bring the car, Dick! I'm going to look at the front of the house."

"Right, boss!"

The police vehicle slowly rolls onto the peaceful boulevard and stops in front while Jack inspects the layout of the well-manicured yard. He wanders down the driveway to the police vehicle, he sits on the hood and gazes at the old McPherson place.

Dick cranes his head from the car window. "What were all those signals about, Jack?"

Spencer Barnes had told Detective Reinhardt that he had heard McPherson argue with his friend Ian Wilcox just prior to the time of murder. He said he heard Wilcox threaten Bryce before storming out of the house. Jack needed to find out where Barnes could have been situated to hear the threat.

"Jog my memory, Willy," says Reinhardt as he points a finger to the right of the old McPherson place. "Who were the neighbors there?"

Cooney reads from his notes. "The Gladstones. Both deceased. They were out of the country at the time of the murder and the house was vacant."

Jack points his finger at the estate on the other side. "So this is where little David grew up?"

Willy again glances at his notes. "Edward Smythe and his wife Irene Sinclair."

"Isn't he the asshole we saw with Captain Maddox yesterday, Jack?" asks Dick Newland.

William Cooney continues to read. "They were vacationing with the McPhersons at the time of the murder. Their house was vacant as well."

Detective Reinhardt removes himself from the hood of the car. "I need to pay them a visit."

*

A resounding roar of dominance emanates from the largest of the lions. People gather around the lair and gaze in awe. Jenny and her mother hurry over to see the king of beasts with head held high and teeth glaring.

"Isn't he amazing, mom!"

The sparkle in the youngster's eyes makes her mother smile.

Before moving on, mother and daughter share an amusing moment watching the cubs playfully rollick about. They will spend the next few hours taking in the sights and sounds of this wonderful place including souvenir shops and refreshment booths.

Entering one of the African exhibits, Jenny squeezes her mom's hand and squeals, "There's Justin!"

Releasing her grip, the little girl runs towards her sister's boyfriend who is standing by the elephant pen. "Justin!" she shouts. "I need to talk to you!"

"Hello, Jenny!" Justin responds with a smile. "What's up?"

By this time, Carol has caught up to her daughter.

"Hello, Mrs. Reinhardt!" says Justin. "Good to see you both at the zoo."

Carol puts a hand on Jenny's shoulder. "She just had to come."

The youngster's excitement is apparent. "I'm doing a speech for school and I need your help! Can I interview you?"

"That's too weird!" remarks Justin. "I'm working on a term paper and need to interview someone."

Jenny is just about to tell Justin about her speech when a man wearing a uniform approaches. "Sorry to interrupt, Justin," says the zoo employee. "Mr. Crawford would like to see you right away."

The little girl's excitement soon changes to disappointment. She looks at Justin with puppy eyes and whimpers, "Do you have to go?"

Carol is quick to amend the situation. "Why don't you come over for Sunday dinner tomorrow, Justin? You and Jenny can talk then."

"That sounds great, Mrs. Reinhardt! Sorry I have to go." He takes a few steps away and turns around. "Check out the new elephant, Jenny! His name is Buster!"

Jenny reluctantly waves goodbye to Justin as he vanishes around the corner of the elephant stronghold.

The twenty foot walls are made of wooden posts woven together with metal strapping. Holes have been cut out at different heights to allow spectators to view the animals within. Jenny and her mom wander over to a window and peek into the pen. The youngster can't help noticing a very strange woman looking in one of the nearby holes.

*

The front door opens and Jack flaunts his credentials. "I'm Detective Reinhardt. Would you be Mr. Smythe?"

"I am Edward Smythe," the elderly man retorts with a hint of snobbery.

A woman stands hidden behind the door. "Who is it, Edward?"

Without taking his eyes away from his caller, Mr. Smythe replies, "It's a policeman, dear."

A frail lady steps from behind the door to have a peek at the detective.

"This is my wife Irene Sinclair."

"I'd like to ask you both a few questions regarding the McPhersons if I may?" asks Jack.

"Oh, my!" exclaims the woman. "It was a terrible thing!"

Detective Reinhardt is invited into their home while Ms. Sinclair continues. "Oh, it was awful. Have a seat, officer. We were vacationing in the Bahamas at this beautiful resort. It was a gorgeous place, wasn't it Edward?"

Jack enters a quaint seating area and takes a chair while Mr. Smythe leans on the fireplace mantel and lights his pipe.

Without waiting for a response from her husband, the woman rambles on. "I remember the phone ringing in our room at an ungodly hour, maybe six in the morning, and it was Helen telling us they had to return home immediately."

"Mrs. McPherson?" Detective Reinhardt needs clarification.

"Yes!" The elderly woman doesn't miss a beat because of the detective's interjection. "Helen said something horrible had happened and they had to leave right away. Well, I insisted that we return home with them. Didn't I dear?"

Her husband answers with a nod of his head.

"We wanted to give them our support and help them through that horrible thing," she tells the detective. "When we got home, we heard about Bryce. We couldn't believe it! We just couldn't believe something like that could happen in our neighborhood. The McPhersons were such nice people."

Ms. Sinclair respires deeply and Jack takes the opportunity to speak. "I'm sure it must have been devastating for both of you."

Mr. Smythe blurts out, "Bryce deserved it!"

His wife is aghast. "You don't mean that, Edward!" She faces Jack. "He doesn't mean that, detective!"

"I most certainly do, Irene!"

Detective Reinhardt would spend the next half hour discussing the despicable character and eventual demise of Bryce McPherson until he mentions their son.

"You know our David?" Ms. Sinclair is pleasantly surprised.

"We attended the same high school," Jack tells them.

"Did you hear that, Edward? He knows our David!"

Mr. Smythe puffs on his pipe and boasts, "We're proud of that boy!"

Jack resists the urge to say what he thinks of little David and stays professional. "Reports say your house was vacant at the time of the murder. Where was David living at that time?"

"He was only nineteen and ..." Smythe is interrupted by his wife.

"He was with those ruffians!" Ms. Sinclair discloses with a tone of disgust.

"David was on location and working undercover on an important assignment. His first published accomplishment if you recall, my dear."

His wife is exasperated. "Edward, he was living with those dreadful street kids and wearing those unsightly clothes. It was awful, detective! David was gone for a whole month."

"All part of the assignment," concludes her husband.

Jack considers this a good time to depart. "Maybe I've asked enough questions for one day. Thank you for all of your input." He rises from his chair and Mr. Smythe accompanies the detective to the front door.

Jack turns and says, "I hope I haven't stirred up any demons."

"Demons!" scoffs Edward Smythe. "What demons could you possibly mean?" Not waiting for an answer, he bids the detective a good day as he closes the door behind him.

*

The red-faced lady sits at the rear of a transit vehicle and smiles as she carries on a silent conversation with her imaginary friends. In her mind's eye, she is with her two young friends and on their way to the shopping mall. Her friends jokingly tease her and she reacts by covering her smile with a white gloved hand.

The bus anchors at the mall's entrance and everyone disembarks including the red-faced lady. The old woman giggles as she hobbles into the huge shopping centre. Once inside, she shakes her head and the giggling stops. There seems to be some confusion as to where to go first. She resists the temptation to turn right and goes left. Her imaginary friends have abandoned her and Anna is by herself.

Jenny and her mom enjoyed their visit to the zoo and are at the shopping mall as planned. Mrs. Reinhardt is picking through clothes in the kid's section and Jenny isn't really interested in any of her mom's selections so far.

Glancing about, the little girl catches a glimpse of a woman over in the next section. It's the same strange woman she had seen earlier at the elephant pen.

"Mom," Jenny whispers with enthusiasm. "Look at that lady over there! I saw her at the zoo today and now she's here!"

Carol continues her fruitless search for an outfit and is oblivious to what her daughter is saying.

Not being able to resist getting a better look at this very odd person, the youngster inches her way closer. Peeking from behind a rack of woman's lingerie, she almost gasps aloud. The woman's face is completely red and she looks very sad.

Jenny feels sorry for the old woman as she fumbles with some merchandise and drops it on the floor. The little girl hurries to pick up the pair of white gloves and hands them to the woman.

"You dropped these," Jenny says timidly.

The red-faced lady takes the gloves and smiles at the little girl. "Bless you, my dear."

"Jenny!" shrieks her mom. Carol is frantic and rushes over to where her daughter is standing. "I've told you never to wander off!"

The old woman turns and waddles away while Carol continues to reprimand her daughter.

"You need to be more careful, young lady! You never know what could happen!" She takes Jenny by the hand and marches her back to the kid's section. Not wanting her mom to be any more upset than she already is, Jenny agrees on an outfit and plans to wear it when Justin comes for supper tomorrow.

Chapter 8

Justin and Shannon sit across from each other at the patio table holding hands and exchanging pleasantries. A nylon umbrella partly shades them from the sun on this glorious Sunday afternoon.

Arrangements have been preplanned. Shannon gets to coddle her boyfriend for the first hour or so and then Jenny gets to sink her claws into him. The little girl is inside the house and keeping a close eye on the action from a kitchen window.

Justin received the good news of a promotion yesterday from Mr. Crawford and is sharing the details with Shannon.

"It's going to be tough living up to their praise and expectations."

Shannon is proud of him and offers words of encouragement. "You'll do just fine, Justin!" She squeezes his hands. "I think it's great!"

They continue with their conversation until Shannon finally peeks over and notices her sister peering from the window.

"Are you ready for the little lioness?"

"I guess so. Let her loose."

Catching sight of her older sister coming towards the house, Jenny quickly retrieves her Ipad and races outside.

"My turn!"

Jenny runs past Shannon and assumes the vacated spot at the patio table across from Justin. She immediately commences her interview.

"When did you start working at the zoo and what do you do there?"

Justin answers each question while the youngster rapidly types. Justin tells her about his duties and the creatures he cares for. Like osmosis, Jenny is absorbing his love and passion for animals.

Jenny asks him about the funniest things that have happened at the zoo.

Being pooped on by the monkeys every day is his immediate response and she giggles as Justin recollects several humorous events involving the different animals.

The Reinhardts have decided to dine outdoors on this sunny afternoon and Jack readies the barbecue. Carol finishes the salad in the kitchen and Shannon walks a tray of plates, utensils and condiments onto the patio.

"Mom wants you to clear the table, Jenny! We need to get ready for supper," says Shannon. "You can finish the interview later."

Gripping her Ipad, Jenny grins at Justin and tells him that she still has lots of questions.

Everyone has gathered around the picnic table and Jack asks his younger daughter if she would like to say grace.

Jenny smiles gratefully while everyone joins hands and bows their head.

"Lord, we are thankful for all we are about to receive. We are fortunate to have Justin with us to share this food and we feel safe with you looking over us." Pausing for just a moment, the little girl adds, "Please keep the animals safe. Amen!"

"That was very nice, Jenny!" her mom says.

After a few minutes of enjoying their meal, Jack starts the conversation. "Justin, I suppose Jenny told you all about the TV program she shouldn't have been watching."

The young man looks confused and shakes his head. "No, Mr. Reinhardt, she didn't." He glances at the little girl for an explanation.

It's not Jenny's turn to speak at the table yet and she looks at her mom for approval. "Go ahead, dear!"

Never before has the youngest risen to such status at the dinner table and Jenny is pleasantly surprised for the opportunity.

"Bad men were killing elephants for their ivory."

"Poachers," Justin responds with a tone of displeasure. "They kill more than just elephants."

"Someone has to stop them," pleads Jenny.

"I know," he agrees. "I read about some poorer African countries having too many elephants and they've legalized the killing for their meat."

Jack puts a huge forkful of chicken to his mouth just as Shannon says, "I can't believe people would eat elephant meat." He puts his fork down and cuts the meat into smaller portions.

"Some people disagree with taking wild animals from their natural habitat and keeping them in cages," continues Justin. "At least zoos care for the animals and are essentially saving them from being slaughtered."

Shannon attempts to sway the topic of conversation. "Speaking of zoos, Justin received some good news yesterday."

All eyes focus on the guest of honour as he explains, "A new elephant arrived yesterday and Mr. Crawford, the director, liked how I handled myself."

"You mean he liked how you handled the elephant," interjects Shannon.

"I guess! Anyway, the zoo's elephant trainer is away right now and I'll be taking over his duties. Mr. Crawford suggests that someday I should attend a school and become a full-time elephant trainer."

"Is that what you want?" asks Jack.

"Not really, Mr. Reinhardt," replies Justin. "I'd rather be an Animal Care Specialist and, maybe later, get into Veterinarian Care."

"I saw Buster!" Jenny blurts out. "He's the biggest elephant in the world!"

Justin smiles as he dips a wedge of bread in his bean sauce. "He's a big one!"

Thinking this would be a perfect opportunity to present her important question, Jenny asks, "Do elephants cry, Justin?"

"Honey, let Justin finish his supper," says her mom. "You can save your questions for later."

Late afternoon clouds have rolled in causing a chill in the air and the Reinhardts have retreated inside. Sitting at the dining room table, they're enjoying the dessert course of apple crisp and vanilla ice cream.

Jenny is very anxious to know the answer to her question and Carol detects her daughter's impatience. "Let Justin finish his dessert, dear!"

"I don't mind if you don't, Mrs. Reinhardt," says Justin. "I enjoy talking about the animals."

Carol shrugs her shoulders and smiles with approval.

Justin knows firsthand that many of the smaller animals in the African exhibits are capable of expressing emotions. He's been feeding and cleaning up after them since he was a young lad. But he isn't too familiar with the larger animals.

"I haven't worked with elephants until yesterday, Jenny. If you let me spend some time with them, I'll know the answer to your question for sure."

His reply has the little girl somewhat dismayed. "Okay," Jenny groans. "My speech isn't due for a while. I guess I can wait."

Carol recognizes her daughter's disappointment. "C'mon, Jenny! You can help me clear the table while Shannon escorts our guest to the living room."

Justin and Shannon sprawl on the couch together and he sighs with some discomfort. "I'm stuffed!"

She snuggles close and the young lovers spend a quiet moment thinking nice thoughts. "Mom and dad are happy with your plans of becoming a veterinarian," says Shannon.

"You think so?"

She answers by kissing him on the cheek and resting her head on his shoulder.

Jenny's interview had been the main focus of conversation at the dinner table and Shannon remembers Justin's important term paper.

"I forgot to ask you about your interview, Justin! Did you talk to the woman with the red face yet?"

Justin perks up. "I saw her a few days ago, but I couldn't catch up to her!"

Shannon giggles. "She must be a fast runner."

"Maybe," he says with a smile. "It was like chasing a shadow! Every time I thought I caught up to her, she wasn't there anymore!"

"Very strange!" remarks his girlfriend.

"The red-faced lady would be perfect for my interview, but Pete says she can't talk."

Just then, Jenny walks into the living room and overhears Justin's last remark about the red-faced lady.

"Yes she can. She talked to me."

Justin swings around. "What? When did she talk to you?"

"Yesterday at the mall," answers Jenny.

Justin can't believe what he is hearing and is very anxious to know. "What did she say?"

Shannon places a soft hand on her boyfriend's shoulder to calm him down. "Relax, Justin! You're going to burst a vein."

He responds by easing back in the couch while Jenny tells them about the red-faced lady dropping a pair of white gloves on the floor and of her running over to pick them up.

"When I handed them to her, she thanked me."

Shannon asks, "What exactly did she say to you, Jenny?"

"Bless you my dear," replies Jenny.

Justin repositions himself on the edge of the couch. Needing reassurance, he takes the little girl's hand and asks calmly, "She can talk, can't she?"

Jenny nods affirmatively.

Jack and Carol Reinhardt hover over the kitchen sink engaged in one of life's domestic pleasures. He prefers to wash and her chafed hands appreciate the gesture.

"I'll have to visit the zoo sometime to watch Justin in action," Jack tells his wife.

"Jenny would love it if you did." She receives another dinner plate from her husband to dry. "What about the case you're working on, Jack? Did you hear anything on the whereabouts of the victim's wife yet?"

His work is always discussed in private and away from the ears of children. A few nights ago, Jack had shared some of the grim details of the McPherson murder mystery with Carol.

Dragging a scouring pad along the length of the greasy barbecue grill, Jack replies, "Nothing yet."

Carol appears disconcerted and she shivers her upper body. "I think it's so creepy!"

"The McPherson case?"

"The thought of it happening on the same day as Jenny's birthday."

"That's right! I never thought of that."

Shannon leads Justin into the kitchen with Jenny close behind. "Justin has to go," she announces.

"So soon?" asks Carol.

Justin explains, "I'm going to pop into work and check on Buster before I head home."

"Did you complete your interview?" asks Jack as he places the shiny grill in the dry sink and wipes his hands with a dish cloth.

Jenny is quick to respond, "We're going to finish the interview at the zoo next Saturday if that's okay with you, mom?"

"You want to go to the zoo again this Saturday?" asks her mother.

"I want to go too, mom!" says Shannon. "Justin is in charge of his first Elephant Walk!"

"After I finish my interview with Justin, he's going to interview the lady with the red face for his term paper," Jenny tells her parents.

Jack questions, "Lady with the red face?"

"You should see the poor woman, Jack," says his wife with empathy.

Pointing to her forehead, Jenny says, "Yeah and she has a tattoo of an elephant right there!"

Carol explains to her husband how they encountered the red-faced lady at the mall yesterday.

"Sounds very strange," remarks Jack.

"Very strange and scary, Mr. Reinhardt!" says Justin. "That's why I want to interview her."

"You should see her, dad!" exclaims Shannon.

"I see enough strange people in my line of work, thank you!" her father replies.

Chapter 9

Detective Reinhardt methodically arranges the clutter of paper-work on his desk as thoughts of the McPherson mystery jump around in his head. Dick and Willy soon fill the entrance to his office and Jack summons them to enter.

"Morning, boss!" greets Newland as the detectives have a seat across form their superior.

"How was your Sunday, Jack?" asks Cooney.

"Just fine, Willy." He prefers to get down to business right away. "Here's what we've got so far, gentlemen. Barnes stops at a bank, goes to the bus station, then you lose him."

Dick looks sheepish and apologizes again. "Sorry, Jack!"

"I want you to keep a close eye on him for the next couple of days," Reinhardt tells his men. "Like I said before, something tells me he knows more than what he told me."

Barnes has already been caught in a lie. The original transcript has the butler in the rear of the house on the night of the murder. Jack knows Barnes had to have his ear pressed against the sliding doors of the den in order to hear Wilcox threaten McPherson.

"We won't lose him again," promises Dick.

"Barnes didn't have a good word to say about the victim," Jack informs the detectives, "and his sentiments are shared by those of Edward Smythe. It appears as though Bryce McPherson was a drinker, an abusive husband and not well-liked. He definitely had a lot of enemies."

"That makes the case more difficult," calculates Cooney.

"That it does, Willy," agrees Jack. "It sounds like he was screwing up at work, screwing around on his wife and his father kept bailing him out of trouble."

Newland snickers. "Sweet deal living in a mansion with mommy and daddy. "What did the neighbors tell you about Anna McPherson, Jack?"

Reinhardt tells the detectives that they didn't see much of her at all. "I guess she never came outside. Barnes said she had some health problems and was taking anti-depressants."

Jill Rosseter enters the office with some papers, hands them to Jack and he thanks her. She turns and, without recognizing the two detectives, leaves the office.

Willy makes the observation and says to his mate, "I don't think she likes you very much."

Jack bends his elbow and peeks at his wristwatch. "I'm going to try and catch Wilcox at home this morning. You guys keep an eye on Barnes and try not to lose him this time."

Detectives Dick and Willy have their orders. They stand and walk towards the door. Dick whispers to his mate, "We better not screw up, Willy!"

"You make it sound like it was my fault," the Scotsman whispers back.

They continue their quiet argument as they exit the office.

*

The city core is surrounded by various ethnic neighborhoods. The city went through a stunning cultural renaissance beginning in the 1950's triggered by waves of Italian immigrants. Joe Lombardi's parents were among them.

Ian Wilcox resides in an apartment above a Chinese restaurant located a few minutes from the police station. With buildings squeezed together, there's little patchwork of green grass in this area of the city.

Jack opens a door adjacent to the restaurant's entrance and walks up a flight of creaking steps. Upon reaching the third floor, the detective knocks on a door displaying the number six. The door opens and he flashes his badge.

"Ian Wilcox?"

Jack eyes a scruffy man in his sixties wearing a blue flannel shirt opened at the front to reveal a black Aerosmith t-shirt underneath and his long grey hair is pulled back into a ponytail.

"I'm clean, man! What's the hassle?" The man definitely looks and sounds as if he's locked in a generation or two gone by.

"I want to ask you a few questions about your old buddy Bryce McPherson," says Reinhardt.

Wilcox acts half asleep and confused. "Bryce?"

Taking a few steps back, he plops down on a well-used couch. He sparks up a cigarette and a puff of smoke fills the dingy one-room apartment. The drawn shades on the windows help to insulate Wilcox from the outside world.

Jack sits on an unstable chair with ripped upholstery and stares at a person who appears to be two valiums and two stiff drinks into the morning.

"I miss him, man!" says Wilcox.

"What can you tell me about him?"

"He shouldn't have gotten married in the first place, man! I told him, but he never listened to anything I had to say. Served the bastard right."

"Why? Why shouldn't he have gotten married?"

He takes a drag from his cigarette. "He was a player, man! He liked the ladies." Wilcox shakes his head. "We were having a blast until he hooked up with that bitch. She killed him and got away with it, man!"

Jack takes his time questioning Wilcox. "I've been told Bryce was abusive. Did he ever hit Anna?"

"He hit everyone with that fucking belt of his," Wilcox is quick to disclose while rubbing the side of his face.

"Did he ever hit you, Ian? You don't mind if I call you Ian?"

"That's my name, man!"

Ian Wilcox rubs the side of his face as if to soothe a pain that won't go away before telling his story.

McPherson and Wilcox entered a mens' club. Not your typical striptease bar but a high-classed establishment. There was no denim casualness to this exotic playpen. Business executives and local celebrities were all well-groomed and impeccably dressed. No chugging draught beer from plastic cups in this place. Everyone sipped flavoured martinis from stemmed glassware or well-aged scotch from tumblers. Hot pink walls, black glass chandeliers and leopard skin sofas were all part of the gaudy ornamentation and tacky elegance.

The two players surveyed the surroundings as they were ushered to their table. A dancer on stage wearing only a white and furry bikini bottom glided suggestively up and down a brass pole while customers gawked and drooled. Another dancer wrapped herself around a chubby client in a well-choreographed lap dance while his friends pawed at the girl and laughed. Other girls wearing slinky garments that revealed their wares weaved through the aisles.

Bryce and Ian sat down and a topless waitress took their order. Wilcox pointed at two elevated cages where dancers painted in zebra stripes performed. "Check out those creatures, man! This is my kind of safari!"

"Let's bungle in the jungle, partner!" McPherson reached across the table and gave Wilcox a high-five.

Their first drink dried up quickly in the scorching heat of eroticism. As Bryce ordered another round, Ian asked, "Where's your wife today?"

"I don't know. The bitch is probably at the zoo with her boyfriend." McPherson looked disturbed. "Don't ask me shit like that!"

Wilcox knew he had hit a sore spot. "Sorry, man!"

They had a few more drinks while Bryce kept his sights on one of the girls. He finally rose from the table and smoothed over to her. His friend watched the hunter and his prey disappear into the executive lounge where anything goes for a price. Wilcox waited impatiently and continued to drink.

McPherson had left his pager on the table and it beeped. He wore it on his belt during work hours and he was supposed to be working now. Wilcox thought it may be of some importance, so he picked up the pager and went to search for his comrade.

The executive lounge had an open area of couches and tables where the cheaper activity went on. Along each wall were cubicles with curtains drawn. This was where the more expensive and nastier enterprises took place.

Wilcox was drunk enough to check each stall and he was successful on his third attempt. He pulled the curtain aside and saw the naked body of a female being ravaged from behind. Bryce had removed his belt and used it to spank her backside.

When McPherson realized his hideaway had been invaded, he lashed out with his belt and struck Wilcox across the face.

"Never interrupt me when I'm hunting!"

Detective Reinhardt watches Wilcox rub his cheek. "What did you do when your best friend hit you with his belt?"

Wilcox's anger is apparent. He grabs for another cigarette and shakes while lighting it. "I told him never to hit me again."

"Did he ever hit you again?"

Wilcox inhales deep in an attempt to calm himself. "Once, man!" he admits. "It was the night he was murdered."

"Tell me about the night of the murder, Ian!"

Once again, Wilcox drifts into the past to tell his story.

The den was dimly lit. The flickering flame of the fireplace engaged with the mounted heads of wildlife on the walls casting spooky shadows throughout the room. McPherson and Wilcox sat on a leather sofa with drink in hand.

"I phoned you to come over because I need someone to talk to." Bryce was in a drunken stupor and he slurred his words.

"What's bothering you, man? You've been acting strange lately." Along with his increase in alcohol consumption, Bryce had become angry and unpleasant to be with. "What's the deal?"

Bryce appeared agitated and raised his voice. "The deal is everybody's an asshole, even you!" He got up with difficulty and staggered to the stereo.

"What's your problem, man?"

"My problem is there's no music." Bryce fumbled with a few albums and chose one. "Remember this song?"

He took the vinyl disk from the cover and placed it on the turntable. The song began and Bryce sang along. "I'll never be your beast of burden." He faced his friend and moved to the centre of the room. "Sing, Ian," he commanded.

Wilcox wasn't in the singing mood. Instead, he watched as Bryce started his elephant dance. Bryce removed his belt, waved it over his head and almost backed into the fireplace. He began dancing more aggressively until he stumbled into the oak desk.

Wilcox jumped to his feet and went to his friend's aid. "C'mon, man! You're going to hurt yourself."

McPherson wheeled about and shouted, "I told you never to interfere when I'm hunting!" At the same time, his belt slapped down on the face and neck of his long time chum.

Wilcox was humiliated and incensed. "I told you never to hit me again with that fucking belt!" He quickly grabbed his coat from the sofa and accelerated to the sliding doors of the den.

"Go on!" yelled McPherson. "Who needs you anyway?"

Before he stormed out of the den, Wilcox turned and glared at his so-called friend. "If I had a gun right now, I'd blast a hole in you!"

"Spencer Barnes thinks you came back and killed McPherson," says Detective Reinhardt.

"I was so pissed off, I could have killed him right then," Wilcox admits. "But I didn't. He was my buddy, man!"

"Who do you think killed him?"

Wilcox is quick to answer, "The bitch of a wife, man! She did it and Barnes helped her. He had a hard-on for Anna and would have done anything for her."

"Including murder?"

Wilcox sparks up another cigarette and puffs a cloud of smoke off to one side. "Oh sure, man! His story about seeing somebody running from the crime scene is a bunch of bullshit. I think she killed Bryce and Barnes set it up like it was a break-in."

"You said Bryce hit everybody with his belt. Did he ever hit Barnes or his wife with his belt?"

"Sure! Like I told you, he hit everybody, man!"

Detective Reinhardt recognizes Ian Wilcox has had enough questions thrown at him for one day. "I have just one last thing, Ian. You mentioned earlier that Anna may have had a boyfriend."

"I don't know, man! Bryce thought she was meeting a guy at the zoo. I think he might have even worked there or something."

"Did this guy have a name?" asks Reinhardt.

Wilcox struggles to recall and shakes his head. "Sorry, man! I can't remember."

Jack is satisfied for now. "I've used up enough of your time, Ian!" He stands and walks towards the door. "I might need to ask you a few more questions later."

Following behind, Wilcox is still struggling to remember. "The guy had a famous last name. It might have been football."

"Lombardi," suggests Jack.

"That's it!" shrieks Wilcox. "Vince Lombardi, man! It ain't over 'til it's over!"

Jack opens the door and begins his descent.

"Nah, he didn't say that." Wilcox rambles to himself as he closes the door behind the detective.

Halfway down the creaking steps, Jack hears Wilcox shout from within his apartment. "If you get knocked down, you gotta get back up!"

Jack thinks to himself. "Vince Lombardi's famous quote is in great contrast to Wilcox's life outcome."

*

The school's library is a brilliant learning environment with splashes of bright colours on picturesque bulletin boards and flashy displays that cover every wall. Jenny's class is enjoying their weekly visit for exchange and renewal of books and resource materials. Most of her classmates are engaged in researching for their speech either on a computer or fingering through the shelves of books while their teacher circulates and supervises.

Sitting at one of the large library desks, Jenny is reading a book on African Wildlife and recording information in her notebook when she senses the presence of Miss Gilmore.

The teacher smiles at Jenny. "You sure have been working hard on your speech. How's it coming?"

"Good," Jenny tells her.

The teacher turns and informs the class, "Ten minutes before recess."

"Would it be all right if I stay in at recess, Miss Gilmore?" asks Jenny.

"Are you sure you don't want to go outside and play with your friends?" Miss Gilmore is always promoting physical exercise and she is reluctant when it comes to having students stay in.

Being one of the top academic students is in her favour and Jenny gives it one last shot. "Please!"

"I guess so, Jenny, but we're not going to make this a habit."

*

Jack lost his appetite about the same time he finished interrogating Ian Wilcox and he missed having lunch. The thought of his future son-in-law's father having any kind of connection to the McPherson case is bizarre and upsetting. He sits at his desk staring vacantly at his notes when two familiar voices can be heard floating down the hallway. Detectives Newland and Cooney are reporting back as ordered.

As they enter the office, Jack tells them, "I called you back in guys because I want you to come with me this afternoon."

"Where we going, boss?" asks Dick.

"I thought we'd go to the bank Barnes went to the other day. You can help me leaf through bank statements."

"How did it go with Wilcox this morning, Jack?" asks Cooney.

"Let's get going," Jack says as he rises from behind his desk. "I'll tell you all about it in the car."

The police cruiser pulls into the 'emergency vehicle' parking spot in front of the huge financial building where the bank is located. Upon entering, Jack talks briefly to the receptionist at the information desk who leads them to an office. The woman in the office invites them in and directs them to have a seat.

"I'm the manager in charge of accounts. How can I help you?"

"We're from the police department," Reinhardt tells her. "I'm Jack." He gestures to the detectives standing behind him. "This is Dick and Willy."

The woman's eyes widen and she appears very suspicious. "Is this a joke?"

Jack immediately recognizes the woman's position.

"Forgive me," he apologizes while presenting his credentials. "I'm Detective Jack Reinhardt. Detective Richard Newland and Detective William Cooney here are about to leave and wait for me outside."

Jack is obviously disconcerted with having to continually use the preferred names of his partners and has finally had enough. Dick and Willy recognize their boss's demeanor and flee the office without uttering a sound.

A more professional introduction relaxes the woman.

"Okay, detective! How can I be of assistance?"

Back outside, Detectives Newland and Cooney lean on the police car and discuss the mood of their superior.

"Jack was sure upset with us in there," says Willy.

Dick nods his head in agreement. "He's always called me Richard. I don't think he likes calling me Dick."

"Or me Willy," says Cooney.

After a few thoughtful moments, Newland stirs from his leaning position and walks away from the car. Cooney follows and they wander to the corner of the street.

"What's down there?" asks Willy pointing to his left.

"It's like the old carnival midways," Dick tells his Scottish friend. "Lots of geeks and freaks."

Newland leads Cooney into a section of town that is a major problem area for the police force. Passing a few homeless beggars and a few more undesirable types staggering about aimlessly, Dick draws his partner's attention to several dives and places of questionable business. He points his finger at a boarded up boutique. "This place was raided last month. Drug bust."

As they continue their stroll up the street, they pass Syd's Smoke Shop and Spa and hear a voice of undefinable gender coming from the doorway. "What's your passion, lovers?"

Twisting their heads in the direction of this strange request, the detectives see a woman with long, flowing hair wearing a mid-length coat. The coat slowly opens to reveal female breasts and male genitalia. "What's your passion, lovers?" the question echoes.

Taken aback, Willy blurts out, "Bloody hell!"

"If that's what you want," says the transvestite, "I'm game for anything."

"Cover yourself up, you freak!" orders Newland.

"The name's Lola."

Dick flashes his police badge, "The name's Detective Newland!"

Lola immediately takes a step back and slams the door behind her. Cooney remains frozen in his tracks until he responds to a tug on his sleeve.

"C'mon, Willy!" says Newland.

The Scotsman appears confused. "Aren't you going to arrest her or whatever it is?"

"Are you kidding! Our jails are already crowded and they sure don't need that kind of entertainment."

Willy is somewhat apprehensive of the surroundings and suggests they head back. Dick complies and the detectives quicken their pace back to the bank.

Cooney appreciates the comfort of leaning against the police car. "Bloody hell!" he repeats. "I can't get over that!"

Newland detects Reinhardt leaving the bank. "Here comes Jack!"

Detective Reinhardt carries a brown envelop under his arm as he approaches. "Let's go, guys. I need to return to the station."

The detectives jump into the car and Willy asks, "What's in the envelope, Jack?"

"I've got printouts of every bank transaction Barnes has made in the last twenty-five years from three bank accounts," Jack tells him. "One of the accounts was opened a few months after the murder. This could make for some interesting reading!"

While Detective Newland drives away from the bank, Jack shifts in his seat to direct his words to both Newland and Cooney. Looking quite stern, he says, "Okay! From now on, it's Richard and William. Do you both understand?"

"Absolutely," answers Newland.

"Aye, Jack!" the Scotsman agrees.

Jack assumes a more comfortable position and leans back in his seat. "So, what did you guys do while I was in the bank?"

"We were hanging out with Lola," Dick tells him.

Willy chuckles. "It was more like she was hanging out with us."

Dick returns his chuckle and starts to sing. "Well I'm not dumb but I can't understand why she walked like a woman and talked like a man."

Willy joins his mate in the chorus. "Oh, my Lola lo-lo-lo-lo Lola lo-lo-lo-lo Lola."

The singing continues until the police car stops in front of the station. Jack gets out and waves to his partners as they drive off. They will return to their stakeout and keep an eye on Barnes.

Walking through the lobby on his way to the elevator, Jack is humming the classic song by The Kinks.

Chapter 10

Jack Reinhardt sips his morning coffee by the office window staring at the gargoyles across the way. He pities their miserable plight and they sit motionless staring back at him. The detective asks himself, "What must they be thinking of me?"

Suddenly, a black bird flies into the window causing him to spill coffee on his shirt. The bird flails its wings in distress before dropping from sight and Jack scrambles for a napkin.

His tie is still dripping wet when Jill enters the office. She takes the napkin and assists her boss in cleaning up.

"You look half asleep. Did you even go home last night?"

Jack had spent hours rummaging through years of bank statements and transactions made by Spencer Barnes. He found nothing unusual with two of the bank accounts. However, Barnes had opened a third account with a deposit of two and a quarter million dollars. This was the same amount Anna McPherson was awarded by the courts after being exonerated in the death of her husband.

The detective made calls to an insurance company and law firm that dealt with Bryce McPherson's affairs. Because Anna had been declared unfit and incapable of making decisions on her own, Barnes was appointed guardian and manager of her financial dealings.

Only one transaction was made in the first year. The amount of two million dollars was paid to the Municipal Zoo. There would be no other activity in the account until a year ago when two monthly transactions started. A seven hundred and fifty dollar payment to the Lawson Development Company and a five hundred dollar withdrawal were negotiated on the first of every month.

The detective's response is delayed. "Morning, Jill!"

She points to the clutter of papers on his desk. "Find anything?"

Jack nods his weary head. "I think so. Are Richard and William here yet?"

"They're right outside." She turns to leave his office. "I'll send them in."

Reinhardt rises from his chair and walks over to the coat rack. As he puts on his jacket, Newland and Cooney enter the office.

"Let's go pay Spencer Barnes a visit, guys."

*

Brightly lit by the mid-morning sun, Justin walks through the main compound of the zoo carrying a bull hook on his way to the elephant pen.

"Playing hooky from school again, Justin?" yells Pete Simpson as he walks towards the young employee.

"It's Wednesday," Justin reminds him. "I only have my evening class."

"That's right. I keep forgetting."

"I thought I'd take Buster for a walk this morning. I might need some help!"

Buster arrived four days ago, and he should be physically and psychologically adjusted to his new environment. Now it's time for some interaction. Justin plans on freeing the enormous beast from his pen and introducing him to the African Jungle where he can mingle with the other elephants. He also plans to work on his term paper. The red-faced lady will surely be at the zoo today.

Pete Simpson accompanies Justin to the elephant pen and together they open the wooden gate. Buster stands in the middle of the confinement and eyes Justin as he approaches while Simpson remains behind.

The huge elephant snorts and bobs his head up and down as if happy to see the young trainer. Justin manipulates the bull hook with precision and Buster responds favourably. Stroking the elephant's trunk, he says softly, "This way, Buster!"

The elephant is led from the pen and down a pathway towards the African Jungle exhibit. The exhibit is equipped with an elephant pit and Buster is introduced to the other inmates without incident. Everything goes according to plan and Justin feels comfortable with Buster's transition.

Leaning on a protective railing overlooking the elephants, Pete Simpson congratulates young Lombardi. "Good job, Justin!"

"Thanks!" Justin races by his supervisor.

"Hey, where you going in such a hurry?"

There's urgency in Justin's voice. "I'll come back later for Buster."

He runs to the locker room and quickly changes into his street clothes. Justin had noticed the red-faced lady watching Buster's introduction to the African Jungle exhibit and he has a plan. He is going to follow her when she leaves the facility.

In a matter of a few short minutes, Justin is in his car by the zoo's exit. The possibility of using this unique woman in his term paper is quite intriguing and he waits with excitement.

The red-faced lady finally stumbles her way through the turnstile and makes her way to the bus stop. She gets on the waiting bus and it pulls away. Justin follows behind as the city transporter makes a dozen or more stops before the red-faced lady gets off.

*

Newland and Cooney remain in the police car while Reinhardt makes his way to the front porch. Just as Jack is about to knock, the door swings open and he is invited inside.

"I was expecting this visit," says a subdued Barnes as he leads the detective into the kitchen.

"You need to explain a few things, Mr. Barnes," Jack tells the Englishman. "I went over your bank statements. Why was there a two million dollar payment to the Municipal Zoo?"

"A donation. Anna wanted to give all of her entitlement to the zoo. I convinced her to keep a small part of it."

Spencer Barnes resembles a proud man standing in front of a firing squad as the questioning continues. "What about the monthly payments to a development company?"

"Rent for Anna."

"Anna is here in the city!" exclaims Jack.

Barnes gives an affirmative nod. "I regret withholding information from the police, Detective Reinhardt, and I only do it to protect her."

Jack is excited about this disclosure and needs to know everything. "Why don't you tell me all about it, Mr. Barnes?"

The butler takes a deep breath before he begins. He explains that Anna had become very distraught during the time leading up to her husband's death and his murder pushed her over the edge. She was placed in a retreat where she received constant supervision. She was found innocent of any crime and left the city shortly after.

"I have no idea where she went and I didn't care to find out," admits Barnes. "All I know is Anna's life now is one of peaceful routine. She rides the bus, visits the zoo and goes to the mall."

"Rent payments started a little over a year ago. Did she just show up at your place one day for help?"

"No," Barnes answers. "I received a phone call from an old friend of hers. He told me Anna had returned to the city and needed help. Together, we made arrangements for her."

The detective asks his next question as if he knows the answer already. "Would that old friend of hers have been Joe Lombardi?"

"Why, yes!" A puzzled expression forms on his face. "How did you know?"

Reinhardt doesn't answer. His job is to ask the questions. "Where does she live exactly?"

Barnes is ashamed of Anna's appalling appearance and it pains him to look at her. "Do you really need to see her, detective?"

"I need to ask her a few questions."

"That will be a problem," Barnes tells him. "She doesn't speak."

*

The red-faced lady proceeds lamely up the sidewalk. Upon reaching her obscure one-level complex, she makes her way along a walkway and into the rear courtyard.

Justin parks on a side street and is in close pursuit. He sneaks into the courtyard, hides behind a dumpster and watches as the red-faced lady reaches her destination.

Young Lombardi needs to collect his thoughts before putting the rest of his plan into place. The interview is very important to him and the red-faced lady is a prime candidate. He needs to gather enough courage to approach unit #6.

From the corner of his eye, he catches sight of a snow white cat making its way towards him. Purring loudly, the cat slinks up to him and rubs its whiskers on his pant leg. Justin picks it up, gives the animal a few strokes and sets it down. He decides to carry out the rest of his plan and the cat follows close behind.

It takes Justin forever to reach the door and he hesitates for a moment before knocking. To his surprise, the door is slightly open.

"Hello!" he tosses the word inside. "Is anyone home?"

The snow white cat jumps onto the window sill and enters the unit through a torn screen.

"Hello!" repeats Justin and he pushes gently on the door.

"Come in and have a seat at the table." The woman's voice is weak and raspy.

Her words send an eerie chill racing through his body. Justin responds by slowly entering the apartment and he sees the old woman bend with difficulty to set a saucer of food on the floor for the hungry cat. Wandering over to a small table by the kitchen sink, he sits in one of only two chairs.

The woman labours to straighten up, then inches to the door and activates the deadbolt. "Her name is Dorothy," the red-faced lady tells her guest as she coughs. "She seems to like you."

Intimidated by her appearance and close proximity, Justin doesn't know what to say. He still can't believe the woman is actually talking to him. There is evidence of a smile on the old woman's face and he forces a grin in return.

"The little girl at the zoo. What's her name?"

Justin needs a moment before answering. "You mean Jenny?"

"Jenny loves the animals." The red-faced lady stoops to drag a hand across the head of her cat and pick up the empty saucer. Again, she struggles to straighten up and she coughs several times.

Sauntering over to the kitchen counter, the old woman places the saucer in the sink.

"I'm going to make some tea. Would you like some?"

"Sure," he replies. Justin figures he'll have time to gain his composure while his hostess prepares the hot beverage.

Looking around the room, he can't help noticing its decrepit state. The walls and ceiling are in need of paint, and the scuffed up floor is missing several tiles. One of the taps at the kitchen sink won't shut off properly and the constant trickle of water has left a permanent orange stain on the chipped porcelain. An old refrigerator and hot plate the old woman uses to boil water are the only appliances. There isn't a television or radio. A rusted radiator by the only window clangs as it provides what little heat there is in the apartment. Besides the kitchen table and two chairs, the only other furniture is a well-used pullout couch that services as her bed. A door to the left of the couch must conceal the bathroom. Justin can only visualize what it must look like.

The old woman places a modest tea set on the table in front of Justin and she invites him to help himself.

"I don't have any sugar and Dorothy just had the last of the cream."

Justin pours tea into a dainty cup and takes a sip. "This is just fine like this."

There is an awkward moment of silence except for the clang of the radiator, the drip of the leaky faucet, the purring of the cat at Justin's feet and the persistent coughing of the old woman. He continues to look around the room in an attempt to avoid eye contact with the red-faced lady and her eyes are fixed on him.

Justin doesn't want to ruin this great opportunity by saying something dumb like "nice place you've got here" or "what's up with the red face". He's decided to let her do the talking while she's in the mood.

The silence is finally broken. "You have your father's personality."

Almost spilling his tea, Justin sets the cup down. "Did you know him well?"

"I was about the same age as the little girl Jenny. My mother took me to the city zoo for the first time. It was after church on a Sunday." The red-faced lady sinks into a memory.

A little girl dressed in white and her mother walked through the turnstile and into the zoo. They smiled at each other as they inhaled the smells and listened to the sounds. The child's eyes illuminated as she gazed about.

"My mother and I walked around for hours," the old woman tells Justin. "The animals were just wonderful." She attempts to conceal a smile with her white-gloved hand and Justin listens intently.

The little girl stood by the monkey cages and giggled at their playful antics when she is startled by a voice that warned, "Don't get too close or they'll pee on you."
The girl turned and looked at a boy who stood next to her. He was a lot taller than her and maybe a year or two older. He carried a bucket and it appeared as though he worked there.
"Who are you?" asked the little girl.
"My name is Joey," he answered. "What's yours?"
"Anna," she told him. "Do you work here?"
"I started a few weeks ago. See these little guys," he pointed his finger at the monkeys. "They might be cute and everything, but they'll pee on you if you get too close."
Anna heeded the warning and took a step back. One of the playful critters shot an amber arch through the screen in her direction just missing her by inches.
"What'd I tell you," Joey said to Anna and they both laughed.
"You're all dressed up like you've been at church," Joey made the observation. "You should wear grubby clothes to the zoo if you want to get close to the animals."

Anna put a finger up to the cage and Joey gave her another warning. "You're white gloves are going to get dirty if you touch the screen."

Young Lombardi wants to ask the red-faced lady a thousand questions right now, but he demonstrates a lot of self-control by remaining silent.

"I saw your father at the zoo many times after that day."

Justin decides it safe to ask. "Your name is Anna?"

"And your name is Justin."

Spinning slowly away from the table, her mood seems to have taken a turn as well. "Why did you follow me here?" she asks in her raspy voice.

Justin is embarrassed to admit his reason and hedges. "I've got this term paper for school and I thought..."

Without allowing him to finish, the old woman walks to the door and unlocks the deadbolt. A gust of cold wind pushes the door open slightly. This is Justin's invitation to leave.

He rises from the chair and walks past the red-faced lady without an exchange of words.

Once outside, the door shuts behind him and he hears the sound of the deadbolt being activated. Justin sadly looks back to express how he feels.

"I'm sorry, Anna!"

*

Detective Reinhardt has finished with Spencer Barnes and is walking towards the police vehicle.

"Here's Jack," Newland informs Cooney.

The passenger door opens and their boss gets in. "Sorry I was so long in there, guys!"

"Where to?" asks Dick.

"Headquarters."

"How did it go in there?" asks Willy.

Jack appears exhausted and just wants to rest for a few minutes. "I'll tell you all about it later if you don't mind." He tilts his seat back and closes his eyes.

"Fair enough," the Scotsman responds.

Newland puts the car in drive and heads back to the station.

Jack will take this opportunity to absorb everything told to him by Barnes. Apparently, Anna McPherson and Joe Lombardi were close friends. Anna made frequent visits to the zoo and this made her husband very jealous. On one occasion, Joe Lombardi and his wife were dinner guests at the McPherson home. If what Barnes says is true, Justin's deceased father has officially become a suspect in the Bryce McPherson murder case.

Detective Reinhardt is roused by street noise and he rubs his eyes. The station is just ahead. What was a thirty minute drive seemed like three minutes.

"That didn't take long," says Jack. "Stop in front, Richard!"

The police car hugs the curb in front of the Federal Building and Newland waits for instructions. He and Cooney are about to be entrusted with a very important task. Their tired supervisor fumbles in his jacket pocket, pulls out a piece of paper and cups it in his hands.

"I need you guys to do something. This is the address of Anna McPherson. Spencer Barnes confirmed that she does indeed live here. Forensics needs a DNA sample."

"Aren't you coming with us, Jack?" asks the Scotsman.

"I've got other stuff I need to do."

Dick is confident. "We can do this, Willy!"

Jack hands the piece of paper over to Newland and wishes them good luck. He gets out of the car and Cooney makes the move to the front seat.

"Be tactful and don't break any rules," he warns them.

"Not to worry, Jack!" says Newland.

Detective Reinhardt closes the door and waves goodbye as the police vehicle spins away.

The tired policeman lifts his head, takes a deep breath and catches sight of a dark cloud slowly rolling in the sky. This solitary cloud suddenly becomes an ominous backdrop for the silhouette of a winged gargoyle atop the building across the street.

Chapter 11

Dick and Willy drive into the small parking lot of the Lawson Apartments complex and leave the police vehicle. While walking towards unit #6, Newland reminds his partner of their plan.

"We'll tell her that the case has been reopened and we need to ask a few questions. Once inside, wait a few minutes and then distract her by knocking something on the floor. That's when I grab something that she's been handling. Got it?"

The Scotsman finds the scheming element of detective work quite invigorating. "Aye!"

The detectives are met on the walkway by a hissing cat.

"Piss off!" exclaims Willy. He makes a kicking motion and chases the snow white cat away.

The detectives get to their destination. Newland knocks on the door with authority and reaches into his breast pocket for his police badge. There's no answer and he raps on the door again. No answer and he twists the doorknob lightly.

"It's locked."

"She's not home. What do we do now?" asks Cooney.

After a moment of thought, Dick suggests they visit the superintendent of the building and ask if he will let them in.

"We'll tell him it's a matter of life and death. Ours if we return to the station without a DNA sample."

Detective Newland taps his knuckles on the superintendent's door, flashes his badge and the detectives are invited inside.

"My name is Gus Tatulis," the bearded man says as he plops down on the couch to resume watching a game show on TV. "How can I help you?"

Dick uses a stern voice. "We need to get inside unit #6. It's a matter of utmost importance."

"You don't say," Tatulis scratches his chest area. "Unit 6 is it?"

"Could you let us in?" asks Dick. "It's very important."

Gus is more interested in his television program than in what Detective Newland has to say.

"Don't pick that one! Did you see that?" The superintendent points at the TV screen. "Any idiot would know it was number three! What a loser!"

Newland wants to get on with business. "Sorry to interrupt you Gus, but we really need to get into that apartment.

Tatulis is somewhat agitated. "Did you try the door?"

"Yes. It was locked."

"If it's locked, then she's in there."

Detective Cooney has been looking out the window all this time. "Not anymore!" He sees a woman leaving unit six and is witnessing the red-faced lady for the first time. "Bloody hell!"

Dick quickly joins his partner by the window and can't believe his eyes. "Holy, shit!"

Gus finds their reaction amusing and chuckles. "She's quite a looker, isn't she?"

"Let's go, Willy!" says Newland with urgency. He opens the door and the two detectives are in hot pursuit.

The red-faced lady makes her way to the front of the building and down the sidewalk to where a bus is just coming to a stop.

Newland shouts, "Anna, wait!"

He races close behind her and is about to touch her shoulder when the woman wheels around to face her pursuers.

The detectives gasp and are taken aback by her unsightly appearance. Frozen in their tracks, they watch as the red-faced lady boards the bus and the bus pulls away.

"I can't believe what I just saw!" Dick finally responds.

"That's Anna McPherson?" the Scotsman asks in disbelief.

"Wait until Jack hears this," says Dick as he gives his partner a tug on the arm. "Let's go!"

The detectives will retrieve a DNA sample from the old woman's apartment before returning to the station.

*

"Excuse me, detective!"

Jack lowers his glasses over the bridge of his nose and sees none other than Doctor David at his office door.

"I heard you paid my parents a visit the other day," snaps Sinclair-Smythe. "What was that all about?"

Detective Reinhardt rises from his desk and invites his guest to come in.

"The McPherson case has been reopened. I have to speak with everyone connected."

"Did you have to include my parents? They don't need this shit at their age."

The detective gestures for Sinclair-Smythe to have a seat.

"Sorry if I upset them. I won't bother them again."

"I should hope not!" the doctor says as he sits. "That's why I came to see you. If there are any more questions, you can ask me."

Jack takes this golden opportunity to use the doctor's knowledge of human behavior to maybe help him understand a few things that are most confusing.

"For years Anna McPherson went missing and now she has resurfaced."

Sinclair-Smythe is quick to respond. "I know very little of her or the McPherson case. I won't be much of a help to you."

"It's not about the case," Jack clarifies. "It's about Anna's state of mind."

The detective's statement captures the interest of the doctor.

"I'm listening."

"I'm trying to figure out why people act or react to certain situations the way they do," says Reinhardt.

"Like murder?"

"Spencer Barnes, the butler at the time, tells me that she hasn't talked since the night of the murder and that she may have deep psychological problems."

This is right up the doctor's alley and he has several theories for the detective to digest. "People suffering from a psychological or biological defect will experience mental

health problems. However, the majority of problems of this sort are usually induced by trauma." He pauses. "Could I get some water?"

Jack gets on the intercom and arranges for some water to be brought in.

"Jill should be here in a minute. Please go on."

"One reason for mental breakdown is internalized failure. A person who is unsuccessful as a wife say, falling short of expectations, may have difficulty coping with failure. Anna's home life led to fatigue, depression and substance abuse so I've been told. She was physically abused as well. A person becomes demoralized and devastated which certainly can stimulate one's mind negatively even to the point of committing murder."

Jill enters the office with a tray and sets it on the desk. She pours a glass of ice water and offers it to Jack's guest. Without a response of appreciation from Sinclair-Smythe, Jill smiles and leaves the office.

Jack is surprised by the doctor's comments. "Are you saying Anna killed her husband?"

"That's exactly what I'm saying." The doctor speaks with confidence. "Anna disappearing for years and not talking isn't a wife grieving in silence and isolation. Her mental problems are brought on by culpability. She can't shake the demons that whisper in her ear." Dr. David concludes, "Putting it in layman's terms, she's crazy with guilt."

Detectives Newland and Cooney race through the office pool on their way to see Jack and stop at the secretary's desk. They've been in an accelerated mode ever since encountering the red-faced lady.

Dick is nearly out of breath as he hands Jill a plastic bag containing used tissues he collected from Anna's apartment.

"Here's the DNA sample Jack wanted." He exhales deeply and hurries off towards Jack's office.

"I'll send it down to forensics immediately," Jill shouts behind him.

Willy has very little time to slouch on the secretary's desk and rushes to catch up with his partner.

"In dealing with matters of this sort you are aware, detective, that most of the killing in the world is done by so-called 'normal' people. They're normal in the sense of not having a psychiatric diagnosis or disorder. Killers are motivated to kill for various reasons. They can be bright, functional, conniving and quite the opposite of being mentally ill.

Dr. David Sinclair-Smythe is engrossed in extending his professional wisdom when Dick and Willy storm into the office.

"Sorry to interrupt, Jack! You're not going to believe this!" exclaims Newland.

"I'm busy right now, Richard," Jack tells his partner, "Can't this wait?"

"But this is really important!" Dick glances at the occupied seat beside Jack. "Maybe the doctor can help figure this one out!"

"What is it?" asks Reinhardt.

Detective Newland is quite animate. "Anna McPherson! You have to see her for yourself!"

"You won't believe it, Jack!" gasps Cooney.

"Her face is hideous," Dick explains. "It's completely red."

"Unbelievable!" exclaims Willy.

Detective Reinhardt looks at his guest in a confused manner and apologizes for the interruption.

"Not to worry," responds the doctor. "I'd like to hear more."

Jack suggests the two detectives calm down and have a seat. "Okay, tell us all about it."

"Her entire face is painted red." Newland deems it necessary to repeat himself. "Her whole face is red, I tell you, and she has a tattoo of an elephant on her forehead!"

Reinhardt asks Cooney for confirmation. "Is that what you saw, William?"

"Unbelievable!" repeats the Scotsman.

Jack looks to the doctor. "What do you make of it, David?"

Sinclair-Smythe demonstrates an air of amusement and he is definitely keen on contributing his expert judgement.

"The colour red is associated with several emotions such as rage, anger, shame and embarrassment. Anna perhaps is angry and most definitely ashamed of herself. That's why she hides behind a mask of red paint. The elephant tattoo is puzzling."

The doctor taps a finger on his chin while basking in his element and he takes a sip of water before continuing with his educated deductions.

"The elephant is a symbol of wisdom, loyalty, strength, fidelity and longevity. I'm not quite sure in Anna's case. In some cultures, elephants are a sign of good luck and fortune. The proverb 'an elephant never forgets' may be the clue."

Again, he taps his chin and the detectives wait intently as the doctor processes another thought.

"That's it! The elephant tattoo is a reminder. Every time Anna looks in a mirror, she is reminded of the horrible crime she committed." A smug display of loftiness discharges from Sinclair-Smythe. "There you have it, detective! You have your suspect, motive and reasons for obscure appearance."

Newland and Cooney are persuaded by the doctor's conviction and nod their head in agreement.

The doctor peeks at his watch. "I must be going. I've got a class to teach this evening."

Jack rises from his chair. "My future son-in-law attends that class."

Sinclair-Smythe ignores what the detective has to say. "I trust my parents will not be bothered with this matter again."

Jack offers his hand, but the doctor is on his way out the door. He lowers his extended hand and waits a moment.

"I don't think that asshole ever calls me by my name."

"What he said is pretty convincing," says Dick. "Anna murdered her husband!"

Jack sits back in his chair and admits, "What he said is very incriminating, but I'm not completely sold." Although sounding impressive, Jack senses inaccuracies in the analysis of a presumptuous and overconfident Sinclair-Smythe.

"Are you going to bring her in, Jack?" asks Cooney.

"Not just yet, William." Detective Reinhardt has years of experience with law actions of this magnitude and matters tend to move in a less hurried and deliberate manner. "We'll need more than that asshole's testimony in court."

"She did it," repeats Dick, "and Barnes is in on it."

"Barnes knows more than he's telling us," admits Jack. "Why don't you guys go back and keep an eye on him?"

"You got it!" answers Dick.

Just as Newland and Cooney are about to leave, Jack says, "I almost forgot! Did you get Anna's DNA sample?"

"We did so," Dick answers proudly. "Jill probably sent it to the lab already."

*

Shannon paces back and forth in her bedroom while using hand gestures and giggling. With cell phone stuck to her ear, she is actively engaged in a spirited conversation with Justin. He's been busy with the new elephant at the zoo and won't have time to meet her at Chapters Restaurant before class tonight.

"That's incredible!" she exclaims as she flops on her bed.

Justin is telling his girlfriend everything that's happened in his life since they last saw each other less than twenty-four hours ago. Listening intently, she leaps from her bed and swings the door open. Without interrupting their chat, she shouts, "I'll be home for supper, mom!"

"Okay, dear!" her mother yells from the kitchen.

Shannon shuts the bedroom door and resumes her position on the bed.

Carol Reinhardt reaches into the cupboard to get dinner plates and hands them to her younger daughter. "Go put these on the dining room table please and set a place for your sister."

"Glad to be of assistance," Jenny playfully responds. The little girl enjoys helping her mom in the kitchen.

Just as she completes setting the table, Jenny hears the side door open. She runs back to the kitchen and leaps into her father's arms.

"Hello, Jenny!" Her father follows with a monster hug.

Carol walks over and gives her husband a kiss. "You're home early, dear!"

"What a day," he says with a sigh.

"Go relax on the couch. The newspaper is on the coffee table."

Jack gives Carol another kiss and wanders into the living room.

It will be an hour until supper and Jenny decides this a good time to finish the rest of her homework. She scurries upstairs on her way to her room and passes her sister coming down.

Shannon enters the living room, leans over the back of the couch and gives her father a kiss on the cheek.

"You're home early."

"Hello, honey! Are you getting ready to go out?"

"Justin is working late, so I'm going to have supper here."

"Oh, good! That gives us time to talk. Come around here and have a seat."

Jack sets the newspaper to one side and Shannon sits beside him on the couch. Removing his spectacles, he asks, "Remember when Justin was over Sunday and you told me about a woman with a red face?"

"Justin told me he went to her place this morning."

"What?" Her father can't believe his ears. "He went to her place!"

Carol races into the room to see what all the excitement is about. "What's going on?"

"Justin went to see the red-faced lady!" he tells his wife. "Did she talk to him, Shannon?"

"I don't know," his daughter answers. "Justin said he'd tell me all about it tonight at school."

Carol notices the confused look on her husband's face. "What is it, Jack?"

Regaining his composure, he asks Shannon, "Why would Justin go to her place?"

"Remember, dad! He wants to interview her for his term paper."

His wife is very concerned and repeats her question. "What is it, Jack?"

"Shannon," he asks, "Could you go and get my pipe from the den?"

"Sure, dad!" His daughter leaves the room to retrieve her dad's pipe.

Jack whispers to Carol, "The red-faced lady is Anna McPherson!"

*

Spencer Barnes makes his way to his car, gets in and backs out of the driveway. Pulling away from quiet suburbia, he is heading for the university section of the city and on his way to school where he attends a Behavioral Sciences course every Wednesday night.

Just minutes later, a police vehicle rolls to a stop a few doors down the street from the home of Spencer Barnes. Dick and Willy have planned a stakeout and will wait patiently for any activity.

*

It's butt break at the university. Students are vacating their classrooms and filling the hallways. Justin is waiting at the regular meeting place when Shannon approaches. They kiss and head for the cafeteria.

Upon their arrival, they sit at a vacant table and Justin asks, "Do you want a coffee or anything?"

"No thanks." Shannon eyes him closely. "You look a little tired."

"I'm a little tired. Buster's a lot of work."

The two love birds talk for great lengths on the phone and always seem to ask the same questions over and over again.

"How's it going with you?" asks Justin.

"My dad was acting kind of weird at supper. He was freaking about the red-faced lady and wanting to know if she talked to you."

Justin looks surprised. "I wonder why your dad wants to know about that?"

"I'm not sure," answers Shannon, "but I want to know. Did she talk to you? What did she say? Was she creepy?"

Her line of questioning has Justin chuckling.

"She did talk to me," he finally divulges.

For the next fifteen minutes, Shannon listens intently to her boyfriend's account of what happened during his encounter with the red-faced lady.

"I blew any chance of an interview," he summarizes.

Shannon squeezes her boyfriend's hand lovingly. "That's too bad."

Justin looks at his watch. "Butt break is just about over. We better get to class."

On the way back, Shannon says, "I almost forgot to ask. How was Sinclair-Smythe's entrance tonight?"

"It was great!" Justin tells her. "He's lecturing on pro athletes and how they deal with fame and fortune at a young age. You should have seen it. The doctor rode onto the stage on a unicycle wearing a baseball shirt, football pants, hockey helmet and he was dribbling a basketball. He pedalled up to one of those kiddie basketball hoops and slam dunked a basket. It was hilarious!"

Shannon laughs and says, "The man is loony!"

Justin leans over and gives her a kiss. "See you after class. I love you!"

"I love you, too!"

Justin races down the hallway and enters the auditorium while Spencer Barnes walks in right behind him.

Chapter 12

Jack marches up to the reception desk and introduces himself to a young woman. She smiles pleasantly, gestures for him to have a seat in the waiting area and leaves her station.

Within seconds, the receptionist returns. "Right this way, Detective Reinhardt!"

Jack follows her to an office door. She raps lightly and opens it for the detective to enter.

A distinguished looking gentleman sits behind a desk. He rises from his chair and approaches his visitor with out-stretched hand.

"Good morning, Detective Reinhardt. Nice to meet you," he says as the two men shake hands. "I'm Samuel Crawford, the director of this fine establishment. Please, come in and have a seat."

Jack sits and Crawford returns to his side of the desk. "How can I be of assistance, detective?"

"First of all," starts Reinhardt. "I'd like to comment on how great of a place this is."

"Well, thank you. Do you come to the zoo on occasion?"

"This is my first time," admits Jack, "but my wife and daughters come. Actually, my oldest daughter dates one of your employees. Justin Lombardi."

Crawford is taken by surprise. "You're Shannon's father!"

Jack is equally surprised. "You know my daughter?"

"We've never met in person, but I've seen her on camera. She is a pretty girl. Justin is lucky young man."

Shannon's father is very proud and he thanks Mr. Crawford for his comments. Jack points to a wall of monitors. "I guess you're able to watch everything that goes on from your office."

"Surveillance cameras are positioned in strategic locations throughout the facility and we have monitors in every building," he tells the detective. "It's a safety feature we feel necessary."

"Of course," agrees Reinhardt.

Samuel Crawford is interested and suspicious. "What do we owe to your first visit, detective?"

"I'd like to ask you a few questions about Anna McPherson." His statement has the director's immediate attention. "What can you tell me about her, Mr. Crawford?"

The director is silent and needs some coaxing from the detective. "Why don't we start with her involvement with Joe Lombardi?"

Crawford is inhibited by the question and can only gaze at the wall of monitors. On one of the screens, Justin can be seen directing Buster through the entrance of the elephant pen on their way back from a morning stroll.

Buster wanders to the middle of the enclosure while Justin muscles with the heavy gates. Just as the second gate is closing, he is startled by Pete Simpson.

"How's it working out with Buster?" asks his superior with a hint of seriousness and concern.

"Just fine."

"The night attendant told me that Buster was unusually restless last night."

The young trainer is somewhat surprised to hear this. "He was just fine on our walk."

Pete hands Justin a file. "This finally came in. It's the elephant's records."

"I'll have to read it later, Pete! I'm going to be late for my morning class as it is."

His supervisor has already gone through the file. Buster, after being captured in the wilds of Africa, originally travelled with a circus. He was abused and became too aggressive for them to handle. He was then handed over to an elephant sanctuary that practiced free-contact dominance which is a standard form of elephant management. Buster's response to being dominated was to lash out at his keepers and he soon earned the reputation as a dangerous elephant.

Pete Simpson is worried for Justin and he wonders if working with Buster is wise. He looks at the elephant rocking back and forth in the middle of the yard.

"Look at his eyes, Justin! You better be careful."

Pete Simpson can be seen on one of the monitors walking away from the elephant pen and the huge gate closing behind him.

Samuel Crawford sits at his desk and says, "You probably know about Anna's substantial donation to the zoo."

Detective Reinhardt nods his head. "Two million dollars."

"She came here all of the time, and Joe and her were good friends." The director appears very appreciative. "We were able to expand the facility with that money,"

"When was the last time you saw her?"

Crawford thinks for a moment. "It had to be a few months before Bryce McPherson's murder. I gather that's what this investigation is all about."

The director rises from his chair and walks over to the wall of monitors. "I spend hours fixed on these screens, detective, and I know everything that goes on here. It's been over twenty-five years since I've seen Anna."

"What do you know about the red-faced lady?" asks Jack.

Again, Crawford is taken by surprise. "You know about her?"

"What's her name?"

"It started about a year ago. She comes here just about every day. Justin's father arranged for her to have a free pass and I don't know who she is."

"Why would Joe arrange for her to have a free pass?"

"I'm not sure, detective, and I didn't pry," says Crawford. "Joe was always helping the less fortunate."

Detective Reinhardt is convinced the director is unaware that the red-faced lady is actually Anna McPherson. He readies to leave and the two men shake hands.

"If anything further develops at this end, I will definitely notify the police," the director says.

Just as he makes this promise, the red-faced lady can be seen on one of the wall screens hobbling to the back of the elephant pen.

*

Justin gently rubs Buster's trunk and looks into the elephant's eyes. "There's nothing wild about you." The young trainer kisses the beast. "I have to go now, Buster. I'll see you after school."

As he moves slowly away from the elephant, Justin is aware of eyes peering through one of the cut-out windows. He nonchalantly makes his way closer.

"Hello, Anna!"

The pair of eyes disappear and Justin races to follow her. Once outside the pen, he sees Anna moving purposefully towards another area of the zoo. She wants him to follow her.

Anna leads him to a secluded spot beyond the fringes of the African Jungle where Joe Lombardi had placed a picnic table under a weeping willow tree. He had adjusted the lens of the closest surveillance camera so that Anna would be hidden from view. This was her personal sanctuary.

Willow branches rustle in the cool October breeze and Anna sits at the picnic table. She coughs several times.

"Are you warm enough, Anna?" asks Justin as he approaches. "I can run back and get a coat for you to wear."

"Sit down," she says in her low, grating voice. "I want to talk with you."

After their first meeting, Justin was sure she would never talk to him again. He anxiously sits across from her at the picnic table without saying a word.

"I haven't talked with anyone for so long," she tells him. "I talk to my cat Dorothy, but she isn't much of a talker." There is a hint of a smile on her rugged face, but she soon coughs it away.

Justin can relate to what she is saying and he smiles in return. His job involves the correspondence of hundreds of animals. He talks and they communicate in an assortment of manifestations like squirting pee or crapping on him.

"You have a term paper?" asks the woman.

"Yes, but I'll find someone else to interview. I'd just like to talk with you and find out more about you and my father."

The cool air makes Anna shiver and she clears her throat. "What is your term paper about?" Anna is curious and seems to be conducting her own interview.

Justin provides the red-faced lady with a quick outline of his course of studies and term paper, and she won't be offended upon hearing the reason she had been chosen as his subject of interview.

The woman covers her mouth with a white-gloved hand as she coughs. "What is the name of your girlfriend?"

"Shannon Reinhardt," he replies.

"She is very pretty." Lowering her head in shame, she adds, "Unlike me."

Justin feels empathy for the red-faced lady and he resists commenting on her appearance.

"You are very much in love," she says. "Are you going to marry her?"

Justin tells his plans of marriage and of a surprise he has for Shannon.

"I'm going to the jewelers tomorrow to arrange for a special ring to be made. Something that she will really like. The jeweler is going to provide me with a gold nugget so I have something to give Shannon when I officially ask her to marry me."

Anna smiles. "How are you going to ask her?"

"I'll invite her to stay the night at my place and set the gold nugget on her pillow. When she notices it, that's when I'll kneel and ask the question."

The red-faced lady appears happy for Justin and he is pleased with his plan. Without giving it much thought, he asks, "Were you ever married?" He immediately fears he's asked something that may chase her away.

"A long time ago." She recalls, "We were once very much in love."

Justin is relieved by her response and he listens contently as the old woman tells her story.

"I was about Shannon's age when my girlfriends and I were in Jamaica."

Three young girls stood in the corner of a crowded and smoky disco. Lights flashed and music blared. They yelled to hear each other talk and they giggled. The girl in the middle was being watched by a guy from across the dance floor.

"I'll take the one in the middle," said Bryce McPherson to his friend Ian Wilcox. "You can have the other two."

Bryce's eyes were fixed on Anna and his friend shouted in his ear. "What makes her the one?"

"I don't know. Maybe it's the white gloves."

With a drink in one hand and cigarette in the other, the paisley shirted McPherson made his way through the crowd towards Anna.

"Would you care to dance?"

Anna looked to her friends for approval and her blonde friend gave her a nudge forward.

Bryce put his cigarette in an ashtray on the nearest table and set his drink down.

"Come on! I won't take you too far from your friends."

He took Anna by the hand and led her onto the crowded dance floor.

Disco tunes all had the same beat and one song seemed to flow into the next. Anna liked to dance and soon they were dancing to the third song in succession. Ian and the two girls joined them and everyone was having a good time.

Suddenly, the music stopped and a voice came over the loud speaker. "Ladies and gentlemen, it's time for our dance contest. Get your partner."

Anna and her two friends started for the sidelines.

Ian tapped Bryce on the arm and said, "Do your elephant dance! I bet they haven't seen anything like that before!"

Bryce didn't need to be coaxed. He caught up to Anna and pulled her back onto the dance floor just as a voice said, "Okay couples, here we go!"

The music started and it was too late to put up a fight. Stuck in the midst of gyrating bodies, Anna was a contestant in a competition and dancing to Lionel Richie's 'All Night Long'.

"Here's Russell!" said the voice over the loud speaker.

Russell, one of the resort program coordinators and special-ist in dance choreography, circulated the dance floor. A tap on *the shoulder and a look of disgust from Russell was a cue to exit the contest. One couple quickly got the throat-cutting gesture and another couple got the nose-squeezing stinko sign.*

Couples were eliminated creating more room on the dance floor. Bryce took advantage and intensified his moves. Russell seemed interested in the oddity of the young man's interpretation and kept passing him by. Onlookers cheered and soon only three couples remained.

Bryce removed his belt and waved it around. Then he looped it around Anna, drew her closer and gave her a kiss on the cheek. Anna was having the time of her life.

When the music stopped, Russell put his hand over each of the three remaining couples. The loudest ovation was for Bryce and his dance partner. Ian shook his friend's hand and the girls ran to congratulate Anna. Anna's smile was priceless.

The red-faced lady continues to shiver. "We took the same flight back from Jamaica and I hummed 'All Night Long' the entire time," she tells Justin. "I couldn't believe we lived in the same city. We dated and then he asked me to marry him."

"That's a great story," concludes Justin.

"Your father thought I was making a big mistake."

Justin can't understand why. "Why would my father think that?"

Anna coughs and tightens the kerchief under her chin. "I'll tell you more, but I'm getting very tired right now."

"Of course, Anna! Let me walk you to the bus stop."

They rise from the picnic table and crouch under the willow branches as they head towards the nearest pathway.

Walking by her side and without giving it much thought, Justin asks, "Did you ever have children?"

The red-faced lady glares at him. Her spirit has mutated for the worse and Justin can see the pain in her eyes.

"I'm sorry, Anna!.

She quickens her pace. "I'll be here Saturday."

The old woman makes her way through the exit on her way to the bus stop.

*

Jack has returned from his visit to the zoo and is glancing at his notes when Jill enters his office.

"Vera called, Jack! She has something for you."

Dr. Vera Hampton has had a few days to examine the remains of Bryce McPherson and may have found something vital to the case.

"Fric and Frac are on their way in," says Jill. "Wait 'til you get a load of them!" She chuckles while leaving the office.

Jack continues to mull over his notes until Newland and Cooney make their way into the office. Both are wearing khaki slacks and cream coloured shirt with a pattern of orange swirls. Dick and Willy eye each other briefly and smile at their boss.

"What do you think, Jack?" asks Newland.

Jack shakes his head with disapproval as he rises from his chair. "Follow me."

"Where we going?" the twins ask in unison.

"Down to the forensic lab. I'm going to have Vera examine your numb skulls."

Dick and Willy look amused as they follow their leader down the hallway.

The elevator door opens to the basement floor and the three detectives emerge.

"Good afternoon, gentlemen!" greets Dr. Hampton.

"Hi, Vera!" returns Jack. "Jill says you may have something for us."

Vera leads Jack over to the table where the remains of Bryce McPherson lay while Dick gives Willy a tour of the lab.

With a sweeping motion of his hand, Dick says, "Look around, Willy! A major part of our crime investigation is done here.

He leads the Scotsman over to a glass partition and points to the examination table on the other side. It's occupied.

"Vera can tell us the last time that guy picked his nose."

While Willy's indoctrination continues, Jack and Vera check samples collected from the McPherson crime scene.

"What did you find?" asks Jack.

Vera lifts a piece of glass with tweezers and shows the detective a lipstick smear.

"I compared this sample with Anna's and it came up negative. It appears McPherson was entertaining another woman on the night he was murdered."

"The lipstick smear wasn't included in the transcript!" exclaims Jack. "I wonder why."

"You must remember, Jack, genetic testing was in its infancy back then. They must have determined the lipstick came from Anna. I don't really know."

"Or maybe it was a botched investigation. What about the elephant paperweight?"

"Inconclusive. No separation of DNA types could be obtained."

She directs his attention to a stained piece of cloth. "I took a number of fibres from the victim's shirt and ran some tests."

Using a process called gel electrophoresis, Vera was able to separate fragments of DNA from small pieces of thread. However, she won't confuse the detective with medical terminology and logistics.

"I found two sets of DNA."

"Whose?" the detective asks.

Their conversation is suddenly interrupted by a commotion in the far corner of the room and Jack will have to wait for the answer to his question.

Dick had been showing his mate the labelled jars of body parts in formaldehyde and the volumes of 'Gray's Anatomy' filled with illustrations of human specimen chopped up into every conceivable anatomical chunk when the Scotsman fell faint on the floor.

Jack rushes over and assists Newland in getting Cooney to his feet.

"You look awfully pale, William!" says Jack. "You better get him outside for some fresh air, Richard!"

Dick escorts his queasy friend through the lobby to the revolving doors leading outside. A steady flow of people move up and down the concrete steps of the Federal Building and the two detectives are nudge to one side.

"Here, Willy! Have a seat and take a couple deep breaths. If that doesn't kill you, you'll be just fine."

Willy sits on the hard step. "I just need a minute, Dick!"

While the Scotsman recovers, Newland takes a deep breath himself. "Mmm, smell those exhaust fumes." He looks down at his disinterested partner. "Isn't it great?"

Looking up the street, Dick notices a familiar sight. "Oh, Christ!" he exclaims. "Here comes the drag queen!"

The Wizard of Ahs is prancing up the congested sidewalk towards the Federal Building and his outfit is simply dazzling. He wears a full length, cherry red coat embellished with furry white trim on the collar and sleeves. Tapered at the waist, the bright coat is made of heavy velvet and has large brass buttons down the front. His black-buttoned spats are the same colour of white as the bouffant hairpiece on the top of his head. Fake eyelashes and red lipstick enhance the hermaphrodite's finest features.

"If this doesn't make you puke, Willy, nothing will!"

The slender and dainty Wizard butterflies up the few steps. "Ah, if it isn't the two dicks."

"Hello, Beverly! What drags you here?" asks Newland.

The Wizard notices the nauseated state of the Scotsman. "Ah, is wee Willy not feeling so well?"

Without answering the question, Dick remarks, "You're a little early for Christmas, Wizard. You look like one of Santa's elves."

The Wizard is quick to respond. "Ah and you look like one of the seven dwarfs, Dopey!"

"Ha! Ha! Ha!" Dick laughs sarcastically.

The observant Wizard notes the similarity of garments worn by the detectives.

"Ah, speaking of drag. Wouldn't it be a real drag if everyone were dressed the same?"

Not waiting for a response, the Wizard is on his way to Captain Maddox's office with a street report and has no time to battle with Newland. He skirts past his antagonist and flits into the Federal Building.

Dick is forever appalled by the Wizard. "Now I know how you feel, Willy! That little fagot makes me ill."

"We should go back in, Dick!" suggests Willy. "I'm feeling better now."

Helping his friend to his feet again, Dick says, "Jack's probably finished down in the lab. Let's go see what he's found out."

"You feeling okay, William?" asks Jack as the detectives enter his office.

"I'm fine now, Jack!" he replies.

The detectives have a seat and Newland asks, "What did Vera have to say, Jack?"

"She did a bunch of tests on the victim's shirt," Reinhardt tells them. "Most of the shirt was covered with the victim's blood. But, in one small area camouflaged by all the blood she found the DNA of a second person. There were tears on the shirt which means someone knelt over the victim and wept."

"Whose tears, Jack?" asks Cooney.

"They were Anna's tears, weren't they?" surmises Newland.

Jack gives confirmation with a nod of his head.

"That means she was there in the room," says the Scotsman.

"And the butler's account of what happened on the night of the murder is all bullshit!" adds Newland.

Again, Reinhardt gives confirmation with the nod of his head. "We need to bring Barnes in for questioning!"

Chapter 13

It's late in the afternoon when Detectives Newland and Cooney lead Spencer Barnes into the interrogation room. The stately Englishman has been spared the indignity of being handcuffed. The detectives grin as they sit Barnes at the lone table. Police work such as the retrieval of a suspect is much more satisfying than a long and futile stakeout.

Dick and Willy leave as Detective Reinhardt enters and sits across from Barnes. The Englishman's posture is slouched and there is an expression of guilt on his face.

"I'll come right to the point, Mr. Barnes," says the detective. "You haven't told us the truth about the night of the murder. Anna was there in the room, wasn't she?"

Spencer Barnes concedes without resistance and his voice shakes with emotion as he discloses events leading up to the death of Bryce McPherson.

"Anna once experienced the joy of life. She was full of vitality," he tells the detective. "She was very loving and passionate."

Barnes makes it quite apparent that he was at one time charmed by Anna's innocence and Jack listens intently to the butler's testimony.

"Bryce took advantage of her vulnerability," says Barnes with a tone of anger in his voice. "He would ridicule her and degrade her, and he was one cruel son of a bitch when he was drunk."

Reinhardt has already documented that Bryce McPherson was a reviling character who wasn't well-liked and whose drinking had become escalated. Jack wants to know more about Anna and her state of mind at the time of the murder.

"How was Anna responding to this cruel treatment?"

"Anna went through endless efforts to please Bryce. Her struggles to keep the marriage going soon resulted in fatigue and depression. She eventually distanced herself from him and everything else."

"Even Joe Lombardi?"

"I told you Lombardi and his wife paid a visit one time. I was serving tea and I couldn't help notice Bryce flirting with Mrs. Lombardi as Anna talked with Mr. Lombardi. That was the last social contact she had. She stopped going to the zoo and became a recluse."

Jack thinks it a good time to discuss the actual crime. "What really happened on the night of the murder, Mr. Barnes?"

The Englishman contemplates for a moment and takes a deep breath. "I've already told you that Bryce was drinking heavily that night and his friend Wilcox stormed out of the house uttering threats."

"You had to have your ear pressed against the door to hear those threats."

"Wilcox pushed me to one side as he left the den and Bryce forcefully slid the door shut in my face," says Barnes. "That's when I returned to my quarters at the rear of the house."

Admitting his close proximity confirms the detective's earlier deduction.

"So, what did you hear them argue about when you were listening at the door?"

Barnes shrugs his shoulders. "It was difficult to hear what led to it. Bryce hit Wilcox with his belt and that's when the shouting became louder."

"Did Bryce ever hit you with his belt?" asks Jack.

The detective's question immediately straightens the Englishman's posture and alters his demeanor. "I was proud to be a servant and I demanded respect."

"You had the opportunity to get rid of McPherson and have the blame put on his friend Wilcox," suggests Reinhardt.

Sounding quite defensive, Barnes says, "As I said, detective, I went to my quarters. It was less than an hour when I returned to the den and saw Anna kneeling over Bryce. Her face and gown were covered in blood." His voice softens as he recollects the sight. "She looked up at me in horror and I didn't know what to think."

"What happened next?"

"My rational judgement was obscured and the situation was certainly desperate," he tells the detective. "I just needed some time to think. I turned off the lights and took Anna upstairs. She had a shower and slipped into bed. I cleaned any smears in the bathroom, collected the bloody clothing and went to the laundry room."

"You were covering up any traces that would link her to the murder."

"It was the only thing I could think of at the time, detective! She needed my protection."

"That was very noble of you, Mr. Barnes. However, it also makes you an accessory to murder."

"But Anna didn't kill him," pleads Barnes. "Don't you understand? She came into the den and found Bryce dead on the floor. The crime had already been committed. Anna must have frightened off the killer."

Spencer Barnes breathes deep before continuing. "After cleaning up, I returned to the den and that's when I saw someone running to the door leading outside. I quickly turned on the light, but didn't get a good look at him." Barnes concludes, "Blood stains leading out onto the patio proved there was an intruder. The killer must have returned to cover up his tracks."

"Did Bryce ever have women over to the house?"

"He was a despicable husband. Anna was always upstairs."

"Was a woman over on the night of the murder?"

"Not that I know of, detective. Why?"

"You don't know about the lipstick smear on a glass?"

Barnes looks confused. "I don't know anything about that!"

"Bryce may have been entertaining a lady friend that night. You didn't hear anything?"

"No, I swear!" Barnes contemplates for a moment. "You mean I might have seen a woman running from the room?"

Jack is sensing why Anna was never convicted for the murder of her husband. The involvement of Spencer Barnes and his testimony has Jack in doubt as to what really happened that dreadful night.

"You're sure Anna hasn't spoken since that night?"

"She decided to do her suffering in silence," the Englishman tells him, "and I haven't heard her speak since that time."

Detective Reinhardt has heard enough for the time being. "Let's take a timeout, Mr. Barnes! I'll send in some coffee."

The Englishman hasn't lost all of his dignity. "I'd rather have tea, detective. Preferably herbal if I may!"

Jack smiles as he rises from the metal chair. "I'll see what I can do, Mr. Barnes!"

The elderly gentleman crosses his arms and rests his head on the table as the detective leaves the room.

Dick and Willy have been listening the entire time. Herbal tea has been ordered and the two detectives follow their leader from the interrogation room. Jack finds the first comfortable seat and wearily plops down.

"I think Anna did it," says Newland. "Barnes made it look like a break-in to cover up for her."

Conscious of the stubble on his chin, Jack massages his face. "How about you, William?"

"Aye, I think she did it too, Jack!"

"Everybody thinks she did it, but we need more," says Reinhardt. "What about the mystery woman who was there that night?"

Jack sags in the chair to contemplate the options. Was the murder of Bryce McPherson simply an act of retaliation by an abused wife or had someone else committed the crime? Was the murder an act of rage by Ian Wilcox who returned to the house to kill his drunken friend? Was the murder a sinister plot devised by a vengeful house attendant? Had Barnes committed the crime and made it look as though the house had been invaded? Who was the mystery woman? It pains him to think of it, but he can't exclude Joe Lombardi as a possible suspect.

Dick breaks the silence. "If only Anna could talk."

Jack is roused, "What did you say?"

"If only Anna could talk."

"You may have something there, Richard! We should bring her in for a written report at some point. But right now, we need to get back to Barnes.

Spencer Barnes stirs in his cold, metal chair restlessly awaiting the return of Detective Reinhardt. The cup of tea on the table in front of him is essentially untouched. The Englishman regards its nasty taste as part of his unpleasant detainment.

The door of the interrogation room opens and Jack enters. Before he has a chance to sit, Spencer Barnes confesses, "I have never told anyone this, detective, but I now feel it necessary."

Reinhardt sits and urges Barnes to go on.

"There was a child," says Barnes. "Anna had this wild notion that having a child would be comforting. Sadly, it didn't turn out that way."

Jack remains surprisingly calm. "What happened?"

"It was a few months before the murder and Anna was well into her pregnancy. They had an argument and Bryce hit her with his belt. I prevented him from chasing her up the stairs and then I went to check on her. I found Anna sprawled on the floor in one of the upstairs bathrooms. She was whimpering and unmistakably suffering from shock. Her dress was torn and she was battered and bruised." The horror of this recollection is evident in his expression.

"Take your time, Mr. Barnes!"

Barnes needs to continue. "The fetus was on the floor in front of her. Mr. McPherson, Bryce's father, came and stood behind me. He commanded me to get rid of the mess."

"You're telling me that Bryce beat his wife causing her to lose the child and Mr. McPherson ordered you to get rid of the evidence. Is that right?"

"I'm ashamed of my actions, detective! I was only following orders," the butler tells him. "I put the fetus in a plastic bag and I put the bag in a small wooden chest which I buried in the backyard." He takes a moment before concluding, "Anna was never the same after that."

Detective Reinhardt is somewhat numbed by this disclosure. Barnes has been deceitful in the past and Jack wonders how much of this story is accurate.

"We need to locate the box, Mr. Barnes. Can you show us where you buried it?"

"Of course," he replies.

Spencer Barnes has confessed to the improper and indecent treatment to human remains which is an indictable offense. Barnes is informed that he will be detained overnight. Detective Reinhardt plans to visit the old McPherson place with Barnes in the morning to possibly unearth new evidence in the case.

*

Jack manipulates the large brass knocker on the front door of the old McPherson estate. Barnes and two members of the Task Force accompany him.

The door swings open. "What brings you back, detective?" asks Patrick Grogan.

"Hello, Mr. Grogan," answers Jack. "I'd like you to meet Spencer Barnes."

The two gentlemen shake hands and reciprocate the pleasure of making an acquaintance.

"We need to take a look in your backyard, Mr. Grogan," Jack tells him. "Something may have been buried back there that could be vital to our case."

Patrick Grogan is unsure and wants to know more. "Just what exactly are you looking for?"

"A box with contents I'd rather not divulge right now. I assure you it's nothing of value to anyone but the police."

Grogan takes a moment. "I understand."

While the two officers retrieve shovels from the trunk of the cruiser, Grogan is pleading for them to be careful and not be too destructive. Detective Reinhardt guarantees they'll do their best and Grogan closes the front door.

The outside of the estate has transformed marginally since the time of the murder. Barnes has no difficulty guiding the police along a flagstone pathway that winds between well-trimmed hedges and into the backyard.

The grass is wet with morning dew and songbirds take flight as Barnes leads them into a botanical paradise. Pointing to a large piece of driftwood in one of the flower beds, he says, "It's still here! This is the spot!"

The two officers with shovels begin to dig where Barnes has suggested while Detective Reinhardt and the butler look on.

"Having lost a child the way she did gave Anna a strong motive for killing her husband," says Jack.

Barnes is quick to respond, "Anna wasn't capable of such a crime!" With sounds of metal shovels hitting rock, he continues, "Even if she was capable, is justice going to be served sending her to prison for the rest of her life? She's confined to a life of misery as it is!"

"That's not for us to decide," says Jack.

"How deep are we going?" one of the officers asks.

"It was a shallow grave," answers Barnes. "Not more than half a meter."

"We're at least that deep now, sir!" the second officer informs him.

Waving a finger, Barnes directs the officers to dig a bit to the left.

"It's difficult not to feel sorry for her," says Reinhardt. "To think a husband would hit his pregnant wife and cause her to lose their child."

"The bastard treated her like dirt," says Barnes. "Anyway, he didn't think the child was his. That's why he hit her."

Jack is surprised. "It wasn't McPherson's child?"

"He didn't think so. He accused Anna of having an affair with Lombardi.

The sounds of digging and dirt being tossed continue.

"No wonder she looks the way she does," says Jack.

"After she lost her baby, she began to abuse herself by taking pills and Bryce took delight in her agony. He would laugh at her and say vicious things to her. I was certain she would attempt to take her own life, so I kept a close watch on her."

"Didn't his parents do anything when all this was going on?"

"His parents turned a blind-eye to most of it."

"Did you ever try to intervene?" asks the detective.

Barnes appears angered by the question.

The butler stood in the foyer and heard screams coming from the den. Suddenly, Anna ran from the sliding doors in hysterics and fled up the flight of stairs. Bryce was in hot pursuit. He wheeled his belt overhead and laughed. Barnes stretched his arm out and prevented Bryce from going upstairs. The belt came down on the butler's arm. Bryce swung a second time but missed his target. He then turned and retreated to the den. Barnes went to check on Anna.

The nose of a shovel strikes an object with a thud and one of the officers shouts excitedly, "I've hit something!"

The officers get to their knees and continue to wipe away loose dirt with their hands until a wooden box is hoisted from its burial site.

Both Jack and Spencer Barnes are wide-eyed as though a pirate's treasure has been found. Unlike a treasure chest, there is no heavy lock to break open. Just a simple metal hasp which Jack directs one of the policemen to manipulate.

The officer snaps the hasp and lifts the lid. His mouth drops as he immediately turns his head and looks at Detective Reinhardt.

"What is it!" exclaims Jack.

Chapter 14

Elephant Walk is the given name for the walking path that leads from the pen to the man-made lake where the animals swim. It provides spectators an up-close experience with the elephants and the animals a chance to display their amazing grace. People stream through the turnstiles and quickly position themselves along the protective handrail that lines each side of the entire walking path.

Amongst the avid crowd are the Reinhardts. This is their first family outing in quite some time and Jenny is especially excited.

Inside the corral, Justin is minutes away from conducting his first 'Elephant Walk and Swim' and he plans to have Buster at his side. Rubbing the elephant's trunk with one hand, he holds a clipboard with the other. Records are kept on each of the animals by attendants and Justin looks concerned. Apparently, Buster had been very agitated through the night and had been scraping his huge tusks on the bars of his stall. This is typical behavior of a disgruntled elephant.

"Is something bothering you?" Justin speaks softly to the elephant as he replaces the clipboard on its hook. He caresses

Buster with both hands. "You're going to do just fine today!" Buster bobs his giant head up and down in response. "Well then, let's go!"

The energy of the crowd is incredible and everyone cheers when the massive gates of the pen open. Children cling to the iron rail like magnets to see the show. Just as planned, Justin leads the procession with Buster at his side. The giant elephant responds to the bull hook and slowly they make their way down the walking path. One by one, the elephants leave the enclosure and follow behind.

Everyone marvels at the size of Buster. Some people are intimidated and take a step back. A few smaller children are frightened and begin to cry. Justin waves to the Reinhardts and blows a kiss to Shannon. They wave in return and Shannon's face is beaming with pride. Jenny tilts her head back as far as she can to gaze at Buster as he passes by and she tugs on her dad's arm. The passion his daughter has for these animals is evident and he gives her a smile.

As the parade continues, the adult elephants are communicating to one another by making deep rumbling noises and it's amusing to watch the playfulness of the babies as they clumsily keep pace with their mothers. Jenny reaches out to touch one of the smaller elephants and her mom pulls the little girl's arm back as a warning to be careful.

Suddenly, the procession comes to an abrupt halt. There seems to be some commotion ahead. Many of the spectators scatter from the handrail and screams of fright fill the air. The Reinhardts are very concerned and Shannon becomes frantic. Jack consoles her and races off to find out the cause of the disturbance.

Within minutes, order is restored and the line of elephants begins to move again. Jack returns to his family and reassures them that everything is fine. One of the older female elephants decided she wanted to be the leader. Buster retaliated and rammed her with his huge head sending her against the handrail.

Jack tries to downplay the situation, but Shannon is still very upset. Joining hands, they make their way through the crowd to watch the rest of the show by the water.

The recreational lake is a highlight of the zoo. It includes a sandy beach by the water's edge, trees and rock formations that provide shade, and a mud hole for the animals to wallow in. Patrons can stand on raised platforms overlooking the area or sit in bleachers closer to the action.

Most of the elephants enjoy a cool dip in the water. The 'Swim' is a happy time and elephants can get very social when they're happy. Spectators watch as these gentle giants entwine their trunks and caress each other. The babies frolic and splash in the shallow water while older members of the group swim several meters from shore. Most people don't realize elephants are actually good swimmers. Their huge body is a floatation device. They move all four legs and their trunk acts as a snorkel.

A zoo attendant opens a duffel bag and tosses a few brightly coloured toys into the water for the younger ones to play with. He rolls a soccer ball in the sand and one of the junior elephants kicks it back to him. A female attendant standing in shallow water scrubs the animals with a giant toothbrush. Another attendant with a large tube pretends to rub lotion on the tummies of sunbathers.

While everyone is enjoying the antics, Justin stands off to one side with Buster. The huge elephant is still agitated and refuses to be included in any social activity. With everything under control, the young trainer decides to escort Buster back to his stall.

Shannon sees them leaving and runs to catch up. Leaning over the handrail, she gives her boyfriend a kiss and Buster looks away. Justin holds her hand and the three of them make their way up the hill.

The 'Elephant Walk and Swim' is nearing an end. The line of elephants makes its way up the walking path. Justin opens the huge gate of the enclosure and the elephants stroll inside one by one. The rest of the Reinhardt family join Shannon just as the gate closes behind the last elephant.

"Are you okay, Shannon?" asks Carol.

"I'm fine, mom!"

Justin walks over to join the Reinhardts. "How did you like the show?"

Jenny can't hold back her excitement and speaks first. "It was fabulous!"

"You had us all worried, son," says Jack.

"Not to worry, Mr. Reinhardt. Buster needs a little work, that's all."

"How come Buster looks so angry?" asks Carol.

"Buster was under a lot of stress at his other homes, Mrs. Reinhardt. I think Buster was often put in chains and treated cruelly."

"That wasn't very nice!" says Jenny.

"No, it wasn't. This place will be good for Buster," Justin tells them. "I just have to look for ways to satisfy his needs."

"What happens if two elephants start fighting?" asks Jack.

Justin explains, "A trainer needs to dominate and show the elephant who the boss is. Even a huge elephant like Buster will accept me as his superior. I was able to distract Buster away from the other elephant today and take control of the situation."

"Buster likes you," Jenny tells him.

"I think so, too. I just need to show him respect and he'll respect me. Not to worry!" His last comment is directed at Shannon.

"Be careful just the same," warns Jack.

"We've planned a family brunch," says Carol. "Would you like to join us, Justin?"

"Thanks, but I need to stay and tend to business."

"Well, we better get going," says Jack. "I need to tend to some things myself later today."

The Reinhardts slowly make their way to the exit and Shannon gives Justin a long hug before racing to catch up to her family.

*

Anna nestles beneath her weeping willow tree in a serene environment surrounded by nature's beauty. Leaves flutter to the ground with every gentle gust of cool air. Birds chirping from tree tops and the distant clamouring of wild beasts augment the sounds. The red-faced lady is at peace here.

"Hello, Anna!" Justin speaks faintly, not wishing to disturb her tranquil spirit.

She tightens slightly and glimpses in his direction.

Justin approaches and drapes a blanket around her shoulders. "This should keep you warm."

"Bless you, my son!" says the appreciative old woman as he sits across from her at the picnic table. "Did you get to the jewelry store?"

"Yes and I got the gold nugget."

She puts a hand to her mouth and coughs. "Shannon is a lucky girl!"

"I bought her younger sister something too," Justin tells Anna. "It's her birthday the end of this month."

"You are so thoughtful." The old woman looks tired and she closes her eyes.

Justin studies her face and tries to see beyond her unsightliness.

Anna slowly unfurls her eyes. "Will you have a big wedding?"

Justin and Shannon have discussed their wedding at length and have decided to base the major moments of their lives with the good of the planet in mind. They have agreed to follow the

3Rs when they get married. They will 'Reciprocate' by giving back to nature. They will 'Rejoice' by connecting with nature and they will 'Respect' nature by using less.

"We're getting married in my backyard," answers Justin. "Shannon has planted some flowers and grasses. It will be nice."

"I'm sure it will be."

After a moment, Justin continues, "I want her to have a special ring. I guess the gold nugget plucked from the ground goes against our vow never to abuse the natural world."

The red-faced lady wipes a drip from her nose with her soiled glove. "I want to show you something special that someone gave to me." She collects a monkey charm which hangs from a gold chain around her neck.

"Did your husband give you that?

The old woman's spirit appears to brighten for a moment.

Anna got off the bus in front of the Municipal Zoo and walked through the turnstile. Her first stop was the monkey cage.

Joe Lombardi had been waiting for her to come. "Hello, Anna!"

"Hello, Joseph! Sorry I'm a bit late."

The teenagers have been meeting like this for a few years now, but today was special. Joe had a present for Anna. "

I've got something for you," he told her as he handed her a small, unwrapped box.

She took the box and opened the lid to see a monkey charm on a gold chain. Anna was surprised and speechless.

"Let me help you put it on," said Joe.

"Not my husband," the red faced lady replies and offers no other information regarding the necklace.

Justin remains in silence as Anna recalls, "My life was great at one time. I had the most elegant wedding and I lived in a millionaire's mansion. My friends and family thought I was the luckiest girl in the world."

The willow branches sway from side to side and Anna shivers. She tightens the blanket around her neck and becomes dispirited. "My world soon would tumble down and the only place I found happiness was here."

Justin wonders about the role his father played in her life. "Did you meet my father here much of the time?"

Visible amongst the wrinkles on her face is a hint of a smile. "Your father was my best friend. He was so kind and thoughtful."

Justin returns her smile and the red-faced lady stares at him with glazed eyes.

"Last time we talked, you asked me if I had any children." Somewhat reluctant she confesses, "I had a son. He would have been just about your age."

Anna stood in the den by the screened door leading to the patio. Her dark hair fluttered with each waft of warm evening air that entered the room. She wore a loose-fitting dress, the kind that any expectant mother would wear.

She seldom entered her husband's domain for the laurels of his hunts hanging on the walls made her uneasy. But, she wanted to be with him tonight.

Bryce sat at his desk with a drink in one hand and a bottle of scotch in the other. He mumbled words under his breath while feeling sorry for himself. The mumbling got louder. "Look at you standing there with your fat gut. How could you do this to me?" She has told him repeatedly that the child is his, but he refuses to believe her.

His nasty comment made her cry and she decided to leave the room.

"Where do you think you're going, you slut?" Bryce quickly rose from his chair. "I'm not done with you yet!"

He grabbed Anna forcefully around the waist, pulled her towards him and squeezed her tightly. "Let's dance." He twisted her from side to side and treated her roughly.

"Stop it!" she pleaded. "You're hurting me!"

Her husband released his grip and shoved her to the floor. "Our dance isn't done yet." Bryce unbuckled his belt and withdrew it from the loops of his pants.

Anna was now hysterical. She struggled to her feet and raced towards the sliding door. Bryce grabbed at her and got a handful of her dress. The dress ripped which caused her to lunge into a table by the door. She slouched momentarily and the belt cracked against her back. She slid the door open and raced out of the room.

Anna stumbled her way up the flight of stairs and into a bathroom where she fell unconscious on the floor. The outstretched arm of the house attendant had stopped Bryce from chasing her.

Sprawled on the bathroom floor in a semi-consciousness state, the images that ensued were out of focus and ill-defined. She saw a shadowy figure at the door and then another figure. She heard the babbling of voices. One of the figures drew near and then away. Then, total silence. She crawled to her bedroom and pulled herself onto the bed. She needed to rest until her head cleared. While she laid there, Anna heard unfamiliar sounds coming from the backyard. She dragged her limp body from the bed to the window. It was late at night and the yard was illuminated by the waxing moon. Still in a transfixed state of mind, Anna thought she could see Spencer Barnes burying something in the flower garden. She felt her tummy and began to weep. Her child was gone.

When she had gathered enough strength, she went to the garden and located the spot where her baby had been buried. She scratched at the loose soil until she found a wooden box. There was a plastic bag inside. Again, she wept.

"It was getting close to sunrise," Anna tells Justin. "There was a weeping willow tree in the backyard much like this one." She glances overhead for a moment. "I wrapped my child in a shawl that I had draped over my shoulders and I buried him beneath the willow tree." Anna rubs her teary eyes and coughs a few times. "I didn't want anyone to know about our special place, so I covered up the empty wooden box before I went into the house."

Justin is hearing much more than he expected and he remains silent while the red-faced lady struggles with the image of her awful past.

"When I die, Justin, I want to rest in a special place. Here!" Her eyes plead with him. "Can you arrange it for me?"

He can't deny her pathetic expression. "I'll try! Let's hope that day doesn't come for a long time."

"That day can't come soon enough," says the old woman.

*

Detective Reinhardt walks into his office where Newland and Cooney have been impatiently biding their time.

Twisting in his chair, Dick asks, "Where have you been all morning?"

Willy, at the same time, leaves his window perch and sits beside his mate.

Lowering himself delicately in his chair, Jack answers, "We had a family outing at the zoo and then a fabulous brunch." He rubs his belly. "I should do that more often."

"That's great, Jack," says Dick, "but what about yesterday?"

Jack has to think for a moment aloud. "What happened yesterday, Richard?"

"Barnes and the wooden box, for God's sake!"

His boss calmly tells them it was empty.

"Empty!" exclaims Newland.

"Empty!" echoes Cooney.

Reinhardt shrugs his shoulders and shakes his head. "It's got me confused. Why would there be an empty box?"

"Where's Barnes?" asks Newland.

"Because there wasn't a body, I had no recourse but to release him." Jack adds, "I need you two guys to keep close tabs on him again."

Detectives Newland and Cooney nod in agreement.

Jack ponders for a moment. "What I can't figure out is why a wooden box if there was no child?"

"Here's an idea," says the Scotsman. "What if there was a child and it never died, or what if there were twins and only one of them died?"

"That's crazy, William," says Jack. "I'm trying to be serious."

"Don't be so silly, Willy!" says Newland and the two of them giggle like school kids.

Chapter 15

Carol Reinhardt is busy restoring order to her kitchen after Sunday's roast beef dinner when she hears a familiar rap on the side door. She wipes her hands on her lime green apron and opens the door. "Come on in, Justin!"

"Hello, Mrs. Reinhardt! Is Shannon ready yet?"

Students of the university are eligible to receive inexpensive dental care at the School of Dentistry on campus. Shannon has an early appointment Monday morning before classes and it will be more convenient staying at Justin's place tonight.

"She should be ready in a few minutes, Justin! Go and make yourself comfortable in the living room." Carol resumes her housework as Justin makes his way to the couch.

Jenny is upstairs working on her speech when she recognizes Justin's voice coming from the kitchen. Thinking he may be here only a few minutes and there's no time to waste, the little girl hurries downstairs. She leaps on the couch almost landing in Justin's lap.

"You seem to be excited, Jenny! How's your speech coming?"

She grins with anticipation. "It's going great! I just need to know the answer to my question. Do elephants cry?"

Justin hedges and Jenny can sense he doesn't have an answer for her.

"Your speech isn't due until November and don't you have a birthday coming up the end of this month?"

Jenny frowns as she nods affirmatively.

Justin then promises to tell Jenny the answer to her question by the end of the month. "It will be a birthday present."

She's a little disappointed but agrees to wait until then. Remembering Justin's plans to interview the red-faced lady, Jenny asks, "How's your term paper coming?"

Acting much less excited about his term paper than Jenny is about her speech, he offers the little girl a deal. "When our projects are both finished, we'll read them to each other."

This sounds like a good plan and they consummate the deal with a handshake just as Shannon descends the stairs carrying her overnight bag.

"I'm ready," she tells Justin. "Let's go! I can't wait to hear what the red-faced lady told you yesterday."

Before her older sister whisks him away, Jenny reminds Justin of his promise. "I need the answer to my question by the end of the month!"

*

Willy lets the dishwater out of the sink while Dick dries the last of the supper dishes. Duties alternate each time they dine at home. Tonight's collation consisted of a frozen lasagna entree oven-heated to perfection with a side of garlic bread and washed down with a bottle of imported lager.

"That was a good supper, don't you think?" Newland asks his roommate.

"Aye and now it's time for dessert." Cooney opens the refrigerator door and retrieves a bottle of his favourite quaff. Holding it to his ear, the Scotsman twists the cap. "I love that sound!"

Dick giggles. "You sure do like your beer." He places the last of the utensils in a drawer. "What are your plans for tonight, Willy?"

"I'll probably just watch a wee bit of TV and go to bed early." Cooney moves to the living room and slumps wearily into the couch. "What have you got planned, Dick?" he shouts over his shoulder.

Newland finishes in the kitchen and joins his friend on the couch.

"I don't know. Maybe I'll write some of my book tonight."

Willy is pleasantly impressed. "You're writing a book?"

"A mystery novel."

Cooney salutes his mate by raising his bottle and taking a healthy swallow. "That's great!" the Scotsman exclaims as he uses his free hand to prevent beer from running down his chin.

"Yeah, I think it's great too. You're the only person that knows. I haven't even told Jack!"

"What's the book about?"

"It's a murder mystery about a serial killer terrorizing the city. The main character is a super cop who finds the bad guy and solves the mystery."

*

Shannon lets her overnight bag slip from her shoulder and sets it on the floor as she plops down on the couch while Justin goes to the kitchen and pours his girlfriend a glass of her favourite Shiraz.

"Have I told you how much I love you lately?" he shouts from the other room and she responds with a giggle. Shannon hopes she never tires of hearing those cherished words.

Justin reaches behind her and plants a kiss on her neck. "Here's your wine, my love."

Shannon is anxious and wants to know all the juicy details of his latest interview. "What did the red-faced lady tell you?"

"Anna," he corrects her.

Shannon complies by rephrasing her question, "What did Anna tell you?"

"She's very sick. Her health, I mean. She's always shivering and coughing, and I can see the pain in her eyes."

"Did you ask her about the red face and elephant tattoo?"

"That face!" he exclaims. "I'm sitting across from her trying not to stare!" He takes a sip of wine. "I haven't had the courage to ask."

Justin tells her about the secret meeting place under the willow tree that his father had arranged for her and of her wish to be buried there. He tells of Anna's failed marriage and the loss of a child while Shannon struggles to absorb the accounts of the woman's tragic life.

"I think she wants to die."

"The poor woman. Are you recording all of this?"

"Not in front of Anna," he tells his girlfriend. "I race to the locker room and write down everything. All of my notes are in my backpack."

"This is turning out to be quite a term paper!"

"More than I anticipated," he admits. "Let's get ready for bed."

Shannon eases her way from the couch and grabs her overnight bag. Justin takes the empty wine glasses from the table and starts for the kitchen.

"I'll clean up in here while you get ready, my love!"

Shannon glides down the hallway and into the main bathroom while Justin sets the glasses by the sink and scurries behind her. He needs to put his plan into action.

The master bedroom has been tidied for the occasion. The four-post bed is covered with a thick, down-filled comforter with fresh, cotton sheets beneath. Justin opens the top drawer of a recently dusted bureau and retrieves the gold nugget which is kept in a velvety ring box. He then runs to Shannon's side of the bed and places the box under her pillow.

Justin has just enough time to freshen up, get naked and slip under the covers before he hears footsteps in the hallway. His heartbeat races as Shannon pauses teasingly at the bedroom doorway.

Wearing a white nightshirt that stops midway down her thighs, her nakedness is visible through the shear material. She winds a length of her long, dark hair around her index finger. "I think I'll get my hair cut. What do you think?"

"Change can only alter perfection."

She giggles and struts seductively towards him. He lifts the covers for her to slide in effortlessly beside him. Her head eases back into the pillow and the lovers passionately embrace.

Their kissing is interrupted when Shannon senses something lumpy by her head. "What's that? I can feel something hard."

"That's me!"

His girlfriend appears to be in some discomfort. "Not you, silly. There's something under my pillow!"

Shannon reaches behind and retrieves the velvety ring box. The hinges of the box are spring-loaded and the lid snaps open. Her eyes soon sparkle like the gold nugget within.

"You can design your own ring with it."

Leaping from the bed, Justin races around to her side. Getting to one knee, he looks her straight in the eyes and proposes. "Will you marry me?"

The betrothed will spend the rest of the night embracing and consummating their love for each other.

*

"You're writing a mystery novel! That's awesome!" Cooney believes his new mate could become an accomplished writer one day and he is very impressed.

"Detective work helps me come up with ideas to write about," says Newland in a modest fashion. "And like I said, you're the only person who knows I'm writing a book."

The Scotsman reaches for the remote on the coffee table and clicks the power button. The television flashes from station to station until it stops at a movie channel.

"Hey, Dick!" exclaims Willy. "It's your wee mate the Wizard!" Cooney has stumbled across the October classic 'The Wizard of Oz'.

Newland appears disgusted by his friend's comment. "Don't remind me of that flamer, Willy. He turns my stomach."

"Ach, look at that!"

The exhilarated roommates gaze at the disturbing scene where the winged monkeys, controlled by the Wicked Witch of the West, set upon Dorothy and her friends. After tearing apart the Scarecrow, the ugly creatures fly off with the little girl and her dog Toto. Both men find the segment quite incredulous.

"Bloody hell!" says Willy as he stares in amazement and takes a swig of his beer.

"Can you believe our parents let us watch this stuff?" says Dick.

Chapter 16

Justin is wearing a morning smile as he waltzes through the compound on his way to the locker room. His thoughts of Shannon are suddenly distracted by loud snorts coming from the elephant pen. Justin races over and opens the gate to see Buster standing alone in the middle of the yard. His ankles are in chains.

Justin drops his backpack on the ground and approaches the elephant with caution. "What's wrong, boy?"

Buster waddles a few steps towards his trainer and gently taps him on the shoulder with his trunk. Justin detects a hint of sadness in the elephant's eyes as he rubs Buster's trunk. "How come you're in chains?"

The majestic elephant jerks his head slightly. He is aware of an intruder.

"Good morning, Justin!" says Pete Simpson.

"How come Buster is outside with shackles on?"

The attendant on duty last night had left a report on Simpson's desk. Apparently, Buster had been resting comfortably when all of a sudden he erupted like an explosive volcano. He was agitated beyond control and the safety gate of his stall had to be activated. It took several employees to strap and chain him. When the elephant was fully subdued, bindings were removed and he was led outside. The chains remained on as a precaution.

"I guess he got too aggressive last night and had to be isolated. Something is definitely wrong with this elephant."

Justin continues to rub Buster's trunk. "Look at him, Pete! He's as gentle as a pussycat." The young trainer's attention has a calming effect on the elephant.

Simpson is impressed by Justin's dominance over this huge creature, but is worried for his young employee.

"The pussycats we have around here aren't very gentle."

"Well, I don't like the idea of chains. I'm getting them off right away."

"You better be careful," Pete warns him.

Turning to lead Buster back to his stall, Justin asks, "Have you seen the red-faced lady this morning, Pete?"

Simpson shakes his head from side to side as if to say no. "Why don't you forget about her, Justin. She'll never talk to you."

*

Pete Simpson makes his way to the entrance gate and playfully says to his longtime friend, "I'm looking for the Keeper of the Zoo."

"That would be me," says Phil Marlow.

"Has the red-faced lady reared her ugly head?"

"About twenty minutes ago. "Why?"

Pete explains that Justin wants to know if she's here and they discuss the young man's futile attempts to use the red-faced lady as a subject for his term paper.

"Maybe we should tell him the truth," suggests Phil.

Pete is adamant with his response. "Absolutely not!"

Marlow rethinks his statement. "I guess you're right."

"You're damn right I'm right! Besides, we made a promise to Joe we'd never tell Justin."

*

Making his way to the secret meeting place, Justin is alarmed by the sight of Anna slumped over the picnic table and he quickens his pace. The noise of crunching leaves underfoot arouses Anna and she lifts her head.

"Thank God! I thought you might be .."

"Dead," she finishes his sentence. "My time is coming soon, my boy!"

Anna is definitely ill and she coughs several times. Justin sits across from her and he is quite concerned for her health. "Are you okay?" he asks.

The old woman's voice is very weak. "Did you give Shannon the gold nugget?"

"Last night," he tells her.

Anna forces a smile and wishes them both a happy life together. "I hope you have lots of healthy babies." She reaches to put her hand on his.

Justin feels her pain. "You told me you lost your child. My father must have wanted to help you through it."

She squeezes his hand and explains that after she lost the baby, she experienced a complete mental breakdown. She stopped going to the zoo and just stayed at home in her room. "I lost contact with the outside world," she tells him.

Bryce sat at his desk in an agitated state and poured another drink of scotch. "Where is that bitch?" he mumbled to himself.

He staggered to the sliding doors and stuck his head out. "Anna!" he shouted. "Anna, get down here!"

Leaving the doors ajar, he retrieved his drink and took a big swallow. He slammed the glass down on the desk.

"Anna!" he shouted again.

Anna grasped the banister with both hands and writhed her way down the winding flight of stairs. The pills have made her groggy and she struggled to reach the den.

"Close the doors and come here," Bryce commanded.

It was an effort making her way into the room and she needed to sit in a chair by the desk. Bryce made his way to the stereo and fumbled with some albums.

"You haven't been in here since we had our last dance. Remember this tune?"

The song 'All Night Long' by Lionel Richie started to play. It was their song and should have brought back fond memories, but it didn't. Bryce wanted to dance and Anna had neither the strength nor the desire to dance with this drunken excuse for a husband. She remained motionless.

Bryce wagged a finger at her. "Look at you! And to think I married something like you! I must have been desperate!"

Anna bowed her head in shame and began to weep.

Bryce waved a hand at the trophies on the wall. "Maybe I should mount your head up there with the other animals."

Anna bent over and put her hands to her ears in an attempt to hear no evil.

While the music blared, Bryce sang and danced about the room. Then, he turned to face Anna and started into his elephant dance. He slowly clumped towards her and unbuckled his belt. He dangled the belt from his nose. He twirled it overhead until it whipped down on Anna's back.

Bryce fell to his knees in front of her and bragged, "I killed them all! I killed the elephants, the tigers and your baby!"

"Stop it!" pleaded Anna.

He laughed a sadistic laugh. "That's right! I killed your baby!"

Again, she pleaded for him to stop.

"Maybe I should have put your baby's head up there on the wall!" He continued to laugh.

She had to make him stop. Anna grabbed the nearest object from the desk and swung as violently as her weakness would allow. The elephant paperweight cracked against his forehead and Bryce crumbled to the floor. Blood spewed from the gash as he laid motionless on the floor.

She sank to the floor beside him and her arms went limp. The paperweight rolled from her hands and onto the floor. She labored to lift Bryce's head onto her lap and she cradled him like a baby. Anna wept without restraint.

Realizing her husband's ugliness, she pushed him away and wailed, "You made me do this, you monster!" Smeared with his blood, Anna picked up the elephant paperweight and tapped her own forehead with it several times. "What have I done? What have I done?"

"I killed my husband," Anna testifies while Justin sits chilled to the marrow and tongue-tied. She attempts to hide behind her gloved hands as she weeps. "I'm so ashamed."

Moments pass before she says, "I ran away and didn't come back for a very, very long time."

The red-faced lady waddled from one attraction to the next. It was her first visit to the zoo in what seemed a lifetime. At the monkey cage, she recalled her first visit as a little girl and she smiled as she watched the playful creatures swing from side to side. One of the mischievous rascals clung to the cage and squirted in her direction. She took a step back and giggled.

"Anna?" Joe Lombardi asked as he approached.

The red-faced lady turned her unsightly appearance away from him.

Joe saw through this hideous disguise and softly said, "Anna."

Anna looked at him in shame. Her words died at the tip of her tongue, but her eyes spoke volumes.

173

"Your father welcomed me back to the zoo and planned this special place for me. He never asked about my past or why I looked this way."

Justin isn't about to ask her either and he remains silent.

"I never spoke to your father. He died without knowing my story and I feel it necessary to tell you."

*

Detectives Newland and Cooney have been instructed to wait in Reinhardt's office while he attends a short meeting with Captain Maddox. Dick swivels in his boss's chair and Willy sits on the window sill. Both men are wearing similar thick striped shirts and blue jeans.

Dick giggles and Willy asks, "What are you laughing at?"

"I was just thinking about last night when you were freaking over 'The Wizard of Oz'."

"I wasn't," says the Scotsman.

"Maybe it was the beers. You sure like your beer."

"There's nothing like a cold beer after work."

Newland deliberates for a moment. "I heard somewhere that true beer drinkers without a doubt appreciate a case of beer. A case of beer has clout because a true beer drinker savours the taste of each beer. Twenty-four times he savours the taste of a case."

Willy nods his head emphatically in total agreement. "Then I must be a true beer drinker."

The detectives enjoy a laugh as Dick places his hands behind his head and both feet on Jack's desk.

"I've been thinking. For my next book, I'm going to write a story about you. It'll be about a young detective from Scotland coming overseas to fight crime."

Cooney is pleasantly surprised and humbled by his friend's declaration. "You're going to write a story about me?"

"The young detective is a mastermind at solving mysteries and when he dies they put his brain in a jar right beside Einstein's."

"Does he have to die?" asks Willy with a hint of disappointment in his voice.

"Not right away. He has to become famous first."

Willy appears somewhat relieved as he peers from the window at the activity on the street.

Dick soon forgets thoughts of his next book and becomes quite interested in his partner's peculiar actions. "What are you doing?"

"I'm looking out the window."

"What are you doing with your chin?" asks Dick.

The Scotsman appears to be tickling his chin with his fingers. "I'm playing with my beard."

"You don't have a beard."

"I used to have a beard," says Willy. "Maybe I'll grow it again."

Dick tells Willy that he once had a beard, but it didn't come in very good. He had very little facial hair under his lower lip and cheeks.

"I looked Amish."

"My beard is pretty thin too."

Cooney continues to look out the window and Newland is quick to change the subject.

"I remember sitting at home in front of a window for hours at a time and staring at the outside world." He removes his feet from the desk and sits up in the chair. "You become judgmental and start blaming everyone else but yourself for all the shit that happens in your life."

Willy nods in agreement "I know what you mean."

"You also get lonely and out of touch with people. One day, I decided to stop feeling sorry for myself and join in. I did all the wrong things over and over again until I got them right." Newland smiles and admits that it's still a work in progress.

"It's a full time job for me as well," says the Scotsman.

"Life is a lot easier when you're less critical of people. I'm a firm believer in the old adage 'don't cast judgment on a person before you've walked a mile in their shoes'."

"Would you walk a mile in the Wizard's shoes?"

Newland looks disgusted. "You keep reminding me of that flamer. Besides, those aren't shoes he wears. They're poofy slippers."

The detectives share another laugh just as they hear footsteps in the hallway. They scamper to their feet and assume the chairs opposite Jack's desk.

Reinhardt enters the office, tosses a collection of papers on his desk and sits down. "Were you sitting in my chair again, Richard? It's still warm."

"All in the line of duty," replies Newland. "What did Maddox have to say?"

"The Wizard got roughed up pretty bad last night," Jack tells them.

"We were just talking about him," says Willy as he turns to face Newland. "Good thing you weren't wearing his poofy slippers last night, Dick!"

The mood has become more serious and neither Dick nor Willy laugh. In fact, they both look a little concerned for the Wizard.

"He should be okay," says Reinhardt. "He'll probably spend a few nights in the hospital."

Jack suggests that he might visit the Wizard later in the day and Newland isn't about to go as far as to visit his protagonist in the hospital.

"What do you want us to do?" asks Newland.

"You guys need to watch Spencer Barnes and follow his every move," Jack tells them. "His stories are getting weirder and I don't trust him." Detective Reinhardt immediately thinks of the empty box in the backyard.

Detectives Newland and Cooney are posted in front of the butler's home and biding their time once again with idle chit-chat. Since Willy's arrival from Scotland, the two have been forging a strong alliance.

Barnes is aware of the unmarked police vehicle parked on the street as he peeks from his bay window.

"The curtain just moved, Dick!" observes Cooney from the car.

"It's no big deal if he knows we're here. Our job is to follow him wherever he goes."

The Scotsman fancies this phase of detective work very tedious. He fidgets in his seat and fumbles with the crotch of his pants in an attempt to get comfortable. "I hope he makes a move soon."

"Hope," says Dick. "Hope is a very powerful and intense feeling."

Willy eyes his partner with a confused expression. "What do you mean?"

"You can hope for something small or something outrageous. The bottom line is, no matter what it is you're hoping for, you have to make it happen."

Cooney giggles. "So you want me to go and drag Barnes out of his house. Is that right?"

"He'll be out soon enough. Seriously though, what is something you really hope for?" he asks his Scottish friend.

Willy is quick to answer. "I hope there's a cold beer in the icebox when we get back to your house."

The detectives share a laugh and Dick promises to stop for beer on the way home from work.

Willy glimpses at the house only to see the curtain oscillate again. He sighs and looks at his partner. "What's something that you hope for, Dick?"

Newland ponders but for a moment before confessing, "I hope to find a pretty girl and get married someday. But, I'm always nervous around women."

Cooney sympathizes with his partner and contemplates the various setbacks he has suffered involving women. "They make me nervous too."

After sitting quietly and brooding over his short comings, the Scotsman reaches into his jacket pocket and retrieves a pill bottle. He twists off the cap and gently shakes a large capsule into the palm of his hand.

"What's that?" asks Dick.

"Glucosamine sulfate. It's for relieving pain in my joints. I feel like blowing up every time I take one of these."

"No shit! It's the size of a grenade!"

Dick watches Cooney choke down the pill with a gulp of bottled water. "I've got a bit of arthritis in my knees."

The Scotsman almost spits up the pill as he notices a car backing out of the driveway. "It's Barnes!"

"Here we go!" Dick turns the ignition key. "Buckle up!"

Chapter 17

Jack feels a warm chill as he enters the forensic lab and notices Dr. Hampton bent over a microscope.

"Hello, Vera! What have you got for me?"

Vera lifts her head and smiles. "I did a check on Anna's samples. They match the DNA on the victim's shirt. She was definitely there in the room."

"I know," says Jack. "The house attendant changed his story. He told me Anna was in the room but maintains she didn't kill her husband."

Dr. Hampton motions for Jack to follow her to the table with McPherson's remains. "I showed you the condition of the skull before," she reminds him. Vera handles the skull and continues. "The blow to the forehead would have resulted in severe bleeding, but it wasn't enough to kill him." Turning the skull over, she runs her finger along the groove in the base of the skull. "We've already agreed that this was the killing blow."

"That eliminates the paperweight as a murder weapon," determines the detective.

"The original report suggests the victim fell and struck the back of his head on the desk. But, the angle of the hit isn't congruent with the fall and my tests are conclusive. Instead of the head coming down on the desk, something came down on the back of the head."

"He was struck from behind."

The doctor nods affirmatively. "The murder weapon was long and narrow and will fit right there." Vera again runs her finger along the groove in the skull. "Like an iron poker."

"There was a fireplace in the room. The killer could have cleaned the poker and replaced it without anyone knowing."

Detective Reinhardt contemplates for a moment. "We know Anna was in the room and the victim was hit from behind with a long, narrow abject."

"That's all I have for you now, Jack! Sounds as if you're no closer to solving the crime than before."

"You've done great, Vera!" The detective pauses for a moment. "I need to see Anna!"

*

Jack makes his way along the cement sidewalk that leads into the courtyard of the Lawson Building. Inspecting the surroundings, he can't help but think the owner of this place goes to no expense in keeping it as run down as possible.

Behind closed doors, Jack can hear men coughing and spitting both of which are symptoms of heavy smokers. The smells of coffee and burnt toast filter the air. A white cat arches its back and hisses at the detective before it runs off.

Reinhardt lightly raps on the door of unit #6. With no response, he notices the torn screen on the window and he peaks into the apartment. It's too dark to make out much of anything.

"Hello! Is anyone in there?"

A repulsive vision from within suddenly materializes just inches from Jack's face. He gasps and vaults backward bumping into someone standing directly behind him. Jack clutches at his heart and prevents it from lunging from his chest.

"You scared me!" he tells to the man.

A dark haired man with thick beard is standing there. He smells of diesel fuel and cigar smoke. "I scared you or did she scare you?"

Jack tries to catch his breath. "Are you the superintendent?"

"Gus Tatulis. And you are?"

"Detective Reinhardt." Jack flashes his credentials. "Does Anna McPherson live here?"

The superintendent nods. "If you mean the old gal with the red face."

"I need to talk with her."

Tatulis eyes the door. She's in there, but she's not going to talk."

Regaining his composure finally, Jack exclaims, "Oh, I know she's in there!"

The nights are getting colder and firing up the time worn heating system is past due.

"I need to get back to work," Tatulis tells the detective.

The superintendent leaves and Jack tentatively returns to the window. Without peering in, he gently speaks. "I'm Detective Reinhardt, Anna! I need to talk to you!" He waits for a moment before adding, "I need to ask you a couple of questions. Could you at least write something down for me?"

The detective waits for a response that won't come.

"You haven't done anything wrong and you're not in any trouble." Jack is trying to be as delicate as he possibly can, but his efforts are futile. "I just need some answers."

Just as Jack slumps on the window sill, he is startled by a hissing, white cat. He takes a few steps back and the cat jumps onto the sill. Hissing at the detective one last time, the cat makes its way through the torn screen and into the apartment. The detective feels helpless and he turns to wander back to the car.

Sitting for a spell before driving away, he recalls the horrible image in the window. A part of him feels sorry for Anna and he decides to leave her alone for now. In the meantime, he needs to focus his attention on Spencer Barnes. Jack believes the butler has more clarity of mind than he lets on and that Barnes is definitely hiding something crucial to the case.

*

Justin and Shannon are sitting in their favourite booth at Checkers Restaurant prior to their Wednesday class. Unzipping a valise by her side, Shannon pulls out a book.

"Don't let me forget to renew this at the school library tonight."

"What is it?"

"It's a book on Celtic Heraldry with pictures of shields and jewelry and stuff." She leafs through the pages and stops at a marked page. 'What do you think of this design?"

Justin examines the picture of a particular ring. "That is very cool!"

Shannon leans over and kisses him. "I am so happy, Justin! Can we look at some designs together?"

"Sure, my love, but tonight isn't good. I have to get to the zoo really early tomorrow morning before school. Spending so much time with Anna has me falling behind in my chores."

Justin sounds very apologetic, but Shannon senses something deeper than just making up for lost time at work. "What's wrong? What did Anna tell you?"

He squeezes Shannon's hand. "You're not going to believe it. She told me she murdered her husband."

"What!" his girlfriend exclaims. "What are you going to do?"

"I don't know," Justin confesses.

*

Detectives Newland and Cooney are posted in front of the butler's home. It was a false alarm last night as Barnes took them grocery shopping. So once again, they find themselves biding time with idle chit-chat and sharing confidential information.

Willy reaches into his jacket pocket and pulls out a chocolate bar.

"What have you got?" asks Dick.

Willy holds it up for his partner to see. "I've got two. Do you want one?"

"I'm good. You go ahead."

Willy quickly strips the candy bar of its wrapper and, holding it at each end, begins to nibble at the coating of chocolate and peanuts.

Dick can't believe his eyes. "What are you doing?"

The Scotsman retrieves a crumb from his lap and puts it in his mouth. "What? I'm eating my candy bar."

"You're eating it like a cob of corn," says Newland. You don't eat a chocolate bar like that. You're supposed to eat it from the end." He takes a few simulated bites from an invisible treat. "That way, you taste all of the flavours at the same time."

"I like the candy in the middle," Cooney tells his mate. "I like to leave the best part for last."

Dick agrees. "I like the candy centre too, but I've never seen anyone eat a chocolate bar like that."

Willy holds his treat in one hand and wipes his fingers of the other on his pants. He then uses that hand to retrieve the second chocolate bar and he hands it to Newland. "Here, try it!"

Curiosity gets the better of Newland and he takes the chocolate bar from his partner. After removing the wrapper, Willy instructs his partner to hold it at each end and start nibbling.

Dick giggles as he soon realizes that half the fun uncovering the candy in the middle is dealing with the gooey mess and he licks chocolate from his lower lip.

"So, once you've eaten the outside and you're left with just the centre." He stops to catch a slipping peanut and he licks it from his palm. "What happens next?"

"Then you eat it!" Willy demonstrates by devouring his candy middle.

Just as Dick is about to enjoy his candy centre, he is startled by a rap on his window. He accidentally drops the sticky candy in his lap and he scrambles to pick it up. His fingers are sticky and everything he touches gets sticky.

"Shit!" he exclaims as it falls to the floor mat.

There's another rap on the driver's side window and Spencer Barnes is peering into the car.

"Can you get it for me, Willy?" asks Newland referring to the candy bar as he activates the power window with his sticky hand.

"I'm not getting it!"

The window lowers and Barnes informs the detectives that he is on his way to the university.

"I'll be there for a few hours. You don't really have to follow me." He leaves and walks to his car.

Dick hurries to find his candy centre. Reaching between his feet, he locates it and picks it up. It's covered in dirt and hair. Like a frightened kid with a lit firecracker, he tosses the fuzzy remains in Willy's lap.

"Here! Take it back!"

"For fuck's sake!" shouts Cooney. He jerks in his seat and swipes at the thing until it hits the floor again.

Barnes backs out of his driveway and starts away leaving the detectives in a sticky situation.

Dick paws at the ignition key and starts the car. Pulling away, he almost hits the far curb. "My hands are stuck to the steering wheel!" he shouts as he frantically catches up to Barnes.

Willy is quite amused by his partner's incitement. Pointing to his own left cheek, the Scotsman says, "You've got chocolate on your face."

Newland naturally wipes at his right cheek with his sticky fingers.

Willy giggles. "Not that side. The other side."

"You're a moron!" Dick wipes the left side of his face with the back of his hand. "Do you know that?"

Keeping pace with the car in front of them, Dick asks for something to wipe his sticky fingers with. Willy has already licked his fingers clean and he hands Dick a box of tissues. Dick grabs a few which immediately stick to his fingers. In his attempt to remove the tissues, they tear and stick to the steering wheel.

Willy chuckles. "Who's the moron, now?"

Newland does a slow burn while coping with his dilemma. He remains quiet until they reach the university. Sure enough, Barnes parks his car and enters the institution.

Willy opens his mouth wide and yawns. "What time is it, Dick?"

"Time to get rid of this mess," replies Dick. "Let's go home. There's no sense wasting any more time here and I could use a hot bath."

*

The wall clock reads 8:30. Doors swing open and the halls soon congest with anxious coeds on their butt break. Some race for the exits to light up a cigarette and others hustle to the cafeteria for refreshments. Justin and Shannon meet at their regular place and head to the library.

Arm and arm, the lovers turn a corner and proceed along a corridor adjoining the Library of Sciences building. Shannon's elbow is accidentally nudged by a tall, elderly man moving in the same direction and obviously in more of a rush. Her book of Celtic Heraldry is knocked to the floor. The gentleman immediately turns and bends to pick up the book.

"Pardon me, miss!" he apologizes in his depleted British accent. "I am so sorry!"

Not slowing for a response, Spencer Barnes continues his brisk pace to the library.

"He's sure in a hurry," says Justin. "You okay?"

"I'm fine." Shannon conducts a quick examination. "I just hope the book is all right."

At the library, Justin finds a table while Shannon visits the main desk. He eyes his girlfriend amorously and then glances about the spacious room. The elderly gentleman who bumped into Shannon is typing away on one of the computers.

"Okay, I renewed the book," says Shannon as she sits beside her boyfriend. "We can look at some of the designs on Sunday if you come for dinner."

"That sound great!"

Shannon smiles at Justin. "How's your class? Did the doctor have another classic entrance?"

Doctor David had entered the stage wearing a black body suit and red mask. A bright spotlight followed his every move while he wielded a large sword. He lunged wildly forward and he made a lot of other moves from side to side as he swung the sword back and forth like a pendulum.

"The audience laughed, but I didn't think it was funny," says Justin.

"What was it all about?"

The lecture, accompanied with theatrical performance, was about Dissociative Identity Disorder (DID) where a person could possess an alter ego or live a double life much like the story of Dr. Jekyll and Mr. Hyde."

"It was very eerie," Justin tells her. "The doctor was talking about masks and how the people behind them can change their behavior."

"That is so strange!"

Justin agrees. "All the time he talked, I couldn't stop thinking of Anna."

Jack sits at his desk poring over a stack of transcripts. These old documents are cold to the touch and he feels a chill. Rubbing his palms together, he puts his hands under his chin as if praying for answers. Glancing down at his wristwatch, it's almost nine o'clock.

"I've been at this for hours," he thinks to himself.

Detective Reinhardt does his best conjecturing at the office and working late is normal. Standing to give his legs a stretch, Jack waggles unsteadily to the window and peers at the downtown area. A line of headlights and the flashing of neon signs illuminate Main Street. The sidewalks are congested with an army of people popping in and out of consumer havens.

He notices a man resting on a heated grate to keep warm and reaching his hungry hand for charity. Victims living on the street are definitely a crucial matter of contention for the police department, but only one of many. Drug wars, gang rivalries, domestic violence and endless crime all contribute. Jack wonders if the police are fighting a losing battle.

Lifting his head skyward, Jack's eyes fix on a damnable gargoyle across the way. "Are you responsible for this?" he asks aloud.

All of a sudden, a red glow blazes from its eyes. With eyes bubbling like a witch's cauldron, the hideous stone rouses from its comatose state and thrashes its wings. One by one, the gargoyles come to life. They are agitated and wrathful.

The winged fiends swoop down and plunge into the bodies of the unexpected, infesting their souls and mutating them into demented and homicidal maniacs. All of Hell breaks loose.

"Ding!" The resounding noise of incoming mail on the computer snaps Jack from his imaginary nightmare. Shaking his head and rubbing his eyes help the detective regain his sensibility. He glances at the building across the street where the gargoyles have returned to their stone perches.

Sitting at the computer, Jack opens his mailbox. A message sent from a university computer is untitled and consists of an attachment only. Jack intently opens the document and an article written by Dr. David Sinclair-Smythe entitled 'It's a Jungle Out There' appears on the screen. He peruses the contents for several minutes and is confused.

Printing a copy of the doctor's journal, the detective will relegate it to the top of his stack of transcripts. Jack is tired and ready to call it quits for the night.

Chapter 18

Dawn breaks with a menacing advent. Ominous rain clouds laze overhead while the hidden morning sun highlights narrow patches of deep purple sky. A storm looms.

The corpulent Pete Simpson paces as swift as he can through the compound on his way to the locker room where Justin is readying himself for his daily chores. Entering the locker room, Pete doffs his hat and gives his raincoat a shake.

"It's starting to drizzle, Justin! It looks like we're in for some shitty weather."

Young Lombardi leans back on the bench and tugs at his boots. Then stands and stomps his feet. "There! Nice and snug."

Zoo animals aren't particularly fond of inclement weather and often huddle in their shelters to stay warm and dry.

"I suppose there won't be much action today. What are your plans for Buster?" his superior asks.

"Hopefully, I can get him outside for some fresh air." Justin realizes that Buster doesn't like being cooped up with the rest of the herd.

Simpson was actually thinking more long term when he asked Justin his plans for Buster. The zoo closes its doors to the public in a few short weeks. He wonders what the off season will have in store for the young elephant trainer and his ill-tempered subordinate.

"Good luck!" Pete says.

*

Detectives Newland and Cooney walk into Jack's office only to see him slouched over his desk.

"Did you get any sleep last night, boss?" asks Dick.

Jack is startled by their entrance and he sits up straight in his chair. "Not a lot," he answers.

"What's that?" Dick is referring to the document in Jack's hands.

Jack turns the wad of papers over and back again. "It's a science journal written by Doctor David."

"The shite?" questions Willy.

Reinhardt confirms with a nod of his head. "It was sent to me by someone last night and I have no idea why." Looking confused, he tosses the journal on the desk and leans back in his chair.

"You asked us to report in this morning, Jack," Dick reminds him.

"Any luck with Barnes?" asks Reinhardt.

"He took us on a couple wild goose chases."

Just as Newland says that, Willy giggles thinking about the sticky situation involving the candy bar.

"Where has he taken you guys?"

"He took us grocery shopping and to the mall," replies Dick.

"And to the university," adds Willy.

Jack sits on the edge of his chair. "When did he take you to the university?"

"Last night," answers Cooney. "Why?"

Detective Reinhardt immediately jumps to his feet. "Let's go!" He grabs the doctor's journal. "This was sent from the university. Barnes definitely knows more than he's been letting on."

The wipers thump from side to side as the rain splashes on the windshield.

"What a crappy day," says Jack.

Newland is very alert at the wheel. "Why would Barnes send you the doctor's journal?"

"That's what I need to know," answers Jack. "As far as I can tell, it has nothing to do with our case."

Jack ponders for a moment until receiving a text message and he checks his phone. It's from Jill. Suddenly, his heart begins beating as loud as the car wipers.

"Drive to the zoo, Richard! Barnes will have to wait."

"What is it?" asks Cooney.

"Jill says there's been an accident. She doesn't know any of the details."

Newland recognizes the seriousness of the call. He activates the siren and speeds in the direction of the zoo.

The police car screeches to a halt and Jack gets out. A mass of reporters and bystanders are huddled at the front entrance. Signs in the ticket windows read 'CLOSED'. Jack pushes his way through the crowd to the main gate.

"This way, Detective Reinhardt!" shouts Philip Marlow, the Keeper of the Gate. "Mr. Crawford would like to see you!"

Jack enters the evacuated facility and splashes his way to the main building where he is met by fellow policeman Detective Scott Shepard.

"Sorry, Jack!" the detective sounds remorseful. "Crawford's waiting for you."

Jack races to the director's office and feels a sudden lump in his chest as he meets Crawford.

"It's not Justin, is it?"

Samuel Crawford walks over to the door , closes it and turns to face the detective.

"I'm so sorry for your family."

Jack is devastated and needs to sit. "How did it happen?"

"We don't know as yet what exactly happened," the zoo director tells him. "There are two conflicting eyewitness accounts."

"Was it the elephant?" Jack wants to know.

Crawford appears partly responsible as he nods affirmatively.

"I need to call my wife."

"By all means, Detective Reinhardt! Take all the time you need." With that, the director leaves Jack alone in the office.

The officer in charge, Detective Scott Shepard, will go public. Standing at the zoo's entrance, he will inform the media of the horrible incident that claimed the life of a young elephant trainer.

*

The red-faced lady is drenched from walking a short distance in the pouring rain and she leaves a trail of dampness behind her as she wanders into the mall. Her favourite department store is busy as always, but there seems to be some commotion in the Entertainment section. The white gloves will have to wait.

An anchorman's voice reverberates from at least a dozen big screen televisions. "More on this breaking news when we return."

Standing by one of the televisions, an older woman talks loud enough for her hearing impaired husband to hear. "Someone was killed at the zoo this morning."

Anna nears the big screen and the woman is repulsed by this red-faced intruder. She tugs on her husband's arm and pulls him away.

The newsman returns following the commercial break. "Welcome back to our special edition of 'Live at 5'. There was a tragic accident at the Municipal Zoo earlier today that resulted in the death of a young man. With more on the story, here's Karen Hubble live on location."

The camera flashes to a woman reporter speaking into a microphone. "I'm standing in front of one of our city's most popular attractions. But on this rainy day, it became the scene of horror when a young trainer was killed by an elephant. An unidentified zoo employee told me that the victim had been working diligently with an unusually aggressive elephant since the animal's arrival just a few weeks ago. An eyewitness at the scene told me the trainer was attempting to stop a fight between two of these giant creatures when one of them turned on him."

The camera then flashes to a man in his mid-thirties with several microphones stuck in his face. "I saw the whole thing," he tells the news media. "The elephant threw the trainer to the ground using his trunk and then crushed him with his huge head. It was shocking to watch. If you ask me, they should put a bullet in that beast right now!"

The broadcast switches back to the Karen Hubble. "With me is Detective Shepard who is in charge of the investigation. Detective Shepard, what can you tell us about what happened?"

The camera focusses on the detective. "A young employee of the zoo was killed by an elephant. That's all we can disclose until further investigation."

His quick departure is momentarily interrupted by eager reporters crowding around. "We won't have anything more to report until we have all the facts."

The detective walks away and the camera returns to Karen Hubble.

"There you have it," summarizes the woman reporter. "A young elephant trainer killed by his own elephant. This has been Karen Hubble reporting live from the Municipal Zoo."

Anna has heard enough. She wanders into Ladies Wear to look at a pair of white gloves.

*

Samuel Crawford enters his office with a young employee. "Detective Reinhardt, I'd like you to meet John Duscharne."

Jack rises from his slouched position to shake the young man's hand.

"If you didn't know already, John, Detective Reinhardt is Shannon's father," says Crawford. "Have a seat," he directs the young man.

"I'm sorry for your daughter's loss, sir!" says Duscharne and Jack forces a smile.

"One eyewitness said the elephant attacked Justin," Crawford tells Jack. "John here has a different story which I believe to be more accurate." The director sits at his desk. "Tell the detective what you saw, John!"

"I was there the first day when Buster came to the zoo and he flung me to the ground. He scares me," Duscharne confesses. "But, Justin! Justin handled Buster with no problem." The young man fights back a tear. "Justin loved that elephant!"

"Go on," the director encourages him.

John takes a deep breath before continuing. "The rain slowed down a bit just around noon hour. Justin took the opportunity to get the elephants outside to get some fresh air and stretch their legs. I was walking by the pen and heard loud grunting. When I looked inside, I saw Buster and Lucy going at each other. Justin tried to stop them." Duscharne pauses a moment to collect his thoughts.

"How did Justin try to stop them, John? Please tell the detective," says Crawford.

"Justin ran behind Buster with the bull hook probably to get into a better position. Just then, Lucy lunged at Buster sending him backwards and pinning Justin against the wall. Justin fell to the ground and didn't move."

The young man recalls the events vividly. "Buster fended off Lucy and went back to help Justin. He gently nudged Justin with his trunk and he rolled him over. Buster wanted Justin to be okay." His eyes become glassy and in a sobbing voice he adds, "That's when the guys ran out and put shackles on Buster. They led him away without any resistance."

"Thanks, John! You can get back to your duties now," says Crawford.

Young Duscharne rises to leave and looks directly at Jack. "I watched them take Buster away, Detective Reinhardt. Buster turned his head to look back at Justin and I swear the elephant was crying."

"I believe you, John," says the detective. "Thank you for being there."

*

Shannon sits at her desk during English Literature class and shares a laugh with the rest of the students. Their professor is reciting a short and personal composition with humorous overtones.

The class is distracted by a knock at the door. It's a secretary from the administration office and she whispers in the professor's ear. The professor immediately approaches Shannon and directs her to gather her things.

"You're wanted at the office."

Shannon makes her way to the office and notices her mom at the end of the hallway. She immediately senses something has gone terribly wrong.

The family van is parked near the main entrance. The sky has opened up and the rain is heavy. Jenny waits with her nose pressed against the steamy window. She watches as her mother and sister exit the building and talk on the front steps.

Shannon screams in dismay and loses all strength in her legs. Carol catches her and holds on tightly. Mom and daughter make their way to the van.

The expression of horror on Jenny's face tells the story. Tears stream down the little girl's cheeks like a lava flow.

*

A very sullen Carol Reinhardt stirs a pot of hot soup on the stove top. Her eyes are red and puffy from crying. She hears someone at the side door and rushes to embrace her husband. "What are we going to do, Jack?" She starts to cry once more.

Jack has always thought himself as being a tough cop, but he has never had to deal with a heart-rending situation as this. He needs to stay strong for his family.

"We'll get through this."

Her husband's voice is reassuring and she squeezes him close. They remain locked together for a moment until Jack breaks the silence.

"Where are the girls?"

Carol releases her hold on him and gives her eyes a quick wipe with the back of her hand. She sniffles and grabs for a tissue.

"They're both upstairs. I gave them something to help them sleep."

"You should get some rest, too!"

"Maybe I should have a hot bath and read in bed for a bit."

Jack brings his wife close and hugs her for a long time before she goes upstairs.

Sitting at the kitchen table with a bowl of soup in front of him, Jack pokes at the vegetables with a spoon and thinks of the tragedy his family must overcome. The ringing of his cell-phone breaks the silence.

"Hello!" He speaks in a whisper.

After an abridged conversation with Samuel Crawford, Jack rises from the table to begin his post-supper clean up. While rinsing the bowl in the sink, he hears footsteps descending the stairs. Shannon appears groggy as she leans against the kitchen entrance.

"I'm sorry, honey! Did my phone wake you?" Jack walks over and holds his daughter in his arms. "Are you okay?"

She doesn't respond immediately and he leads her to the table. "Have a seat, Shannon." He lowers himself in the chair next to her and speaks in a tender voice. "That was Samuel Crawford on the phone. He said he would take care of all the arrangements."

"No, I'm going to take care of everything! Justin and I had an agreement!"

His daughter tells him of their plans for a green funeral and where they would be buried.

"Are you sure you want to do this?"

"I made a promise to Justin. I'm very sure!"

Jack is impressed with his daughter's fortitude. He holds her hands and they feel cold and clammy.

"You need to get back upstairs before you catch cold."

Nodding in agreement, Shannon starts to leave the kitchen.

"Justin has some notes in his backpack you might want to read," she tells her father.

Chapter 19

The morning after Justin's death is worse than a nasty hang-over to say the least. Jack drags his sluggish body from bed and ponderously readies himself for work. He feels it necessary to report today and his colleagues will pick him up.

Jack leaves the house quietly by way of the side door and gets into the waiting police vehicle. The car then drives away leaving a comatose household behind.

"Is everything all right this morning, Jack?" asks Newland.

"Everything will be fine. It's just going to take some time."

It's still raining and the car wipers thump like a heavy heart.

"Drive to the zoo, Richard! We need to pick up Justin's backpack."

Black clouds lay over the Municipal Zoo like a wet satin sheet. The facility remains closed for business and a small group of people stand at the front entrance with pickets that read 'Save Buster' and 'Let the Elephant Live' among a few others.

Jack is met by Pete Simpson who will escort the detective to Crawford's office. "What's that all about?" asks Reinhardt referring to the picketers.

"Animal Rights activists," replies Simpson. "They swoop in whenever there's an incident involving one of the animals. There will be a lot more of them showing up in the next few days."

"I hadn't thought about the elephant. What's going to happen to Buster?"

"In most cases, when a worker has been killed, the animal is put down."

The door to Crawford's office is open and Pete Simpson allows the detective to enter before him.

"Please have a seat, Detective Reinhardt," says the director. "That will be all, Pete! Thank you!"

Simpson closes the door and Jack sits in the only chair available. The other chair is occupied by Justin's backpack.

"My family appreciates your offer to handle the funeral arrangements, Mr. Crawford!"

"I feel that it's our obligation, detective."

Jack then tells the director of the agreement his daughter and Justin had, of the green funeral, and how Shannon wants to look after everything.

"Of course," agrees Crawford. "Tell her she has our full financial support."

"That's very reassuring. Thank you so much!"

Crawford directs the detective's attention to the chair beside him with a wave of his hand. "Here's the backpack you've requested, Detective Reinhardt!"

Jack rises from his chair and inquires about the fate of the elephant. "If you don't mind me asking, Mr. Crawford, what's going to happen to Buster?"

"His fate won't be decided until the coroner's inquest is completed and we've thoroughly assessed the situation."

"If your employee's account of what happened is true ..." starts Reinhardt.

Crawford politely interrupts. "We're talking about an elephant with a history of aggression, detective. We never want this to happen again."

"Of course not," agrees Jack and he leaves the office.

Detective Reinhardt sits in the police car and looks down at the backpack in his lap. Then, he looks up at the people gathering by the entrance waving signs and chanting 'save the elephant'. This is all too much for him to absorb at once.

"I'm going to work at home today if you guys don't mind."

Both Newland and Cooney understand and are in total agreement of Jack's decision.

*

Carol is straightening the comforter and fluffing the pillows when Jack walks into their bedroom.

"Home from work already, dear!"

"Hello, my love! I thought it would be a good idea to hang around here today and the weekend as well."

The two lovers embrace. "I'm glad and the girls will enjoy having their father close by."

"Are they in their rooms?"

"Shannon has been on the phone for nearly two hours making preparations."

Jack holds his wife affectionately. "She is an amazing young lady."

Changing into more comfortable clothes, his morning coffee is way overdue and he has some interesting reading ahead of him.

*

Detectives Newland and Cooney sit in the police car waiting for some action from Spencer Barnes and have lots of time to converse.

"We need to have Jack's back," says Dick.

Willy looks confused. "What do you mean?"

"He needs our support right now. We have to be there for him and help him through this. And we can't keep acting like screw-ups."

"What do you think we should do?"

"I don't really know, Willy! You're the great detective in my next book. Give me something to write about. Help me out!"

Willy is quick to respond. "You need to change. We both need to change."

"Where do we start?"

"Before we start, we need to stop feeling sorry for ourselves and be more positive."

"I know," agrees Dick. "I'm always making jokes. I guess it's my way of masking my own inefficiencies."

"Once we do that, I think changing our outlook on things is probably the best thing we could do."

"How do we do that?"

"The other day you mentioned how you were becoming less critical of people and that you were a firm believer in not judging a person until you walked in their shoes. Still, you condemn the Wizard."

"The Wizard is such a flamer!"

"He is strange, but he doesn't seem to have a problem doing his own thing. Maybe we need to feel more comfortable in our own skin and do our own thing."

"Are you saying we shouldn't dress the same anymore?" asks Dick.

"I'm saying maybe we should take a lesson from the Wizard.

"I could try to put aside our differences and not act unreasonable when I see him."

"If you talk rational to him and try to see things from his point of view, you may find out that you both have something in common."

Newland perks up. "I could show Jill how I've changed and maybe reconnect with her in a more positive way this time."

"Good luck with that," says Willy.

＊

Jack couldn't resist examining Justin's notes from beginning to end and over a second time. The notes reveal the whereabouts of a child's grave which explains the empty wooden box. The detective has already notified headquarters. The child's remains will be excavated and shipped to forensics later in the day.

"She can talk!" he mutters to himself. "She admits to killing her husband."

Jack wonders if Justin's interviews with the red-faced lady have finally brought closure to his cold case mystery. He gazes again at the notes in his hand. He needs to be sure.

"Dad." The soft voice belongs to his older daughter. "How is it going?"

"Just fine. How are you feeling?"

"I'm okay! I just wanted to tell you that the funeral is on Monday."

Jack invites Shannon to have a seat. "Do you know what's in these notes?"

"I haven't read them," admits his daughter, "but Justin has told me everything."

Shannon tells her father of how Justin and the red-faced lady met on occasion in a special place at the zoo, and of the old woman's relationship with Justin's father.

"I hope the notes help you solve your case."

Jack pulls Shannon in for a loving embrace. "I am so proud of you."

She looks over her father's shoulder and notices the science journal on the desk. "How come you have the doctor's journal?"

Swiveling in his chair, Jack picks up the document. "Do you know about this? Someone sent me this from the university the other night and I have no idea why."

Shannon tells her father all about Dr. David Sinclaire-Smythe and his infamous antics. She tells her father about the doctor's entrance as a punk rocker and how he included the maintenance guy, Mike Wheeler, on stage with him.

"Justin told me the journal was all about the doctor's exploits as a member of a street gang."

"Maybe this Wheeler guy sent me the journal."

While Jack contemplates the idea, Shannon needs to make a few more calls and excuses herself from the study.

Justin and Shannon had talked on numerous occasions about issues including personal health and the environment. They were eating healthier foods and exercising regularly. They had agreed to choose economically friendly alternatives where special events were concerned such as their wedding. It was their intention to have a green funeral as well. Shannon will fulfill a lovers' wish.

There will be no toxic emissions from an embalming or cremation process. The expensive wood and metal of a casket, the grave liners and protective vault, and fancy headstone will all be eliminated. Justin's body will be wrapped in a simple linen shroud and placed in a biodegradable box. A name plate attached to a stone will rest on the ground to identify his burial plot.

Shannon has contacted a cemetery that dedicates a special area for green funerals. Away from the eerie rows of tombstones, it's more of a conservation area where families are encouraged to plant a tree and flowers by the grave site. All of the arrangements have been made. Battling heartbreak and sorrow, Shannon's fight is indeed remarkable.

Jenny is curled up on the couch in the living with a book resting on her lap. She finds it hard to concentrate and she hasn't turned a page for some time. She tried to watch television early, but only gazed vacantly at the screen. Today definitely wasn't a fun day away from school.

Carol enters the room and informs Jenny that she just finished talking to her teacher on the phone.

"Miss Gilmore said your friends missed you today and everyone hopes you're okay."

"That was nice of them."

Carol reaches for the remote. "She wants you to watch the news."

Her mom finds the local news channel and they watch 'Live at Five' for several minutes until a story of interest catches their attention. People are demonstrating in front of the Municipal Zoo and a woman reporter is forced to shout to be heard over the noise. What she is saying is alarming to Jenny.

Jack is mulling over his pile of papers when he hears his younger daughter squeal. He jumps to his feet and runs to the living room where he sees Carol and Jenny on the couch. "What's all the commotion?"

"They might kill Buster, dad!"

Jack puts his arm around her and the little girl is just shaking.

"Justin wouldn't want them to hurt him! He loved Buster!"

"I know he did and Mr. Crawford at the zoo knows it was an accident. He said he would try to help Buster."

"You can help Buster too," says her mom.

"What do you mean?"

"Miss Gilmore said to get your speech ready for Tuesday. She has a surprise for you when you get back to school."

Jenny has a pretty good idea of what Miss Gilmore has planned and she needs to talk with her older sister. Racing upstairs, she finds Shannon in her room.

"Shannon, I need to ask you something."

"What is it, Jenny?"

"Do you blame Buster for what happened?"

"Absolutely not! Justin loved that elephant and Buster loved Justin."

Jenny tells her sister about the people in front of the zoo waving signs that read 'Save Buster' and 'Let Buster Live'.

"I want to go and help!"

Shannon gives her blessing. "You go and save that elephant, Jenny!"

Chapter 20

Dr. Vera Hampton had spent her entire weekend inspecting human remains, analyzing DNA samples and scrutinizing records. It's now Monday and she's still hard at it. She places a test tube of coloured liquid in a machine connected to a computer and types on the keypad. Vera then puts another test tube in a second machine.

A middle-aged man in a white lab coat carrying a file folder approaches. "You look a little tired today, Vera!"

The man is supervising coroner Dr. Theodore Leimann who presides over autopsies performed on all cadavers wheeled into the basement and who endorses all death certificates.

"Hi, Ted!" The doctor slouches in her chair. "What day is it?"

"It's that bad, is it? Well, here's something else to add to the pile." He places the file folder on her desk. "Here's the young Lombardi boy."

Dr. Hampton looks confused. "I've been at this so long, I think I'm seeing double. Take a look at this and tell me what you see."

Dr. Leimann bends closer to the computer monitor. "I see chromosomes with similar linear arrangements."

"Would you say they are a match?"

"What do the genetic markers say?"

"I haven't gotten that far yet," she tells him. Sliding her chair over to the second sample, she asks, "How about this one?"

He again leans in to get a closer look. "They are similar as well."

Dr. Vera Hampton appears somewhat relieved. "Maybe I'm not seeing double after all."

"Something smells very earthy," says Dr. Leimann.

Vera points to a soiled plastic bag on the table a few feet away. "The remains of an unborn child buried over twenty-five years ago."

"Boy or girl?"

"I call him Baby John."

"I'll let you get back to your work, Vera," says Dr. Leimann. "I know how busy you are."

Vera thanks Ted for his help and does just that. Getting back to work means looking for similarities in composition of all DNA samples connected to the McPherson case and checking the genetic markers. She has hours of work ahead of her.

She hears the footsteps of a lab assistant walking past her work station. "Dean, could you get a file for me?"

"What's the name, Dr. Hampton?"

"Joe Lombardi. It should still be in Recent Files. No rush."

"Sure, Dr. Hampton!"

Vera hits enter on the keypad and a message 'profiles match' pops on the screen.

"Very interesting!" she mutters to herself. "Jack's not going to believe this!"

*

The rainy weather reflects the dismal spirit of the congregation. Hundreds of onlookers watch six pallbearers dressed in a blue uniform carry an unadorned box from the tiny chapel. They are followed by the Reinhardt family and a few close friends.

The box is placed on a horse-drawn wagon which the pallbearers will walk alongside. The wagon starts to move ahead and people begin to fall in behind. The procession moves slowly down a paved lane and onto a natural path leading to Justin's final resting place.

Upon reaching the site of interment, the pallbearers lower the box from the wagon and set it on the ground. Mourners move closer and huddle around. A non-denominational cleric presides over the ceremony and Peter Simpson will deliver the eulogy.

Simpson talks of Justin's many accomplishments in a reduced lifetime and his testimonial is interrupted momentarily when a taxi screeches to a halt. A woman dressed in black gets out and makes her way up the dirt trail towards the service.

Philip Marlow nudges Samuel Crawford and they watch as the woman approaches. Along with a few other veteran employees, they don't appear overly impressed with her arrival.

Shannon has been clutching a rose to her heart since leaving the chapel. She steps forward and places the flower on the wooden box. In her other hand, she squeezes her gold nugget. Jack puts a hand on his daughter's shoulder as a sign of fatherly support. Carol pulls Jenny close and hugs her dearly. They are Justin's family and they share his loss.

The service is simple. There will be no vigil or celebration of life. Some people will mingle for a short time and reminisce. Others will wander back to their cars with their own memories of Justin.

Jack walks over to shake the hand of each pallbearer and to thank them for their source of strength. Samuel Crawford, accompanied by the woman who arrived late, walks over to Jack.

"Detective Reinhardt, I'd like you to meet Rita Lombardi."

Carol watches the introduction from several meters away. Jack shakes the woman's hand and points in her direction.

Shannon notices as well and walks over to her mom. "Who is that woman dad is talking to?"

Jenny, still holding her mom's hand, is catching raindrops in her mouth when she sees the red-faced lady at a distance. Drenched with rain, Anna is standing on the other side of an iron gate with her face pressed against the bars. Jenny tugs on her mother's arm.

Carol's conversation with Shannon is interrupted. "What is it, Jenny?"

"Anna! She's over there!" Jenny points to the gate.

Her mom looks, but nobody is there. "Where, dear?"

The little girl looks confused. "She was just there by the gate. I saw her!"

"Your daughter is a lovely girl, Detective Reinhardt," says Rita Lombardi. "You should be very proud."

"I was proud of Justin as well."

Mrs. Lombardi hangs her head in shame. "It's a long story. I could share it with your daughter if she wants to hear it."

"I'll see what she says. In the meantime, Mrs. Lombardi, I need to ask you a few questions."

"Questions about what?"

"I need to ask you about your relationship with Bryce and Anna McPherson."

Immediately, the woman's face turns pale and her demeanor changes for the worse. Gritting her teeth, she speaks in a loud whisper. "I detested them!"

Jack is somewhat surprised by her reaction and he realizes this is neither the time nor the place. He gets the address where she can be reached and he returns to his family.

"Who is that woman?" Carol asks her husband upon his return.

Jack looks directly at Shannon. "It's Justin's mother and she wants to speak with you."

"Oh, Jack!" mutters Carol.

"I have nothing I want to say to her." Shannon is adamant. "And there's nothing I want to hear from her either."

*

Large raindrops splash in the puddles that flood the courtyard of the Lawson housing complex. Unit # 6 is dimly lit and the shadow of someone inside moves past the window.

Anna waddles to the counter and prepares a gourmet dinner of canned beef with liver for her cat. It hurts to cough and she winces in pain. Her apartment is cold and dank, and her clothes are soaked. The old boiler system has malfunctioned and the heat to her apartment has been cut off.

Placing the dish of cat food on the floor, Dorothy shows her appreciation by licking the hand of her keeper. Anna is aware of her failing health.

"I have to find you a good home. I know a little girl who would take good care of you."

Wiping the counter with a well-used rag, she bends to put the empty cat food can in the garbage beneath the sink and the bag is overflowing with kitchen scraps. She shuffles to the door with garbage bag in hand and turns to see a contented cat licking her whiskers and fur.

"I have to go to my special place tomorrow, Dorothy! Maybe the rain will stop!"

The red-faced lady leaves her door and trudges towards the dumpster. On the way, she wobbles and drops the garbage bag. Collapsing in a puddle of water, Dorothy scurries over and licks Anna's face.

Chapter 21

The gargoyles high atop the building across the busy street are weathering yet another wet downpour. Jack is late getting to work on Tuesday and he hardly has any time to sip his coffee by the window and converse with them.

"What to do first?" he thinks aloud.

Jill leans into his office. "Vera is on line 1, Jack!"

Jack thanks his secretary and presses speaker phone.

"Hello, Vera! How's everything going down there?"

"Hectic as usual, but getting very interesting. I need you to get me one more DNA sample."

"Who's?"

"The wife of Joe Lombardi is the final piece to the puzzle. Do you know her whereabouts, Jack?"

Detectives Newland and Cooney have entered the office and Jack motions for them to be quiet and have a seat.

"It just so happens she's in town," Jack tells Vera.

"I thought she might be attending the funeral."

"I'll try to get that sample to you later today."

"Great! I'll have something definite for you in a few days."

"Talk to you later, Jack!"

"Bye, Vera!"

Jack ends his conversation with Dr. Hampton. He takes a pencil and crosses out something on a pad of paper. "One down and four to go," he mutters to himself.

Reinhardt finally takes notice of his counterparts sitting contently across from him and he can't believe how impeccably dressed they are in dissimilar outfits. Newland's navy coloured sports jacket is without any decorative adornment and his tie is a delicate mauve with a pattern of silver and white swirls. A pale blue dress shirt and charcoal grey slacks complete the ensemble. Cooney wears a light grey suit with a hint of black and white flecks. A plain white shirt is background for a tie of soft pink, grey and white stripes.

"You guys are looking quite dapper this morning. What gives?"

"William and I have been talking and we've decided to make some changes. I like how you call me Richard and from now on we are Richard and William."

The Scotsman is all smiles. "Every girl's crazy about a sharp dressed man."

Their usual silly and impulsive behavior which Jack is accustomed to has been replaced with a more refined character. Jack is impressed, but also suspicious.

"Where are we off to first, Jack?" asks William.

Jack looks down at his list. "First, we need to see Anna. Then, we need to get a DNA sample from Rita Lombardi." He immediately recognizes their confusion at the mention of Rita Lombardi's name and explains, "She showed up at the funeral yesterday. She's staying at a motel in the south end."

*

The signal for recess resonates loudly in the classroom. The sound would be displeasing to the ear of most people, but the students erupt with excitement every time it blasts. As the students rush for the exit, Miss Gilmore calls for Jenny to come to her desk.

The little girl approaches and the teacher asks, "Did you get a chance to watch the news the other day?"

"Do you want me to go to the zoo?"

"If you believe animals should have rights just like people do, then I think you should go."

"I can make my sign right now!" Jenny says with excitement.

"Is your speech ready?"

Miss Gilmore tells her that arrangements have been made to give her speech in front of the television camera today at noon time.

Jenny can't believe her ears. "I'm going to be on T.V.?" She had ideas of raising a sign at the zoo, but not this. "Do you think anyone will listen to a kid?"

"It's young people who shape our world for the future. You could make all the difference, Jenny!"

"I don't know if I can do this, Miss Gilmore."

"Sure you can." Her teacher is full of encouragement. "Go and make your sign. We have to leave in an hour."

Jenny races over to the art centre to make her sign. She knows exactly what she wants to say.

*

The police vehicle pulls into the parking lot of the Lawson Housing Complex. Jack gets out and heads towards Anna's apartment, but is intercepted on the way.

"She's not there!" shouts the superintendent from his front door.

"Do you know where she went?"

"The ambulance came and took her away last night."

"Which hospital did they take her to?" There is urgency in the detective's voice.

The elevator door on the third floor of University Hospital opens and Detective Reinhardt marches to the nurse's station. Flashing his credentials, he asks a nurse, "Where can I find Anna McPherson?"

The nurse looks at a clipboard and has some difficulty locating Anna's name. "You said McPherson?"

"The woman with the red face."

The nurse tosses the clipboard on the desk. "Just one moment, detective!"

She hurries down the hall and into a room. Within seconds, she returns with a man wearing hospital apparel. The man introduces himself as Dr. Sandhu and Jack is invited into a quiet area where they can talk.

"We have been referring to her as the elephant woman," the doctor tells Jack. "She arrived without identification and we haven't received any information on who she is as yet."

"Her name is Anna McPherson. How is she?"

"We've had time to administer a few tests," the doctor tells him. "She suffers from emphysema and tuberculosis. Both diseases are typical of homeless people living without shelter and a warm place. Does she live on the street?"

"No, but she lives in a rundown housing complex. How bad is her condition?"

"Her condition is very serious, Detective Reinhardt."

"Can I see her?"

Dr. Sandhu nods. "Wait right here. I'll get Nurse Riley."

A veteran nurse of many years of service motions for the detective to follow her. Walking down a corridor, Nurse Riley asks, "So, her name is Anna?"

"Yes," answers Jack.

"We cleaned Anna up a bit. You might not recognize her."

Jack immediately recalls his first sighting of Anna. "That's quite all right!"

"Dr. Sandhu requests that Anna not get excited. She's having difficulty with her breathing." The nurse leads the detective into a room.

Anna has been placed in hospital care with shared occupancy. Two of the bed dwellers have visitors and a third is glued to a wall-mounted television set. A privacy curtain wraps around a fourth bed where Anna rests.

Nurse Riley opens the curtain slightly, pokes her head in and whispers, "There's someone here to see you, Anna!" She slides the curtain open further and quietly departs.

Detective Reinhardt inches closer to observe an old and wrinkled woman with her head buried in a pillow. An oxygen mask is strapped to her face and intravenous tubes are connected to her left arm. He sees the pain in her tired eyes as she gives him a glance.

Jack introduces himself, but she already knows who he is.

"If I ask you a few questions, could you nod your head yes or no for me?"

There is no response from Anna and he senses any effort to get her to respond will be useless.

Sounds of the news network can be heard coming from the television and a woman's voice. "This is Karen Hubble live on location at the Municipal Zoo where an employee was recently killed by one of the elephants."

Jack is distracted by the TV and he steps back to watch.

"Protesters remain on the picket line in their struggle to save Buster the elephant. Today, their efforts are strengthened by the support of a grade seven student from Lincoln Public School. Jenny Reinhardt was a friend of the young man who was killed. Let's hear what Jenny has to say."

"That's my daughter!" exclaims Jack. "Could you please turn it up?"

He opens the screen wide so Anna can watch. "Could you tilt the TV a bit this way?" The patient in the bed across from Anna graciously complies.

When the camera focusses on Jenny, the little girl is standing by herself and holding the sign she had made at school.

"I wrote a speech on the slaughter of elephants and how the killing of these magnificent creatures has to stop or they will be gone forever." She wipes a raindrop from the end of her nose. "When I was doing my research, I learned about some horrible things happening in poor countries over in Africa. Some people are killing elephants for food and other people at war are killing elephants for their ivory to pay for weapons. I feel glad and fortunate that I don't live there. But now, some people in our own city want to kill an elephant and that makes me sad." Jenny hasn't any cue cards. She is speaking straight from her heart.

"What a cute girl," says one of the patients who is quickly shushed by another.

"We need to realize that elephants are capable of feelings, too," says Jenny. "I read a story of a mother's love for her family. She was shot and not quite dead. When the hunter went to shoot one of her calves, the dying mom with all the strength that she had left, lifted her trunk and put it on the hunter's arm. He saw the pain in her eyes and didn't shoot."

Jenny is very emotional as she continues. "Justin Lombardi, the elephant trainer who was killed, was my friend and he helped me write my speech. He loved animals and he loved Buster. I know Justin wouldn't want Buster killed."

Her eyes are glassy and she gives her nose another swipe. "I wrote my speech to save all of the elephants, but that's an awful lot to ask. So, I'm only asking for one elephant to be saved." A group of activists join Jenny on camera and repeat the chant. "Save Buster! Save Buster!"

The camera switches to the woman reporter. "I spoke with Jenny Reinhardt off-camera and she told me that the future of elephants lies with the wisdom of people and it starts right here with Buster. I'm Karen Hubble reporting for 'Live at 5'."

The station's anchorman finalizes the story. "Jenny Reinhardt is an impressive young lady with a clear message. Her sign reads 'please don't kill Buster'. We have more to come when we return."

The patient in bed three turns the volume down on his television. "What a smart little girl."

Jack returns to Anna's bedside and detects a glimmer in her tired eyes. With all of her strength, she lifts her right arm and points in the direction of the TV.

"That was my daughter," Reinhardt proudly boasts.

Anna curls her index finger in a summoning motion.

"You want me to come closer?"

Anna weakly turns her head back and forth as if to say, "No!" She again points to the television set.

"My daughter? You want my daughter to come here?"

Anna weakly nods her head signaling yes.

*

A neon sign flashes 'VACANCY' as the police car pulls into a quaint motor inn. Jack's attempts to dodge raindrops are unsuccessful as he holds the collar of his jacket high around his neck and runs towards one of the units. He raps on the door and Rita Lombardi soon allows the detective entry.

Rita sits on the corner of the bed with drink in hand. There's a half empty bottle of whiskey on the dresser beside her.

"I take it your daughter didn't want to talk with me," says Rita. The alcohol is definitely impairing her speech.

Jack sits at a table across from her and immediately gets down to work. "Mrs. Lombardi, I need to ask you about the McPhersons."

"I hate them!" The anger in her words is practically visible. "They ruined my life!"

"Let's go back to the very beginning when you first met them. Can we do that?"

She reaches for the whiskey bottle and fills her glass. Then adds an ice cube and swirls it around with circular motions of a finger. "It was the first and only time I saw them together. Joe and I were invited over to their place."

Spencer Barnes placed a tea set on the table in front of Joe and Rita Lombardi. The guests nibbled from a tray of snacks as the house attendant poured expresso into four tiny cups. Conversation was minimal. Joe had never met Bryce and they didn't have much in common except for Anna. Anna had never met Rita and Rita was unfamiliar with her hosts.

The room was very quiet when Barnes left.

Anna leaned towards Joe and they talked about the animals while Bryce got to know Mrs. Lombardi. Rita kept looking over at her husband who was completely involved with Anna.

"I didn't realize when we got married that Joe had a special relationship with Anna McPherson," Rita tells Jack. "Joe would mention her now and again, but I didn't know they were meeting frequently at the zoo." She wiggles to adjust the hem of her blue dress. "I saw the way Joe and Anna looked at each other that night and I knew they were in love."

"What did Bryce and you talk about?"

"He seemed to be interested in me and complimented me on how I looked. He said he wanted to meet with me and that he had something very important to tell me."

"Did you meet with him?"

"I went to his place a few nights later. He told me he would always leave the patio door open for me whenever I wanted to come and talk."

"What did Bryce tell you?"

"He told me that Joe and Anna were lovers and that she was pregnant with his child. I was devastated and vulnerable." Her anger mixes with shame as she continues. "We had a few drinks and we had sex."

Jack knows how Bryce McPherson manipulated people and he listens in contempt of Rita's actions.

"It went on for a while. I would go over to his place and sneak in through the patio. Nobody knew!"

Reinhardt now knows Rita is the mystery woman. "You were there on the night of the murder?"

"I was there," says Rita.

Rita Lombardi tapped lightly on the patio door and entered the den where Bryce sat at his desk. She made herself a drink and moved seductively towards him. She set her glass on the desk, straddled him in the chair and gave him a big kiss.

Bryce turned his head to avoid being kissed and pushed Rita to the floor. He stood over her and kicked at her.

"Go on, get out of here you miserable slut!"

"Did you kill him?" asks Jack.

"I could have killed him at that moment," admits Rita. "I got to my feet, grabbed my glass and threw it at him. Then, I ran out of the house crying." Rita takes a gulp of whiskey. "The bastard was alive when I left."

"I'll need a DNA sample, Mrs. Lombardi."

Her eyes light up with bitterness. Rita spits into a tissue and throws it at the detective. "There! Have a party!"

Jack takes a plastic bag from his pocket and picks up the dampened tissue. "I'll need you to stay in town until further notice."

She swallows the rest of her drink and sneers at him. "I'm not going anywhere but to Hell!"

Jack opens the door to leave. "My daughter is right. You have nothing to say to her."

As he makes his way to the police car, the detective hears a whiskey glass smash against the door.

"How did that go?" asks Newland as Reinhardt slides into the passenger seat.

Jack looks at both of his men. "She is one resentful woman and definitely a suspect!"

Chapter 22

With head in hands and elbows on his desk, Jack sits and contemplates. Thoughts of the McPherson case are racing about in his head like the people on the busy street below his window.

Newland and Cooney enter the office and Jack recognizes their presence. "Good morning, guys!"

"Good morning, Jack!" they echo in turn.

Reinhardt looks up and is quite impressed. Not only are both detectives well-dressed in dissimilar outfits, they have obviously paid a visit to a stylist. Richard's hair is cut short and parted on the left side. William is sporting a perm of neat curls and there is evidence of whiskers on his chin. Many of the interchangeable characteristics once shared by the two are no longer apparent.

"What's the plan of action for today?" asks Newland.

Jack hands Dick a piece of paper. "I want you to run this over to Howard and have him look up these names."

Detective Newland takes the paper and gives it a quick glance. "A&W, Little Caesar, Big Mac. It looks like a fast food order?"

"I get hungry every time I read the doctor's journal," says Jack.

His witticism doesn't receive even a moderate chuckle from his unresponsive partners and he explains, "These are the nicknames of the street kids that the doctor writes about in his journal. Tell Howard he'll have to go back twenty-five years or more."

"Right!" says Newland.

"Then take a ride out to the motor inn and keep an eye on Rita Lombardi. Make sure she doesn't skip town," he tells them. "In the meantime, I'll be at the hospital with my daughter Jenny. She's going to talk with Anna.."

*

Jack is mindful of Jenny's maturity and he is confident she will perform well. Sitting in the hospital waiting room, he feels it necessary to give her last minute fatherly instructions.

"Don't be afraid, dear! Anna is very sick. She might be wearing an oxygen mask and there might be tubes in her arms."

"I'm not afraid," Jenny reassures her father. "Does she still have her red face?"

Jack shakes his head to answer no. "I don't know what she might tell you. If you get frightened, you come and get me."

"Did she do something bad?"

"I don't really know and that's why I'm not sure you should go in there."

Nurse Riley pokes her head into the waiting room. "Anna is ready to see you, Jenny!"

The little girl gets to her feet and grabs her backpack.

"You can leave that here with me," her dad says.

Jenny puts the backpack over her right shoulder. "I've got something I want to give Anna."

Her father smiles, "I'll be right here if you need me."

Jenny wouldn't admit to her father, but she is nervous. Nurse Riley leads her into an ill-ventilated chamber and the heavy door creaks shut behind them.

A female patient shrieks. "It's the little girl on the news!"

Her approach has Jenny visibly apprehensive and a second patient comes to her rescue. "Don't be afraid! What you did yesterday was incredible."

The little girl gives an appreciative smile and relaxes somewhat as Nurse Riley leads her to where Anna's lies. Staring at a closed curtain, Jenny hears a weak cough from within and is momentarily paralyzed. Nurse Riley gives her a nudge of encouragement and leaves the stuffy room.

Jenny eventually finds the courage to part the curtain ever so slightly. A frail woman looks at the little girl with tired eyes and she smiles. Jenny returns the old woman's smile and inches her way to Anna's bedside. She's not frightened any more.

"I'm Jenny."

Anna is respiring without the aid of an oxygen mask. "Come closer." She whispers only to the air that surrounds her and Jenny needs to lean in to hear what she is saying.

The old woman weakly reaches across her body and offers her left hand. At first touch, Anna's hand feels rough and clammy, but Jenny quickly senses her tenderness.

The female patient in the room shrieks a second time. "The sun is shining!"

Gathering by the window, people in the room are bright and cheerful as they gaze at the glowing ball of energy in the sky. It has been over a week since they have experienced this wonderful sight.

Anna squeezes Jenny's hand and the little girl gets closer to listen.

"When the sky is crying, you see the sun. Don't you, Jenny?"

"My mom says the rain is the tears of angels and the sun will eventually shine and make things better."

Anna smiles. "Always see the sun, my little one."

Jenny releases her hold on Anna's hand. "I brought you something." She takes a gift from her backpack and puts it on the bed.

The old woman smiles and Jenny realizes Anna needs help to open it. The little girl tugs at the ribbon and peels away the wrapping to reveal a pair of white gloves. She helps the old woman put them on and grabs a tissue from her backpack to wipe the tears trickling down Anna's cheeks.

"I have something for you," Anna unfurls her right hand to reveal a gold necklace with a monkey charm. "Someone very special gave this to me and I want you to have it."

Jenny is reluctant but grateful. She knows accepting the gift is the right thing to do. "Thank you very much, but why me?"

"You are special, my dear! You love the animals just as Justin did and it was Justin's father who gave this to me."

Jenny takes the charm and holds it near to her. "I'll wear it forever," she tells the old woman.

Anna squeezes the little girl's hand one final time. "There's something I want you to do for me. Come closer, my dear."

Jenny leans close to hear Anna's whisper.

*

After driving his younger daughter home, Jack returns to his office where Howie Hirsch greets him.

"Hello, Jack!" Hirsch holds a list of names and numbers in his hand. "I've got most of the information you were looking for!"

"Have a seat and let's hear what you've got."

Howie sits across from Reinhardt and reads from his list. "A&W - real name Anders Wisselink. He's been in and out of prison for the past fifteen years mostly for armed robbery. You can find him at the County Detention Centre."

"Sounds like a bad dude. Who's next?"

Howie glances at his list. "Little Caesar – real name Lawrence 'Louie' Cassals. Not so lucky. They called it a gang related slaying in the newspaper. Found him in an alley with multiple stab wounds."

"I don't understand it."

"Understand what?" asks Hirsch.

"These guys were part of a street gang that Dr. Sinclair-Smythe wrote about in his journal," Jack tells him. "There was no mention of weapons or violence."

"Years on the street may have turned them into hardened criminals," suggests Howie.

"I guess you're right, Howard! What else have you got?"

Hirsch hands him the list of names and addresses. "Here, Jack! They're all there except for Big Mac." Hirsch looks somewhat defeated. "I couldn't find a thing on him."

Reinhardt smiles. "Big Mac, real name Mike Wheeler. He's the maintenance foreman at the university."

Howie Hirsch is totally confused. "How did you ...?"

"My daughter Shannon," Jack tells him. "She told me that Big Mac and Doctor David are still good chums."

"Do you want me to run his name through and see what comes up?" asks the computer geek.

"You've done a great job already, Howard! I know where to find him."

Hirsch rises from his chair to leave and tells the detective to enjoy the rest of his day.

Detective Reinhardt intends to do just that. He quickly finishes his paper work and will return home for an enjoyable family supper.

The Reinhardts have kept their family unit glued together over the past few troublesome days. Carol especially took it upon herself to soothe the grief and pain felt by her daughters and husband with tender loving care. At the same time, each family member has regarded the others with empathy and compassion. The Reinhardt household remains solemn.

Following their family supper, Jack shared many details of his work with his wife. His perplexity was obvious to her and he complained of a minor headache. Carol administered two non-prescription tablets which provided a calming influence and Jack was able to sleep without too much discomfort.

Chapter 23

Jack quickly bites into a piece of toast and washes it down with a sip of coffee.

"I can't believe I'm so late," he tells Carol. It sounds like a complaint, but he actually enjoys the luxury of sleeping in.

Carol recognizes her husband's pretense and suggests he drive Jenny to school this morning.

"Take the van," she insists.

"Come on, Jenny!" Jack shouts from the kitchen. "You're going to be late!"

The sun is shining bright and the school yard is filled with children at play. The Reinhart's van stops in front and Jenny leans over to give her father a kiss.

"Thanks for the ride, dad!"

Jack squeezes her hand and tells her how proud she makes him feel.

The school bell rings and children race for the doors.

"There's the bell," says her father. "Off you go!"

Noisy children with rosy cheeks and runny noses pile into the school. Kicking off their boots, they hang their coats on designated hooks and race into their classrooms leaving the hallways silent and muddy.

The grade sevens are a responsible group of youngsters. With limited prompting, they get out their journals and start to write.

Miss Gilmore waits until all is calm. "Everyone, put your pencils down. I need your attention please."

The students respond by putting their pencils down to listen. Their teacher tells them she has something to share with them before morning announcements.

"We're all aware of Jenny's appearance on the news and of her fight to save Buster." She walks to her desk and picks up a newspaper. "Well, guess who is on the front page this morning?"

Miss Gilmore unfolds the newspaper to display the bold headline 'Buster Saved' for everyone to see. She then reads, "Jenny Reinhardt, a grade seven student at Lincoln Public School deserves much of the credit for saving the life of Buster the elephant."

Cheers of elation fill the room and many of Jenny's classmates leap from their desks to congratulate her. The beam on Jenny's face is priceless.

*

Jack is somewhat apprehensive about coming into work so late and having his morning routine altered. He'll have to forgo standing by his office window sipping coffee and talking to the gargoyles across the street.

Not seeing Jill at her secretarial station as he walks by is unusual. Jack continues down the hallway to his office and stops dead in his tracks. Many of his colleagues and team members are there and cheer his arrival.

Reinhardt is totally surprised. "What's going on?"

Captain Maddox hands him the morning newspaper. "Congratulations, Jack!"

The captain is followed by others wishing Jack the same salutation while the detective peruses the front page.

"Thank you everyone!" he says as they depart one by one.

"How's it feel to be the father of a celebrity, Jack?" asks his secretary.

The proud father looks at his daughter's picture on the front page. "It feels wonderful, Jill!" Newland and Cooney slap their partner on the back as he walks over to his chair and sits. "I need time to absorb all this."

Jack reads from the newspaper. "The heartfelt words spoken by Jenny Reinhardt touched everyone involved and ultimately brought about the final decision to spare the elephant."

"Your daughter is a local hero," says William.

"Heroine," says Richard and his mate stands corrected.

Before Jill leaves the office, she informs her boss that the zoo's director phoned earlier and would like to speak with him sometime today.

"Great!" says Jack. "I need to hear what Samuel Crawford has to say about all of this." He looks over to Richard and William. "After our visit to the zoo, we need to pay Barnes a visit. I'm sure he's the one who sent me the doctor's journal."

*

"Come right in, Detective Reinhardt!" invites Samuel Crawford. "Glad you could make it!"

"Looks like the zoo is busy today," says Jack.

The director chuckles. "We finally have a sunny day. It rained so much this past week we were thinking of building an ark for the animals."

"I noticed the crowd of people by the elephant pen."

"All hoping to get a glimpse of Buster and that's not going to happen. The elephant is going through a series of tests and treatments right now."

"I read in the newspaper Buster might have a condition that I didn't quite understand."

"Have a seat, detective," offers the director and both gentlemen sit. "It's possible that Buster was in the throes of a behavioural phenomenon called musth at the time of the tragedy. Musth is a hormonal imbalance that causes male elephants to act aggressively. It can be treated and we're hoping Buster's condition is only temporary."

"So, it wasn't really my daughter Jenny who saved Buster."

"On the contrary," says Crawford. "Her inspiring message had us searching for alternatives and a specialist was brought in to examine Buster. Jenny is quite an amazing little girl."

"She is indeed!" agrees a proud father.

"There is another reason why I wanted you to come. It's about your investigation," says the director. "I haven't been totally honest with you, detective! I was sworn to secrecy but it doesn't really matter now."

Detective Reinhardt is very interested in what Samuel Crawford has to tell him and the director continues. "Joe Lombardi was a good friend and confided in me. Joe suspected his wife was having an affair and he told me that he may not have been Justin's biological father. I swore never to say anything to Justin."

"Did Joe mention who he thought might have been Justin's real father?"

Crawford shakes his head in a negative response. "Also, I need to tell you that Anna McPherson is the red-faced lady."

"That much we do know, Mr. Crawford! Justin talked with her and his backpack is full of notes from interviews he had with her."

"But I was told she couldn't speak!" exclaims Crawford.

"She chooses not to speak," Jack corrects him. "But she spoke to Justin and she spoke to my daughter Jenny."

The director is at a loss for words as Reinhardt picks up the backpack and bids him good day.

Detective Reinhardt is given a wave by the Keeper of the Gate as he leaves the zoo on his way to the waiting police car.

"Wish Shannon the best from all of us!" yells Marlow.

Jack returns the wave and now plans to pay the butler a visit.

*

Following their short visit with Spencer Barnes, the detectives decide to forgo the noise and congestion of a busy restaurant. They negotiate the drive-thru of a familiar fast-food chain and return to the police station to have their lunch.

The hungry detectives hustle to the large table in the conference room and start tearing away at the paper bags like scrounging junkyard dogs.

After a few huge bites of his juicy hamburger, Newland mumbles, "So what did Barnes have to say, Jack?"

"Don't talk with your mouth full," Cooney warns his mate.

Richard takes a deep swallow and sticks the straw of his drink between his lips. Rinsing his mouth with root beer, he apologizes to William. "Sorry!"

In a more domestic fashion before answering, Jack sets his food on the foil wrapper and swipes a napkin across his greasy lips. "First of all, I told him about Anna being hospitalized. He wasn't surprised. Then, I asked him about the journal. He was the one who sent it."

"Did he say why?" asks Newland.

"He seems to think there's a hidden clue in it somewhere," replies Jack. "He thinks the neighbor's kid knows something about McPherson's murder."

"The shite? What would he possibly know?" asks William.

"More of the butler's bullshit if you ask me," says Richard. "I've said it all along. Anna killed her husband and Barnes is covering up for her."

"He's certainly tough to figure out," says Jack. "We'll go to the hospital when Anna is well enough to talk."

"If she talks," Cooney points out.

The detectives continue devouring the contents of each paper bag when Jill enters the conference room.

"The Wizard is here to see you, Jack."

Newland flinches with abjection and Cooney, detecting Richard's discomfort, reminds his mate to mind his manners. Reinhardt finishes nibbling on a deep-fried onion ring and tells his secretary to send him in.

Within a few seconds, the effeminate snitch glides into the room. He appears much less flamboyant than usual dressed in casual attire. There is evidence of bruising on his face from the beating he took last week.

"Ah, it's the trilogy of terror."

"Looks like you've recovered from your injuries, Wizard!" says Jack. "I've got a list of names back in my office I want you to look at."

The Wizard acknowledges Reinhardt with a limp-wristed wave of his hand, but is preoccupied with Newland's appearance. Inching closer, the Wizard touches the crinkled cotton fabric of the detective's suit.

"Is that seersucker, sucka? You look good Dickie boy!"

Newland struggles somewhat to keep his composure. "It's an affordable imitation and I prefer to be called Richard."

The Wizard glances at Cooney and back to Newland. He is legitimately impressed with the detectives' tidy pretense and individuality.

"Ah, I do declare! You gentlemen look gooo-ood!"

William compliments his fashion critic. "You look nice too, Wizard!"

"Ah, you're just teasing me. Don't tease me, now. Are you teasing me?"

Newland echoes Cooney's compliment just as Jack rises from his chair.

"Let's go to my office, Wizard!"

"Ah, Jack, I do look nice, don't I?"

Jack encourages the Wizard to follow him with a tug on his elbow.

"Ah, and they look good, too! Are they teasing me?"

Richard and William are quite amused by the Wizard repeating himself as he leaves the room.

*

"Roll down the window and ask this guy where the maintenance shop is," Jack instructs Richard.

The police car stops at the gate and a security guard leaves the shack.

"How can I help you gentlemen?"

Detective Newland converses with the guard who goes through a series of hand signals. After thanking the guard for his assistance, Newland follows his directions to the Progress Building where the university's maintenance shop occupies the basement floor. Richard and William will again wait in the car while Jack carries on the investigation.

Jack folds the doctor's journal under his arm and enters the modern building. Inspecting the spacious lobby, there's a service desk situated in the middle with an information board mounted overhead. Jack walks over and peruses the list of names, departments and floors where the various services can be located.

"Can I help you?" asks a white-haired lady sitting at the desk. The creases on her face are as pronounces as the blue veins in her hands.

"I'm looking for Mike Wheeler," answers Jack. "Would I find him downstairs?"

The elderly woman points a crooked finger towards the elevators. "Basement floor, turn right. He's at the end of the hall."

Reinhardt thanks her and walks to the elevator. Pressing the down button, he hears the elderly woman make an all-call.

"Mike Wheeler, you're wanted in the maintenance shop. Mike Wheeler to the maintenance shop."

Riding the elevator to the basement, Jack turns right. The door to the office at the end of the hall is open and he calls out, "Anyone here?"

A tall, balding man emerges from an adjacent work area. "Hello!"

"Mike Wheeler?" asks Jack.

"Yes," the maintenance man replies.

Detective Reinhardt commences with his professional rules of conduct. Flashing his badge, he introduces himself and the two exchange a firm handshake. Using a tone of authority, Jack informs Wheeler that he is here on official police business.

"I'd like to ask you a few questions if I may?"

Wheeler consents to the questioning and sits in a chair by his desk.

"I understand you and Doctor David Sinclaire-Smythe have a close relationship which began a long time ago. Is that correct?"

"I've worked here for over twenty years now. It was David who got me the job."

Jack tosses the doctor's journal on the desk. "Have you ever seen this before?"

The maintenance man takes a closer look. "I'm familiar with it."

"You're Big Mac?"

Wheeler confesses, "I am!"

"The journal was sent to me for some reason. Why do you think someone wants the journal in the hands of the police department?"

"Beats me. Did you ask David about it?"

"Not yet," admits Jack.

"Maybe the police need David's help with something. I know he's helped them in the past."

Reinhardt moves about the room deliberately and inspects the surroundings like a good cop should. He will pay close attention to how Wheeler responds to his next question.

"Have you ever heard of the name Bryce McPherson before?"

Wheeler calmly answers, "No, who's he?"

Jack is convinced the maintenance man has nothing to help the cause.

"It's nothing. I've taken up enough of your time."

Mike Wheeler rises from his chair and the two men duplicate the firm handshake.

Turning to leave the room, Detective Reinhardt catches a glimpse of a silver object mounted above the doorway. The angle of reflection from a ceiling light hitting the silver object caused a momentary sparkle.

"Is that you're good luck charm above the door?"

"Something like that. Most people have a horseshoe, but I have that."

The silver object resembles a tire iron, but smaller and made of chrome. It appears to be a decorative ornament or an award of some sort.

"Did you win it?" asks the detective.

The maintenance man appears humble. "It's a long story,"

"Okay," says Jack. "Thanks again for your time."

Mike Wheeler watches from the door as the detective drifts down the hallway and disappears out of sight.

"Any luck?" asks Newland as Jack gets into the police car.

"That was a waste of time," answers Reinhardt. "Wheeler doesn't know anything. Let's go back to the station."

Chapter 24

The morning sky is an amazing blend of bright orange and pink tones. Jack stands by his window mesmerized by the glow. It appears as though off in the distance the city is on fire. In the foreground, the gargoyles slumber with their constant stares and sinister grins.

"They know something I don't," Reinhardt thinks to himself.

Feeling frustrated with the lack of progress in the McPherson case, Jack sits in his chair and rummages through the papers on the desk. He locates a telephone number and places a call. Detectives Newland and Cooney enter the office just as he hangs up.

"I've just made arrangements for a visit with A&W. Are we all set, guys?"

Tired of continually sitting and waiting for Barnes or Rita Lombardi to make a move, his partners are up for the task.

Richard replies, "Let's do it!"

The detectives present their credentials at the gate and the steel barrier of the correctional facility yawns wide for them to enter. The police car comes to a halt in front of the maximum security building and Jack is met by a uniformed guard.

Reinhardt is escorted inside and led to a small room where he will await the arrival of Anders Wisselink. The room is typical of penal institutions and much like the interrogation cubicle at the police station. Dull and uncomfortable, a wooden table and two metal chairs take up all the floor space. A surveillance camera is mounted high in one corner and a two-way mirror is constructed into the inner wall.

Jack sits in one of the hard chairs and tosses the doctor's journal onto the table. Any slight movement or sound in this hollow chasm causes a reverberant clatter.

The detective has only a short time to enjoy the surroundings when the door of the room opens. The doorway is darkened by two figures. A guard nudges the prisoner into the room, closes the door behind him and will observe from outside.

Jack remains in his chair while confronted by a man who is unmistakably suffering from numerous years of physical abuse. He resembles a cross between an aging rock star without make-up and a burned-out drug user wallowing in the gutters of Hell.

Reinhardt introduces himself and asks discreetly, "What do I call you?"

"A&W! You can call me A&W! You know, like in the root beer! Yeah, that's me! A&W!"

Not only does he ramble in repetitive verse, Anders Wisselink twitches and blinks as he rants. His hands would flail about if it wasn't for the handcuffs.

The sound of metal grating on tile swells the tiny room as the prisoner kicks the chair from under the table and sits across from Jack.

"You look familiar. Do I know you? How about the time we ripped off that '65 Chevelle. The red one with white soft-top! You look familiar! Do I know you?"

"You don't know me, A&W, but I know some of your friends," Jack tells him.

"Me and my friends sure had fun cruising in that car! Yeah, it was a '65 Chevelle! Man, you look familiar! You sure I don't know you?"

Jack easily recognizes the difficult task of conversing with A&W and will take it slow. "I need to ask you a few questions about your friends. What can you tell me about Little Caesar?"

"Little Caesar! Little Caesar was a good man! Yeah, tough! He was a good man! Got killed! Too bad! He was a good man! Tough, you know!"

The prisoner continues to twitch and blink while the detective gazes with watchful eyes. "Did Little Caesar ever kill anyone?" asks Jack.

A&W squirms in his chair and answers vehemently, "He was tough, man! Got into some tough shit! You didn't want to mess with LC! I miss him, man! He was tough!"

Jack continues the interrogation. "What about Big Mac?"

A&W convulses with each question. "Big Mac was a good man! Liked shiny things! He was a good man!" He appears agitated as he continues, "He quit us! He was a quitter! Not like LC! He wasn't a quitter! He was tough!"

"Why did Big Mac quit your gang?"

A&W jerks his head and exposes the whites of his eyes. "He was a quitter! Got soft! I hated him for that! He quit us! Liked shiny things but he was too soft!" He slams his cuffed hands on the table. "He was a quitter!"

Jack allows the prisoner time to calm himself before asking his next question. Bending forward in his chair, he twists the doctor's journal to face A&W. "Have you ever seen this before?"

A&W leans well back in his chair and then thrusts forward until his nose is inches from the document.

"Where's the small print! I'm not signing anything! Are you trying to trick me! Everybody tries to trick me!" He discharges a sinister laugh and peers up at the detective. "Everybody tries to trick me!"

"Do you remember Timbit?" asks Jack. "He was a member of your gang for a very short time."

A&W rolls his eyes and appears disengaged. Then he giggles as he squeezes his thumb and index finger together. "Squishy, squishy! Very soft! Timbits are very squishy!"

Detective Reinhardt explains to the one-time gang leader that Timbit was actually David Sinclair-Smythe, a university student posing as a street kid in order to infiltrate 'The Family'. The document on the table was an account of his running with the pack.

A&W is quite disturbed. "Timbit was soft! Too many questions! I knew he wasn't one of us! Too squishy! Big Mac let us down! Too soft! Not like Little Caesar! He was tough! Got killed! I miss him, man!"

Jack is confident that A&W knows nothing of the doctor's journal and asking more questions would be futile. He looks in the direction of the two-way mirror and waves a hand. The prison guard enters the room and helps the prisoner to his feet.

"Subway Harvey!" starts A&W. "He was a good man! Yeah, pretty tough too! He's dead! I miss him, man!" A&W continues to ramble on about Subway Harvey while being led out of the room.

Again, Jack feels frustrated with the lack of progress in the McPherson case. He sits and considers his visit with A&W a wasted effort.

*

The elevator door opens on the basement floor of the Federal Building. The forensic lab always sends a chill through the detective's body and Jack shivers as he approaches Dr. Hampton.

"Good afternoon, Vera! You look tired."

The pathologist has toiled for days with DNA samples. Testing includes working with various chromosomes and their groupings of phosphate, nitrogen and carbon sugars; ordering and joining amino acids to possibly form a protein; structuring and arranging molecules; matching and mismatching all genetic materials.

"Everybody tells me I look tired." says Vera.

Records and samples have been flying over her desk like crazy. She kept detecting similarities in the composition of certain profiles and thought she was seeing double at one point.

"I'm exhausted, Jack!" Vera leads Jack to a table. "The good news is all tests have been completed and the results are finalized."

"What did you find out?"

On the table lay coloured cards representing six DNA samples related to the McPherson case. They have been labelled and strategically arranged.

"I was a visual-spatial learner at school. It helps me to move around objects to solve problems. It's sort of a game. Do want to play?"

Jack smiles. "Sure!"

"As you can see, the red card is marked Anna and the blue card Bryce." She points to the cards directly below. "The pink card is Rita and the light blue card is Joe Lombardi. The two yellow cards at the bottom are Justin and Baby John."

"Baby John is Anna's unborn child," determines the detective.

"Yes," says Vera. She picks up Justin's card and waves it over the others. "Where should I put him?"

Jack points. "Beside Rita and Joe!"

"Based on the DNA markers, the probability of this match is zero percent," says the pathologist. "Joe Lombardi was not the biological father of Justin."

Vera rearranges the cards and places Justin's card beside Rita and Bryce.

"There's your match!"

Detective Reinhardt is dumbfounded. "Are you kidding! Justin was fathered by Bryce McPherson! Joe Lombardi wasn't Justin's father!"

Vera allows him to absorb the news. At the same time, Jack is remembering Samuel Crawford alluding to the fact that Joe himself questioned being Justin's real father.

Dr. Hampton then hands Jack the card of Baby John. "Where does this go?"

Jack takes the card and immediately places it beside the cards of Anna and Joe.

Vera slowly replaces Joe's card with the card of Bryce.

"Bryce McPherson fathered both children," she tells him.

Jack stands frozen with his mouth wide open.

After a short moment of silence, Vera asks, "What are you thinking, Jack?"

The detective shakes his head in disgust. "The miserable bastard killed one of his kids and never got to know how great a kid Justin was!"

"It's pretty sad," says Dr. Hampton. "What's your next move?"

"I need to ask Rita Lombardi a few more questions."

*

It's late in the afternoon when Detective Reinhardt knocks lightly on the motel door. Rita Lombardi lets him in and is the first to speak.

"I guess you have the DNA results, detective."

Jack is pleasantly surprised to find Rita still sober. Her speech isn't impaired and she appears much less spiteful.

"I do," he says as he sits in a chair. The detective waits for a moment before questioning the suspect. "I'm shocked to find out that Bryce McPherson was Justin's biological father. You have some explaining to do."

Rita is quick to respond. "The first night I went to see Bryce, he told me Anna was pregnant with Joe's child." She remains standing. "I hated my husband for that and having sex with Bryce was my way of retaliating."

"Did you ever question Joe about that?"

"Of course, and he denied it," answers Rita. "I knew he was lying and I continued to see Bryce." She sits on the corner of the bed. "Bryce told me Anna lost her child and that's when I told him I was pregnant with his child."

"How did Bryce respond?"

"He didn't believe me."

"So, what did you do?"

"I told you I went to his place one last time to plead with him. That's when he threw me down and called me names."

"You ran back to Joe and told him the child was his," determines the detective.

Rita shamefully nods her head. "Joe made me do it. I despised him for what he did to me."

Jack fills in the rest of the story. "You gave birth to Justin, stuck around for a year or two, and then skipped town."

"I made a huge mistake," admits Rita, "and I couldn't cope. I ran away and I've been running from something I can't escape ever since it happened."

"You sure did make a mistake. We did testing on Anna's unborn child. Bryce was the father, not Joe."

Rita leaps from the bed and races to the dresser drawer where she retrieves a bottle of whiskey. She seems confused as she fumbles for a glass. After chugging an unhealthy portion, she slams the glass down.

"You mean to tell me that bastard lied to me about Joe being the father?"

There's no need for Jack to answer and Rita's eyes once again illuminate with rage.

"You were one of his victims just like Anna was," says Jack. "He treated women like prey."

Rita continues to swallow whiskey while the detective tells her of Anna's reappearance and activities, and how she has been a prisoner for all these years.

"Anna's wounds aren't any deeper than mine. She just masks her sorrows with red paint." She takes another unhealthy gulp. "I drown mine!"

"Who do you think killed Bryce?"

"I envy her! I just wish I had been the one to kill the bastard!"

Chapter 25

Knowledge of the DNA testing only frustrates Jack. He sits at his desk and mulls over the case. Rita Lombardi certainly had motive and she admitted being there on the night Bryce was killed. A lipstick smear on a broken glass proved that much, but it isn't conclusive evidence in court.

The weekend rolls by without any further contribution to the case and Monday comes. Jack again spents most of the day leafing through Justin's notes and the doctor's journal. He's convinced Spencer Barnes is withholding vital information and he isn't sure about Ian Wilcox. The detective plans on speaking with both of them soon. Anna McPherson lies in a hospital bed and remains too ill to have visitors.

Two more frustrating work days will coast by without progress.

Lying in his cozy bed on Tuesday evening, Jack reads the doctor's journal for a countless time. His wife slips between the sheets and cuddles against him.

"Any luck, my love?"

He closes the document, places it on the night stand and snuggles beside her. "The house attendant is positive the journal has some connection, but I can't find it."

"How do they survive?" asks Carol.

"How does who survive?"

"The street kids. I can't imagine young kids having to live on the streets."

Jack is quick to answer. "They beg, borrow with no intent to repay, and steal. They're always breaking into places and they'll take anything they can get money for in return."

"I feel sorry for them!" says his wife.

"I feel sorry for some of them. Some of them are runaways and innocent delinquents. Others are criminals who terrorize the streets and are capable of murder."

"Do you want me to turn out the light, Jack?"

"Sure! I have to get some sleep!"

A couple of hours elapse and Jack hasn't slept a wink. His mind is a revolving door allowing thoughts in and out. Suddenly, Jack sits up in bed. "That's it!"

Carol is roused and groggy. "What's the matter, honey?"

Her husband is ecstatic. "I just figured it out!"

"Figured what out?"

"Who killed Bryce McPherson!"

Jack jumps out of bed and races into the bathroom to shower.

*

Detective Reinhardt, flanked by Newland and Cooney, storm into the lobby of the Progress Building. The white-haired receptionist picks up the phone, makes an all-call and points her crooked finger to the elevator. The detectives are on a mission and they take the stairs to the basement.

Without missing a step, they march to the end of the narrow hallway until darkening the doorway of the maintenance room. Mike Wheeler sits at his desk and doesn't appear overly surprised to see Detective Reinhardt.

"Did you forget to ask me something, detective?"

"Actually, I have a lot more questions to ask, Mr. Wheeler! You need to come with us to the station."

Wheeler remains placid. "Am I being arrested for something?"

"Should you be?"

Mike Wheeler thinks it wise not to answer the detective. Remaining silent, Detective Newland places handcuffs on him while Cooney reads him his rights.

Jack glances at an empty space above the doorway where Wheeler's good luck charm had been mounted.

"Where is it, Mr. Wheeler?"

The maintenance man undoubtedly expected a return visit from the Law and thought it best to eliminate his shiny award from plain view. He concedes without a fight and answers the detective.

"It's in the top drawer of my desk."

Jack retrieves the tire iron and Big Mac is led from the maintenance shop.

*

The police station is buzzing with activity as industrious workers swarm about engaged in their areas of expertise. Mike Wheeler is taken directly to the interrogation room while Newland and Cooney deliver the possible murder weapon to the forensic lab.

Wheeler sits across from Detective Reinhardt and pleads his innocence. Jack continues with his line of questioning until alerted by a text message on his phone. An expression of confidence overwhelms the detective.

"We have the murder weapon, Mr. Wheeler! The tire iron is a perfect match to the wound suffered by the victim."

The accused drops his chin and appears defeated.

"You look tired, Mike! It's over. Why don't you tell me all about it?"

It was dark, but not just because the moon was hidden by the blackened sky. Evil lurked this Devil's Night. Only something bad could happen on a night like this. Murder perhaps!

David Sinclair-Smythe aka Timbit had told Big Mac of an easy break-in next door to his parents' home. The occupants would be away except for a drunken son, his strung out wife and a butler who resided in the rear of the house.

"I waited by the front gate until all the lights were out," says Wheeler.

"Where was David?" asks Jack.

"He waited at his house. He wasn't comfortable with the situation and didn't want to be involved in a robbery."

"But he was involved."

"Well, like I said, I waited until the lights went out and then I went to the house."

Big Mac crept to the rear of the house and onto the patio. He would manipulate his shiny tire iron to pry open the French door, but the door was unlocked. He used a pocket flashlight which provided just enough light to move about the den without knocking anything over. A smoldering fireplace projected grotesque images on the walls and the big man was frightened. He squeezed the tire iron securely in his right hand.

The flashlight pointed to a huge, oak desk and Big Mac shuffled his feet towards it. Suddenly, someone or something grabbed his pant leg and he swung at whatever laid on the floor beside him. Alarmed by the sound of sliding doors, he retreated to the patio and into the night.

After a few hours, Mike Wheeler has provided a full confession and Detective Reinhardt leaves the interrogation room.

He stretches his arms, arches his back and smiles at his partners. Detective Newland and Cooney congratulate their boss with a pat on the back.

"We heard it all, Jack!" says Newland.

"What's next?" asks the Scotsman.

An expression of bemusement crosses the detective's face. "I think you're going to enjoy this, William!"

*

Tonight's entrance is regarded by many students to be the doctor's finest ever as Sinclair-Smythe duplicates Elvis Presley's last stage performance with brilliance. It's a lesson in Behavioral Science entitled 'Fame, Fortune and Forfeiture' with a focus on the ultimate cost of greatness.

The doctor's costume includes a black wig and bushy sideburns, white flared pants and high-collared jacket with shiny trim and sequins. Multi-coloured scarves hang from his neck and a guitar dangles loosely at his side.

The King's most celebrated songs continuously embrace the auditorium while Sinclair-Smythe lip-syncs. Following each tune, he tosses a coloured scarf into the cheering audience causing students in the front rows to brawl over the souvenir. After flinging the last scarf to his adoring fans, the doctor struts to the middle of the stage and is ready to lecture.

"Success inevitably resulted in drug use and abuse which led to Elvis's demise," starts Sinclair-Smythe. "The King of Rock and Roll was playing the numbers game." The doctor strums his guitar and sings. "One for the money, two for the show, three to get ready and." He strums the guitar once again before dramatically concluding, "Four to go."

Just then, the rear doors of the auditorium crash open and a uniformed security guard leads three detectives down the flight of stairs towards the stage. Dr. David is appalled by the audacity of someone interrupting his pageantry and remains speechless. Onlookers sit confused as the policemen ascend the stage and overhead microphones amplify the ensuing arrest.

"David Sinclair-Smythe," begins Jack. "You are wanted in connection with the murder of Bryce McPherson. You need to come with us." Reinhardt gets some gratification in purposely eliminating the dignified title of Doctor.

While Newland reads the doctor his rights and Cooney slaps the cuffs on him, a student with kinky hair and bad case of acne rises from his seat. He recognizes the bust as part of the doctor's performance and begins to clap in appreciation. A few more students follow suit and then a few more. Amid the cheers of adoring fans, Sinclair-Smythe is taken into custody.

Cooney takes the doctor by his right arm. "Right this way, you little shite!" he says as he leads the suspect from the stage and up the aisle.

Reinhardt leads the doctor by his left arm and detects how insubstantial and yielding Sinclair-Smythe really is. "Squishy, squishy! Timbits are soft and squishy!" he mutters to himself.

Students fill the aisle and the security guard fights his way through the mob in an attempt to make way for Doctor David's departure.

As the star of the show is escorted to the top of the stairs and through the exit, Newland's voice comes over the sound system. "Elvis has left the building!"

Hurrying up the stairs and pushing his way through the congestion, Newland passes a kinky-haired student with acne who can be heard saying, "Now he's performing exits! The man is a lunatic, I tell you!"

Chapter 26

One by one, team members meet in the conference room where they will bring closure to the Bryce McPherson cold-case mystery. Howie Hirsch strolls over to Jill and comments favourably on her choice of perfume. Vera sits and chats about coronary procedures with Chief Inspector Burgess. Detectives Newland and Cooney stand by the window and nibble aggressively on complimentary doughnuts. Members of the team share a sense of gratification for solving a crime and all are awaiting the arrival of Detective Jack Reinhardt.

"Good morning, all!" says Jack as he enters the room accompanied by a tall, slender gentleman. "For those who don't know him already, this is Spencer Barnes." Jack offers his guest a chair and tells them, "I've invited Mr. Barnes to join us this morning to shed light on what really happened on the night when Bryce McPherson was murdered."

All team members assemble at the table and Jack readies himself to disclose the events.

"First of all, I'd like to thank everyone for their unrelenting efforts and for a job well done." Smiling faces acknowledge their accomplishments while Jack continues. "It was Mr.

Barnes who sent me the doctor's journal and that journal was his undoing." Jack turns to face their guest.

The stately Englishman is poised with legs crossed and arms folded. He speaks eloquently.

"When Anna resurfaced, I had no experience in dealing with her condition and decided to take a night course in Behavioural Science at the university." Barnes speaks eloquently and has everyone's attention. "To my surprise, David Sinclair-Smythe whom I disliked as the kid next door was the lecturer."

Barnes adjusts his position in the chair slightly and clears his throat before continuing. "During one of his classes, the doctor was reunited with one of the gang members."

Detective Reinhardt clarifies, "The journal documents the exploits of Sinclair-Smythe masquerading as a member of a street gang called 'The Family'."

"The journal was written around the same time Bryce was murdered," Barnes tells them. "I couldn't resist the thought that it may contain the answer, so I sent it to the police."

"I thought the journal was just adding to the pile of paper-work until I met with Anders Wisselink," says Jack. "He was the leader of the street gang Sinclair-Smythe wrote about and he provided the hidden clue Mr. Barnes alludes to."

"Which was?" asks Dr. Hampton.

"Big Mac liked shiny things, Vera!" answers Jack.

Dr. Hampton, along with other team members, looks confused and Detective Reinhardt feels it time to disclose precisely what unfolded that dark night.

"Bryce McPherson was an abusive husband and a drinker. Anna McPherson was grief stricken over the loss of her child and zonked out half the time on pills. She was physically, mentally and emotionally tormented by her husband. Is that accurate, Mr. Barnes?"

"Her love of life had lost its spark and I believed she was suicidal," replies the former house attendant. "I kept a close eye on her."

"On the night of the murder, Bryce was drinking heavily," Jack tells them. "His friend Ian Wilcox dropped by, they got into an argument and Wilcox stormed out of the house threatening to kill Bryce. Rita Lombardi shows up and tells Bryce he's the father of her unborn child. They have an argument and she runs out of the house wanting to kill him. Soon after, Bryce summoned for Anna to join him in the den where he continued her torment." Again, the detective looks to Barnes.

"When I entered the den," says the Englishman, "Bryce was motionless on the floor and Anna knelt at his side. She held the paperweight in both hands and my only thought was she had killed him. I turned off the lights and escorted her upstairs."

"Mr. Barnes would clean her up and return to the den about an hour later to clean up in there," says Jack.

"When I returned, there was someone in the room," says Barnes. "By the time I turned on the light, the intruder had fled onto the patio and into the darkness. I initially thought Anna had killed her husband, but I was now convinced the real killer had just fled the scene." Barnes admits submissively, "Not wanting Anna to be involved in any way, I told police Anna was upstairs the whole time."

"You took a big chance perjuring yourself, Mr. Barnes," says Chief Burgess.

"I wasn't thinking of myself, sir! Only of Anna."

"There wasn't hard evidence to accuse any of the possible suspects and investigators in the case more or less treated it as a botched robbery attempt that inevitably resulted in an unsolved murder," says Detective Reinhardt.

Jack pours ice water into a glass and takes a sip before continuing. "Which brings us to Sinclair-Smythe's journal and my visit with Anders Wisselink aka A&W. Amongst his insane gibberish, A&W kept repeating that Big Mac liked shiny things and the doctor's journal mentions that Big Mac wore shiny things on his belt. When I went to the university to ask Mike Wheeler aka Big Mac some questions, I saw a shiny ornament shaped like a tire iron mounted over the doorway of his office. I thought it was an award of some kind, but it turns out he stole if from an auto body shop he had broken into."

Jack again sips from his water glass. "Anyway, Sinclair-Smythe wrote about the gang breaking into places and stealing merchandise to sell for money. Big Mac's ornamental tire iron would have been a perfect tool to jimmy locks and pry open windows. Unfortunately, it turned into a murder weapon."

"David Sinclair-Smythe set up the McPherson home for a break-in?" asks Chief Burgess.

"He would wait next door while Big Mac carried out the plan," says Jack. "Bryce had regained consciousness but remained on the floor. He grabbed the intruder by the leg and Big Mac swung the tire iron. That's when Mr. Barnes returned to the den."

"I followed the intruder onto the patio and noticed a light on at the neighbor's place," says Barnes. "I just thought they must have lights on a timer while on vacation."

"Big Mac raced over to join his accomplice," Reinhardt tells them, "and would relay the bad news. David stopped his masquerade immediately and Big Mac would soon quit 'The Family'."

"The doctor's arrogance was his downfall," concludes Spencer Barnes. "He coerced Mike Wheeler from hiding and I just happened to be there the night they were reunited."

Chief Burgess rises from his chair to once again congratulate Detective Reinhardt. "I know this case had a personal connection, Jack! Take all the time you need," he says before leaving the conference room.

"If I am permitted to do so, Detective Reinhardt," asks Barnes, "I would like to be the one who breaks the news to Anna?"

"By all means," replies Jack.

256

"Speaking of Anna," says the secretary, "I'm interested in knowing why she painted her face red and had the elephant tattoo."

"Mr. Barnes?" asks Jack.

"I needed to know myself and that's precisely why I took Sinclair-Smythe's class," says Barnes. "Anna truly believed she had killed her husband and she thought it necessary to transcend the boundaries of her real self in order to deal with it. She chose to hide behind a mask that reflected the last real image she had of herself. A face covered in blood and holding an elephant paperweight to her forehead was that image."

"But she looks so ugly," remarks Detective Newland.

"It was her situation in life that was ugly," responds Spencer Barnes. "Anna was once a beautiful young woman. Hard to believe, isn't it?"

"It's a sad story," Jack concludes. "Anna McPherson served a life sentence of misery for a crime she didn't commit!"

*

The three detectives negotiate their way through the crowded airport to the departure gate. Detective Cooney and the remains of Bryce McPherson are to be flown back to Scotland shortly.

Richard knew this day was forthcoming but hadn't planned well for its arrival. He dodges someone's travelling case on wheels and says, "I just don't see why William has to leave in such a rush, Jack!"

"Chief says William is to report back immediately. It seems as though William here is being missed by the Glasgow City Police."

Richard looks at his mate. "I'm not surprised."

The detectives continue to weave through the congestion to a waiting area. Jack hustles off to the washroom leaving the two friends to sit and reminisce.

In their short time as roommates, the two have grown from being cardboard copies into their individual selves. Together, they have shared and learned to deal with life's ups and downs.

"I'm going to miss having you around," says Richard. "You helped me to find myself."

"You helped me too, Richard. I enjoyed having you as a mate."

Their intimate conversation is eventually interrupted. Jack approaches and peers at his watch.

"It's just about time to board your flight, William!"

Cooney rises from his seat and flings his carry-on tote over his shoulder.

"That sounds like a hockey bag full of beer caps. What have you got in there?" asks Reinhardt.

"It's my going away gift from Richard."

Newland pipes up. "He's not to open it until he gets to Scotland."

"You'll be happy to get back home," says Jack.

"Aye!" The Scotsman's response is dubious.

Richard embraces his mate in a masculine hug and slaps him on the back.

"Thanks for all of your help, William," says Jack and they share a firm handshake.

Detective Reinhardt's first impression of William, who preferred to be known as Coon, had been less than complimentary. Now, Jack has the most respect for the detective from Scotland.

"I hope we meet again, William," says Richard. "We have to meet again! I'm writing a book about you!"

The Scotsman slowly walks to the gate and glances back. "Give me a shout and let me know how the book is coming." With a smile and a wave of his hand, William Cooney steps out of sight.

"What is that jingling noise in his bag?" asks Jack.

"Beer caps," answers Richard. "One for every beer he drank at my place."

"He's going to get detained for sure!" Jack's comment has Richard smiling.

Detectives Reinhardt and Newland use their credentials to acquire entrance to the roof where they can watch the takeoff.

"You're writing a book?" asks Jack who appears pleasantly surprised. "Is it a fiction?"

"No, true story about a Scottish detective who solves crimes and becomes famous."

"William is the detective in your book?"

"He's the wisest man I ever met," says Newland. "He reminded me of the lyrics of a Beatles tune 'take a sad song and make it better'. I looked at my life and knew I had to make changes." Richard takes a moment to recall. "William also told me that if I felt good about doing something then why stop. The bottom line is to be happy!"

The detectives watch as Cooney's plane rolls forward to begin the staging process.

"I certainly do agree with the changes you've made lately," says Jack.

"I feel better about myself and I owe it all to William."

The airplane taxis on the runway and comes to a momentary stop. At the same time, Jack's cellphone chimes.

"Hello, Jill!"

Listening to what his secretary has to say, he watches the tires of the plane leave the tarmac.

"There goes my best friend," says Richard. "I'm going to miss him."

Jack ends his call and they watch as the airplane performs a complete circle before entering its flight pattern.

"What did Jill have to say?" asks Richard.

Jack stares at the sky. "She wanted us to know that Anna passed away a few minutes ago."

Like Anna's soul ascending to heaven, the airplane becomes smaller and smaller until vanishing into the blue yonder.

"This whole thing is very strange," says Newland.

"What's strange, Richard?"

"The remains of Bryce McPherson depart for Scotland on the same date of his murder twenty-five years earlier. And now Anna dies on the same day."

"It is a strange coincidence," admits Jack. "What I find most disturbing, it's my daughter's birthday today."

Chapter 27

Carol Reinhardt vigorously stirs a bowl of cake batter and pours it into a pan while the aroma of spaghetti sauce with meat balls overpowers the entire house.

Her older daughter enters the kitchen and inhales deeply.

"It smells good in here, mom!"

"I'm preparing Jenny's favorite."

Shannon sticks her finger into the empty bowl and retrieves a small taste of batter. "Where is the birthday girl?"

"She ran upstairs right after school to work on her speech. She has to give it next week."

Carol carefully lifts the cake pan with both hands and walks over to the oven.

"Could you get the door for me, please?"

Shannon complies with her mom's request and asks, "Has Jenny got friends coming over?"

Sliding the cake pan into the oven, Carol closes the door and sets the timer.

"Your teenage sister has informed me that she's now too old for birthday parties." Carol gives the spaghetti sauce a stir. "She also says she's too old to go trick-or-treating tomorrow night."

Jenny stands in front of the full length mirror in her parent's bedroom practicing her speech. When she comes to the part where she gives mention of Justin and his love for Buster, Jenny's eyes fill with tears and she has trouble continuing.

"I'll never be able to get through this without messing up," she thinks to herself.

She starts from the beginning again although this time, she is interrupted by her sister's voice coming from the bottom of the stairs.

"Jenny, it's time to ice the cake!"

The birthday girl dips the wooden spoon into a bowl of chocolate icing and uses short strokes to spread the decadent mixture over the top of the cake. She continues to operate the wooden spoon with delicate precision, dipping into the bowl and smoothing the icing until the entire cake is covered.

"Good job, Jenny!" says Shannon. "Can I lick the spoon?"

"Sure! I get the bowl!"

Shannon daintily tastes the icing from the wooden spoon while Jenny plunges her face into the bowl.

Coming up for air, the little girl's face is covered with chocolate. "This icing is good, mom."

"I can see how you're enjoying it."

The three of them are giggling and having a good time when the side door opens and Jack enters.

"It looks like everyone is having a good time without me."

"Hello, honey!" says Carol and she walks over to kiss her husband.

"We were just decorating my birthday cake, dad!" Jenny gives him a chocolatey smile.

"You should have saved some icing for the cake," says her father.

"Go and wash up for supper girls," their mother tells them. "And then set the table."

"I'm starving!" says Jack. "It smells like spaghetti!"

His wife smiles. "You're always hungry when you solve a case. How did it go today?"

"Don't say anything to Jenny to spoil her birthday, but Anna passed away this afternoon. We should wait until tomorrow at least to say anything."

"That's so sad, Jack!"

A family effort of kitchen clean-up after supper is followed by a relaxing time in the living room which includes the opening of birthday presents.

Carol snuggles on the couch beside Jack and sips from her tea cup. Jack stretches an arm across his wife's shoulders and, at the same time, feels the weight of the McPherson case lifted from his own shoulders. Jenny has already opened her gift from Shannon, a board game which the two sisters are playing.

"You win again, Jenny!" says Shannon and her sister is all smiles having won a third game in a row.

Their parents are highly amused and Jack says, "She must be cheating to win every time."

"Check for extra cards up her sleeve, Shannon," says her mom.

The room fills with giggles as the newest addition to the family, a snow white cat, rubs its whiskers on the little girl's leg and purrs loudly. Jenny lifts the cat and administers a loving hug.

"You know I'm not cheating, don't you Dorothy?"

"Why don't you open this?" suggests her mom as she hands Jenny a nicely wrapped gift. "It's from your dad and I."

Jenny sets Dorothy gently on the floor beside her and opens her birthday present.

"A watch!" she exclaims with excitement.

Carol helps her daughter with the new watch and explains some of its features. Holding her wrist high in the air, the little girl admires the fit while her older sister runs upstairs.

Returning momentarily, Shannon hands one last present to Jenny.

"This is from Justin."

With eyes bulging, Jenny accepts the gift and puts it on her lap.

"What could it be?"

"Open it, sweetheart," encourages her mom.

Jenny slowly and methodically removes the ribbon and paper. Setting the wrapping in a neat pile on the floor next to Dorothy, she gradually lifts the lid of the box and peeks under the tissue paper. Her eyes bulge out even further.

"What is it?" asks her father.

"Just a minute!" Jenny carefully sets the box on the coffee table and races to the stairs. "I have to get something from my bedroom."

Everyone adorns identical expressions of uncertainty until Jenny's return. She has white gloves on her hands, the same white gloves she only wears to church on Sundays. She picks up the box and places it on her lap once again.

"I don't want to get fingerprints on it," Jenny tells them.

Shannon and her mom are entertained by the little girl's actions while Jack appears less amused. He considers the white gloves a potentially bad omen.

Jenny reaches into the box with both gloved hands and raises a glass statue depicting a young elephant resting on its hind haunches. A closer look reveals a blue-tinted tear rolling down one side of its face.

"Justin answered my question just like he promised," says Jenny.

epilogue

A young woman lies asleep in her soft bed next to her husband. She is slightly roused by a dream and she twists under the black satin sheets.

A bright light permeates the fluffy layers of white cloud and a heavy mist blankets the calm waters of the lake save the tiny ripples that lazily make their way to the sandy beach. All is tranquil.

Suddenly, there's a bubbling mass of confusion out on the lake. Huge waves erupt and race towards the shore. Crashing against the rocks, the raging waters send a cascade of spray high into the air. A young matriarch emerges from the tempest, raises its noble head and lets out a deafening trumpet blast. A lightning bolt flashes from a hunter's gun and rips a hole in the elephant's chest. Blood splatters from the wound turning the water red.

The young woman's eyes open wide and she sits straight up in her bed. Sweat beads on her brow as she shivers. Damp as if splashed by the tumultuous waves in her dream, she clutches a monkey charm which dangles from her neck.

"Are you all right, Jenny?" asks her husband as he wraps his arms around her.

Without an answer, he eases her back into her pillow and holds her tight. Eventually, she falls asleep.

Jenny awakens to the pit-a-pat of raindrops hitting the tin roof of the hut. Stimulated by this soothing sound, she reaches for her husband but the place beside her is unoccupied.

She rises from her berth and steps barefoot to a glassless window. Sticking out her tongue to catch the raindrops, she's not at all concerned about the grey sky. A voice from within is saying, "Always see the sun, my little one."

Jenny lives with her husband John in a one room bungalow camped in an obscure rural district a few miles from Molepolole, Botswana. She is the veterinarian of a sanctuary which is the focal point of a two and a half million hectare wildlife preserve. As a child, Jenny had dreams of a place not far from here.

She had met her husband at university and John is now an accomplished photographer and inspiring filmmaker who is currently working on a wildlife documentary. They were summoned to Africa two years ago and have plans to stay for many more.

John makes his way across the compound and catches sight of his lovely wife at the window.

"Are you sticking your tongue out at me?"

"I'm catching raindrops," answers Jenny and she giggles.

Her husband stretches his arms high into the air. "Take a look around, my love. We're living in paradise!"

Jenny thinks to herself before responding. Paradise can't be just a place. It must also be a condition people put themselves into that gives them total satisfaction. That's what paradise really is.

"Yes we are, my love!"

The rain suddenly stops and Jenny points skyward. "Look! The sun is starting to shine!"

As the bright sun makes its way from behind the clouds, the animals in the sanctuary come out of hiding and the cheerful sounds of nature fill the camp.

John smiles as he beholds the twinkle of sunshine in Jenny's eyes.

CPSIA information can be obtained at www.ICGtesting.com
Printed in the USA
LVOW08s2039080716

495653LV00001B/3/P